KNUT

Tom Mallin

Available:

Verbivoracious Festschrift Vol.1—Christine Brooke-Rose
Verbivoracious Festschrift Vol.2—Gilbert Adair
(Edited by G.N. Forester and M.J. Nicholls)
The Languages of Love — Christine Brooke-Rose
The Sycamore Tree — Christine Brooke-Rose
Go When You See the Green Man Walking — Christine Brooke-Rose
Three Novels — Rosalyn Drexler

Forthcoming reprint titles:

Next
The Dear Deceit
The Middlemen
Xorandor/Verbivore

by Christine Brooke-Rose

Erowina

by Tom Mallin

other Verbivoracious titles @

www.verbivoraciouspress.org

KNUT

Tom Mallin

Verbivoracious Press

Glentrees, 13 Mt Sinai Lane, Singapore

This edition published in Great Britain & Singapore

by Verbivoracious Press

www.verbivoraciouspress.org

ISBN: 978-981-09-2165- 1

Printed and bound in Great Britain & Singapore

First published in Great Britain by Allison & Busby 1971.

Introduction

Rupert Mallin

Tom Mallin—1927 to 1977

"If I start to make anything with my hands, I know I can do it (but) I destroy myself," Tom explained to journalist Michael McNay in a *Guardian* interview January 26, 1971.

Tom Mallin's brief life was a tightrope between talent and destruction.

Tom Mather Mallin was born in the Black Country in 1927. Following his father's fatal heart attack at the wheel of a new car in 1933 (Clifford Vincent was a leading seller for Dunlop), Tom was thereafter "charitably educated" at the Royal Masonic School, Hertfordshire. Ideally, the school both taught the classics and vocational skills. Tom spent over ten years boarding, which he loathed, and developed a terrible stammer, a condition that resulted in frequent bullying. Through masonic connections, King George VI's speech therapist Lionel Logue cured the boy's stammer, for which the child was grateful.[1] He won a scholarship to Birmingham School of Art in 1943 and from there a scholarship to the Royal College of Art in 1945.

However, national service in the army intervened. He was impressive in training—from rifle shooter to parachuting. He appeared to be rising in the ranks until his posting to the Middle East challenged that progress

---

1 Tom Mallin's letter, circa 1939, quoted in 'The King's Speech'—the diaries of Lionel Logue—by Mark Logue and Peter Conradi—*Quercus 2010*

and changed his life. Eventually, his talents were recognised and he spent some time working at the Cairo Museum. Rumour persists about Tom's time in the army. Had he produced posters for Arab nationalists by design or mistake? Faced with redeployment, had he jumped ship to remain in the Middle East? He once said that he dyed his demob suit red and joined an Anarchist group on his return to London in 1947. The truth or an over-active imagination? He had his passport withdrawn for a number of years.[2]

What is also known is that he walked out of the Royal College of Art after two weeks and began studying at the Anglo-French Arts Centre in St John's Wood (The Anglo-French survived from 1945-51). The Anglo-French had a bohemian edge (Tom grew his hair long and was spat at in the street because of his appearance). Here Courbet fused with Picasso, reflecting the 'New Realists' of Paris at the time—a group of artists working out of a slaughterhouse, which appealed to him. The son of a grand mason, Tom embraced realism, in its widest sense, not merely to cast off his upbringing but in the hope society could grow more egalitarian and open.

In 1949 Tom married artist Muriel George. He took a menial job at an art gallery in Bond Street where he trained as a picture restorer, later specialising in 16th and 17th Century Italian paintings. In 1955 he, his wife and two boys, Simon and Rupert, moved to Clare in Suffolk—moving into a redundant pub with crumbling stables. The stables were slowly turned into studios. Until 1963 Tom worked in Bond Street during the week, only returning at the weekends to paint and do up the property.

Apart from his restoration work, Tom produced a massive body of visual art—drawings, illustrations, cartoons, etchings, paintings, furniture and sculpture. Many of the life-size figurative sculptures he buried beneath the lawn. He could produce the work but was seized by artistic doubt, probably fuelled by the precision of his restoration work.[3]

What is not a myth is the motivation for his writing. In 1963, after a

---

2 I have been in touch with a leading Military Historian, who has uncovered documents but nothing is conclusive.

small party at the house, a female friend left her diary behind. One entry read: "Tom says he is going to write. It's just another daydream." He began writing that day, with the statement to the effect painted on the back of his desk.

Back at the Royal Masonic School, English had been Tom's favourite subject and he read whenever his hands were not engaged. Writing enabled Tom to balance between his ability and the destructive forces of it. It wasn't until 1970 that Tom Mallin could write full time, with the support of his wife. Tom was very active in the campaign for Public Lending Rights and taught literacy in the village. Within a few years, five of his novels were published, nine radio plays broadcast and several of his plays were performed in theatres in London, Edinburgh and New York. His early death in 1977 left many unread manuscripts, including 47 short stories.

Tom Mallin—The Reader

From the outset, Tom's reading was wide ranging. He read Greek and Roman classic works from an early age and enjoyed the Gothic novel as evidenced by his volumes of Edgar Allan Poe, Tolstoy, and Mary Shelley's *Frankenstein.*

As a young adult he read at least three novels a week—thrillers, crime novels and literary works. Drawn more to literary realism and its offshoots, Tom read Balzac, Dostoyevsky, Tugenev, Zola, George Eliot, Dickens, etc. He read all the Modern Classics from Orwell to Gunter Grass; and the Emerging Classics—from Algernon Blackwood to Camus and Genet. He was drawn to the play scripts of Strindberg and the films of Bergman.

Tom was also fascinated in non-fiction books. There were many Victorian medical books like *Gray's Anatomy* on the shelves. He read some histories but preferred books like Mayhew's London. Because of his previous calling as a painter and then picture restorer, he read many books on artists and art history from Ancient to Modern. The only books I never

---

3 Much of Tom's artistic output is now in private collections in the UK and Europe.

saw Tom read nor did I discover on his shelves were biographies and autobiographies.

Knut and the Gothic Novel

In my view, Tom used the genre of the gothic novel as a vehicle for parody. Obviously, Karen is not 'the stupid servant' of early gothic novels. In the cold northern crumbling mansion of the aristocrat, the grand gymnasium becomes a playroom for children—it becomes its opposite. There are many examples of this subversion.

Why the violence? However the surface appears, there is always the violence beneath, occasionally puncturing the veneer but bubbling always. Tom, via his schooling and some terrible experiences in the army, had the surface perfection of his art stood on its head in 1947. Returning to take up a scholarship at the Royal College of Art his first task was to draw plaster casts of great classical figures he had seen for real in the Cairo Museum. His exit from this institution within days of entering runs like this:

TUTOR: Mallin, your drawing is too dark. Are you pressing too heavily on your pencil?
MALLIN: No—it's a 4B pencil.

Tom walked away. The RCA wanted no harsh shadows in the art produced there—no dark shadows across the culture.

Tom's association with the Parisian "New Realists" took off. What appealed to him was their fusion of realism and abstraction in looking beneath the surface, personally, politically and culturally. It is therefore a large irony that Tom Mallin then earned his living as a picture restorer for over twenty years where his work was in restoring the surface of paint. However, in his writing Tom once again fused realism and abstraction to look beyond appearances, beneath the surface.

PART ONE: OUT OF CONTEXT

Filled with the pain of love and my head bowed in shame, I listened to the written words become obscene in her vaulted mouth. Her active tongue and bright pink lips enunciated each syllable with a precision which, while making audible the childish content of my secret manuscript, seemed to be a particularly brittle and articulate condemnation.

Around my nose and on my upper lip, a light perspiration felt suddenly chill. It was tangible evidence of my embarrassment.

"'I am surprised to find I am'?"

She cocked her head on one side and gave me a searching look with her bright, mauve eyes. It was as if, suddenly illuminated, she had discovered I was an independent being and was uneasy to find before her a familiar whose presence was an unwelcome surprise and one which she resented. My pride hurt, and no stranger to dark moods, I allowed a shadow to blacken my sullen look while I stared down at the carpet. It was possible she thought of me as a threat to her authority which, up until that moment, had gone unchallenged, or, and more likely, that I, as an emerging male, posed a problem which would force her to think upon her own sexuality; an idea which I confess excited me greatly.

When she repeated what I had written, I thought I detected a respect which previously had been lacking. It could equally have been an acknowledgement of my uncertain entry into adulthood.

"'I am surprised to find I am'?"

"Free to be, yes. There is an overwhelming sense of relief now that she is dead . . ."

A sudden and prolonged fit of coughing, caused by the accidental swallowing of my own saliva into my lungs, bent me double while the green liquid swilled and bubbled in my watery chest. When it subsided, I hastened to wipe my eyes and sniffed back a few nasal tears which had been on the point of escaping from the tip of my nose. Her hand, which had rubbed my back, patted my shoulder and, after an affectionate squeeze, withdrew to smooth the page of my manuscript. The exertion of my coughing had blocked both ears, muffling sounds in the darkening room. I inserted a little finger into one ear and yawned my mouth open until my jaws clicked and the hiss of silence filled my head.

"Don't expect to feel buoyed for long, Knut. The elders' attitude could be far worse and you may yet come to wish she were still alive . . . "

"Never!"

". . . or I dead."

My heart hesitated, seemed to shrivel and then deliberately, like an unborn child, it turned clumsily over and, with a kick, sent the blood surging up into my face so that I found myself having to breathe more quickly. Katya pretended not to have noticed. On the other hand, she could have been hiding her amusement as she bent her head low over the page and, in silence, continued to read.

'Drawn from my mother's womb on a long, tenuous cord, I was suspended in a grey nimbus and have remained there, like a hardening leg of pork dangling from the kitchen rafter, until today, when I was cut down for the feast of a lifetime.'

"Oh, you poor little piggy. When was this?"

'I should explain that it was my mother, Madlin Strobl, who did the devouring.'

"You make her out to have been some sort of praying mantis."

"Helga said Morag ate her own babies."

"Good grief! Helga's a peasant. She's so steeped in traditional superstition that . . . Knut, it's a tale she tells to frighten children. Those sicked-up balls of fur were the hairs Morag licked off herself and swallowed. Not kittens. Really!" With her eyes, she sought patience from the heavens.

"You're so gullible, Knut."

"Aunt Estrild gave birth to a rabbit."

"Yes, but that was different."

'Like the female bluebottle which lays her eggs on the juiciest part of the meat, my mother dug her ovipositor into my being and laid the worms of degeneration so that, before I was a day old and suspended in limbo to putrefy, I became the vector of an alien abnormality.'

"Knut dear, you're not abnormal. And you mustn't blame Madlin for your illness."

"Not my sick mind?"

"She wasn't evil. Selfish, maybe, but not evil. Not unless . . ."

I snorted down my nose to indicate my disagreement and revealed, I hoped, the contempt I felt for my dead mother by a suitable and pained expression. But Katya was enclosed by her thoughts and my defiance went unnoticed. When, later, she spoke, it was as if she were at the other end of a long corridor and was walking towards me slowly, remembering her thoughts aloud.

"In the darker corners of this house there have been committed things far more horrible than your imagination could invent, Knut. Things which have distorted personality and blackened souls. But Madlin was innocent of this. On the other hand," she flashed me a smile and spun like a baller-ina, "if you have the shameful thoughts which come to us all, not to worry. And don't dramatise everything so."

"You're talking gibberish. And may I have my notebook back. Please." I stood for a long time with my hand outstretched. In the end, I had to snatch the book from her. "And I wish you wouldn't criticise me so. If you persist," I turned my back to hide a flash of malice, "I might write hor-rible things about you out of spite."

"Who will there be to read them? Karen? I certainly shall not. Besides, you know less than nothing about the real me. And you will never know, because I am not so foolish as to write them down."

"You will not be able to resist taking a peek. And do you know why?

Because, my dearest Katya, you are vain."

Katya stamped her foot.

"That's the unkindest thing you could have said about me, Knut. I'm deeply hurt. Write your beastly book. I shan't read it. Ever."

A week later I drew a line beneath the offending passage and began all over again.

'Madlin Strobl, my mother, was capable of the most outrageous acts against me, her only son.'

After some deliberation, I crossed out the word son and wrote daughter. If I was to write an autobiography, it was essential to be accurate.

'Like a night witch, she would enter the nursery and, lifting my eyelids, place a wriggling earwig beneath each so that I awoke to a world filled with dancing sparks. At other times, she would half crush two captive flies and put one in each ear where they lay buzzing and tickling, filling my head with sounds. If I cried out, she clapped her hand, cupped full of insects, over my mouth, so when I screamed, after she had left, they flew out like dark spittle.'

"What's troubling you?"

"It is a sickness which can be diagnosed."

"Then consult Borge and have him cure you."

"It is a butcher I need. One who keeps his knife sharp on the steel hung from his belt. A butcher whose face is like bleeding pork."

"Oh dear, Knut. Have you got a castration complex?"

I was acutely embarrassed by her reference to that part of my body and tried to push past her but she caught hold of my sleeve.

"Knut darling. I'm sorry. It was very stupid of me. I should have more respect for your sense of, well—drama. God knows, both of us are suffering, but you mustn't allow this feeling for tragedy to become a madness. You're not so ill that death is the only alternative. Please. Put such thoughts out of your mind. If only for my sake." Gently, she pulled me to her, kissed my lips and, with the back of her hand, stroked my cheek. "We've only got each other." I pushed her from me and with more violence than I had intended.

"I have repeatedly asked you never to touch me!"

"I'm sorry. As you wish." Rolling her handkerchief into a small tight ball, she dabbed the end of her nose. "Ever since Madlin's death—" she hesitated, either to search for a precise turn of phrase or because she had seen the trembling in my hands and limbs. "We should be drawing closer together, not be at loggerheads. And I repeat. I am determined to leave. And shall. At the first opportunity. Think what it will be like living here on your own without me."

Imagine I could, and I burst into tears.

Cradled in her enfolding arms, I was lulled. It seemed that I had been crying all my life and would continue to do so.

"I'll stay," she whispered into my hair. "For a little while at least."

When the door closed, I looked down. Through my tears, the notebook looked like a slab of crystallised anorthosite rock which had become strangely limp, like cloth. I opened it and a tear rolled off my cheek and splashed onto the large, looping pothooks of someone else's hand. It was Katya's writing. The diluted ink enlarged into blue, marbled pools which I had to blot with my sleeve.

Undoubtedly beautiful, Knut has the luminous skin of a consumptive but, being born old, he has been denied a maturing youth to firm his looks. Large-eyed, gentle and with the slowest of lazy smiles, he can evoke a sadness which is disturbing; especially to women who, in his presence, yearn to become his mistress, sister, or, and best, his mother. Surrounded by such incestuous attention, deprived of natural love and his innocence irrevocably scored, Knut is not to be expected to be other than resentful of my affection and hostile towards me, his only friend. Which is a pity. Of all men, Knut is the one I most love. It is this shared pain which will be our undoing.

I caught up with her on the floor below in the long, dark corridor and outside what used to be the music room. I thrust the damp pages in front of her face.

"Lies! All lies!"

Katya took the notebook from me and closed it.

"I have never lied to you, Knut. Ever. I may have avoided answering you sometimes, yes, but that was to shield you from pain. Have you ever been so considerate of my feelings? Or as honest? Mmm? I think not. You have been deliberately untruthful. The disguise you have worn to mask your emotion has been transparently thin. What's wrong with love? God, we've had little enough of it."

It was like having run naked from a maniac only to discover on rounding the next corner he was barring the path with a drawn dagger directed towards one's dropping bowels.

"I didn't want you to think less of me."

"Knut, the weaknesses which truth sometimes reveals are not necessarily unattractive. And love, never."

"At times," I said, trying to outstare her, "I felt you would have preferred me to have been effeminate."

I could not have dug a more effective pit between us and into which either of us could have been unbalanced and fallen to our extinction.

Katya's indignation raged across her face, and my apology plummeted like a stone. I waited in vain for the reverberation to come echoing back but she slammed out of the room. The silence she left in her wake was more stringent than a hand slap. Dejected, I could have wished for a more merciful admonishment at her hands. As it was, there was still most of the day to be lived through.

The following afternoon, Katya surprised me by taking my hand and pulling me into the empty ballroom. In the cold, in the weak light which filtered through one of the half-opened shutters, we danced a curious scuffle to the music in our heads whilst beneath our feet the old floorboards creaked and our breath steamed from our mouths.

"We are like two snails."

I pulled a face at the thought of slimy bodies entwining about each other but Katya pointed over my shoulder, indicating the trail our footsteps were making in the dust and I understood her allusion.

Suddenly, she stopped, gripped my shoulders and looked into my face.

"Come away with me, Knut. Before disgrace forces us to leave. We're too proud to stomach being ejected by the elders."

"They wouldn't dare."

"Together we form a more effective opposition but not as long as we remain in this house. Will you?"

"You might desert me."

"For God's sake, Knut, I'm asking you to help me! I'm begging you."

Seizing her hand, I pressed it to my lips, kissing her palm and inhaling the acidity of her slight perspiration.

"Someone's coming!" She snatched her hand away and, running swiftly and silently to the mirrored wall, disappeared through the concealed door.

The "somebody" was Marcel, walking on the balls of his feet, his right eye red and watering from the draughts which blew through the many keyholes. He entered the ballroom and stood looking at me and at the footprints in the dust. Plainly visible were the tiptoed steps left by Katya when she had fled the ballroom.

"I beg your pardon, Master Knut. I thought I heard music."

"It was a tarantella," I said, pairing his preposterous lie.

"Oh, and, Marcel, from now on I wish to be addressed as Herr Strobl. For as long, that is, as you remain in our employ."

Marcel's face betrayed no emotion, but under his heavy lids his eyes darkened and seemed to contract.

"Herr Baldric wishes to see you in the study, Herr Strobl."

"Alone?"

"I expect Fräulein Katya will have run into him by now," and he deliberately followed the path of Katya's footsteps to the mirrored door with his eyes. I had no alternative but to leave as he waited patiently by the door, holding it open for me.

Katya was stood looking out of the study window at the perpetual, snow-covered winter landscape which isolated us from other human habitation.

"Come in, Knut." I closed the door and gave my uncle a perfunctory bow. I felt more secure greeting him in this manner. A handshake would have betrayed my instinctive dislike of the man. "Sit down. You too, Katya."

We didn't, but Uncle Ira seemed not to notice. Katya turned round.

"You've only got to admit to writing it, Knut . . ."

"That's enough, young woman. Now, Knut. As your guardian—and for the next three years as required by law—I am responsible, not only for your moral rectitude but your physical well-being. The latter I need hardly remind you has been a worry to us all for as long as I can remember. You were sickly as a child and, contrary to all expectations, have been dogged by ill health ever since. Perhaps this is your punishment. I know your mother, God rest her soul, believed it was a judgement upon her for a dissolute youth."

I balked at the mention of my mother's youth. It had never occurred to me that she had ever been young. I wanted to snigger.

"However, that's not what troubles me. As I said, I am responsible for your spiritual and moral rectitude."

While he waffled on I racked my brains to think what I had written which might have come into his hands. My notebook was safe in its hiding place. Of that I was certain. Only Katya knew of its existence. It was impossible that he had come upon it by chance. If he had gone snooping and winkled it out I stood to argue the morality of such questionable conduct and might be able to nullify any objection he may have had regarding the content of the book.

"You can imagine my consternation when I read it. And I admit to reading it. I have a duty. Just as I would were I your father. And as your father would have been, I was horrified, that you, a Strobl, heir to an estate, could write such a disgusting letter."

I had written no letter! I was about to protest when Katya stiffened and gave an almost imperceptible warning frown.

"Do you deny that this is your handwriting?" He took from off the desk and unfolded several sheets of ruled paper and handed them to me. I leafed through them quickly and managed to take in such disjointed words as, "your adoring eyes", "longing", "the closeness of your body", "to kiss kisses", "my desperate need", "eternity", "aching for", and, paradoxically, "I would sooner die". The letter was addressed to "My Darling Baby", and signed "K." All the sheets were in the unmistakable handwriting of my darling Katya.

"Well? Do you admit to writing that disgusting letter?"

"Yes, sir. I wrote this letter. May I ask how you came by it, sir?"

"It fell from Karen's pocket when she was serving at table." He saw my puzzled look. "She denied you had written it. Naturally. But a maid, Knut. A maid! And at your age. How long has this, this 'affair' been going on between you, eh? And don't say only a few weeks. In so short a time a man could not be so compromised by his animal instincts that he found it necessary to write such, such a . . ." Lost for words, he waved the letter in the air. "I wouldn't write such a letter to my own wife, sir!"

"May I beg of you that Katya be asked to leave?"

"Certainly not! Her presence here is to shame you. To shame you into the realisation that what you are about is wicked. Not only have you corrupted a serving girl, though as likely as not it was she who initiated your degradation, but you have discredited yourself in the eyes of your elders as the future heir to the Strobl estate."

Katya took a step forward.

"Karen will be dismissed?"

"Unfortunately, she must remain. She is Helga's ward. Bastard daughter, I shouldn't wonder. To some extent, our hands are tied by Frau Axell, who incidentally knows nothing of this, and mustn't. The shock would kill her. So I warn you, Knut, if you think to continue this obscene liaison you will be ostracised by the elders, and for the rest of your life."

He continued to admonish me for nearly half an hour, during which time he extracted from me the promise to have nothing to do with Karen ever again, to repent of my ways and to try and live in uprightness in the future. Not finding it difficult, because I was not forced to lie, I promised him I would, and convinced him. Ironically, Katya was given the task of supervising me, of staying close and making sure I did not try to make Contact with "that kitchen slut" ever again. Her earnestness nearly made me explode with laughter.

Before I was dismissed, Uncle Ira said it would be to my credit if I showed a contriteness by staying in my room. The longer my penitence, the more impressed he would be with my determination to conduct myself in the future, not only as a gentleman, but as a Christian gentleman.

I left with my head suitably bowed in shame and shut the door behind me with the meekness befitting a penitent.

Halfway up the stairs on the second floor, a breathless Katya caught up with me. I turned round.

"You got me into a pretty pickle, Katya," I growled. "I've got to stay closeted for at least a fortnight!"

Katya seized my hand and pressed it against her bosom. In her grip, my knuckles cracked.

"I could eat you!" and she dragged my hand behind her so that my arm was about her waist.

"What I don't understand, Katya, is how Karen came by the letter."

"Goose. She was my postbox," and she laughed. "Yes. My little postbox."

 You were very foolish to trust such a letter to Karen. Unsealed too."

"You didn't read it. You couldn't possibly have read it."

"I saw enough to know why Uncle Ira was alarmed."

Katya stopped and put her head on my shoulder. "Yes. I was very naughty to write such a foolish letter."

We drew closer together and I looked down into the dark well of the staircase feeling my mood and gesture to be entirely unreal.

"Will you write me another letter, Katya? Mmm? I will search under my pillow every night."

"Never. Ever." She disengaged herself, pecked at my cheek and ran down the stairs with her skirts flying. "But that's not a promise, mind."

I made my way up the rest of the stairway, placing one foot carefully in front of the other. I was disturbed. Much as I wanted her love, the possibility of it becoming reality was frightening.

'One is born innocent. One does not fight off the temptation to sin in order to remain good. Goodness, like sinfulness, is proffered and taken with the milkiness at one's mother's breast.

Thus it was as a babe, when I gnawed my mother's dugs with bare gums, the nourishment I sucked was a bitter pus which oozed into my soft mouth, infecting me.'

Granoise wet-nursed you. K.S.

"I wish you would refrain from pencilling in snippets of information."

When Katya looked up, her mouth wide open, I looked down. I found the pink, wet interior of her mouth exciting. I heard her strong white teeth bite into the hard toast. "Besides, Katya, you have not considered the possibility that my autobiography might be fictional. A sort of autofiction."

Katya's teeth crunched into the biscuiting toast. It sounded as if she were chewing crushed pumice stone.

"It won't work, Knut. Self-medication is often as dangerous as the disease it seeks to treat."

"Katya, and for the last time, if you must write, begin your own book."

In reply, Katya heaped even more jam on the corner of toast still left to eat.

Breakfast was a meal I detested and went without; the elders, too, although some ate it in their rooms off silver trays balanced on their bony knees while they sat propped up in bed. Katya, always neatly and freshly dressed, smelling sweet and looking crisp, took hers, and with great relish, in the breakfast-room. Generally she ate hard toast and jam, very like an Englishman would be served. In order to be with her and share the liveliness with which she began each day, I would sit opposite to her sipping herbal tea into which other remedies had been stirred. It was a loathsome brew and, while I sipped it, I could not help but imagine I was drinking stale urine. I even had an image of the wizened old woman from whom the herbalist had squeezed the golden liquid. Not unnaturally, I never finished the concoction but let it grow cold in the glass and an oily skin develop on the surface.

"Your breath smells foul this morning, Knut." I covered my mouth with a hand and held my breath. "Are you feverish?"

"I awoke in a sweat during the early hours," I said, speaking down, into my sleeve.

"I guessed as much. And your cough?"

"Dry. But I'm not on the trot."

Karen entered with a silver tray held and pressed against her bosom. For a fleeting moment she looked like a breast-plated amazon but far too delicate and light-stepping to engage in battle with a deadly male.

The embarrassment I felt when I had first confronted Karen, after the two weeks in the wilderness of my room, had long passed and Katya and I were again on the friendliest of terms with her; only pretending an arrogant and cool disdain a subservient maid warrants when an elder was in the vicinity or the hateful Marcel and his watchful eye lurked around the corner. Having grown up with Karen and being the same age made it difficult to be other than on the friendliest of terms with her; especially as she had, from all accounts, conducted herself with admirable dignity and great courage when wrongfully accused by Ira of improper and licentious conduct.

"Try and persuade Knut he should go back to bed, Karen."

Karen came and stood against me, pressing herself into my arm. I could distinctly feel the slight pout of her stomach, the slope to her groin and the rise of her parted thighs. Her warmth permeated the cloth of my jacket and her stomach undulated against me while she breathed. When she laid a cool hand on my brow, I tried to remain respectful in thought and not tremble, but it was difficult; infidelity seemed so temptingly pleasurable, despite Ira's warning and the inevitable wrath of Katya's affronted possessiveness.

"His temple is very cool."

"Borg said a fall in temperature was a clear sign all was not well, didn't he?"

"I'll make up his bed."

Before I could protest, Karen had clattered down the tray and left the room.

"I'm damned if I'm going to be ordered about!"

"Don't be difficult, Knut. Besides, think how much more pleasurable it will be to do your writing tucked up in bed."

"But I'm always sat in bed. And dammit; I haven't long finished a two-week stint purging myself of lust!"

My excitement exploded into a hurtful and very dry fit of coughing. When I was through, I wiped my eyes and cradled my sweating brow on my hand.

"I shall come and take my morning cup of chocolate with you, Knut. Would you like that? And in the afternoon, I will read to you."

"Make it a promise."

"Why not? There is little else to do in this damned house."

But it was very dark when she eventually came to my bedside.

"I'm sorry, Knut darling. Truly."

Two months later I was sat at the window of my room feeling very much better and enjoying have Katya fuss round me, tucking in the rugs. When I was sufficiently cocooned and the window opened to let in the curative air, Katya took hold of the notebook I was clutching.

"Last week you said tomorrow. What do you say today?"

"You haven't given your lapdog his cube of sugar to balance."

Katya kissed the tip of my nose.

"Beast," and she eased the manuscript out of my grip.

"It's in no sort of order. I have written as the memories came to me."

"I'm not bothered."

"Well, read it in your room. And don't pencil comments in the margin."

PART TWO: THE MANUSCRIPT

"Whistle, boy. Whistle."

"Yes, Helga."

It was always "that damned boy's dog" or "that boy and his damned dog", never Knut or Hubbard.

"We've progressed. Downwards. At least, I thought we had."

"Pardon?"

"Keep whistling. I said, downwards. When I was a young girl, we slept above the animals. The ground floor was given over to the animals. Mostly chickens. Some geese. And the horse. A pig. A cow or, if you couldn't afford that, a goat. And the horse. Their heat was supposed to keep us warm in the winter but it was really because no one could afford to build extra sheds. Not if one had only a little land to farm. But the stink! It was the smell I detested. I suppose I should have got used to it, but I never did. It got into our hair and clung to our clothes. We smelt like urinals. We looked like them, and some—well there were some who behaved like animals. The townspeople would have nothing to do with us, except take our money. It was said they washed it when the shop closed for the night. They were mean enough. But it was hard on us poor girls, having the young lads sniff and turn up their noses at us. It was humiliating but it didn't prevent them from misbehaving."

Helga slipped the crimped pie into the log-fired oven, kneed the door shut and wiped her hand on her voluminous apron.

"I thought those days were gone for ever, but here you are reminding me of them."

"I haven't spoken!"

"Whistle! You are making me remember the times I'd rather forget."

"I?"

"And that damned dog of yours. It ought to be chained to a cleat in the yard, not allowed down here with us humans. If I was your mother . . ."

I wouldn't have objected. The moist cheese was grating into soft curls and falling silently onto the rising pile.

"I'm going into the larder to wipe the jars of pickled cabbage. If you so much as pause for breath, I shall know what you're up to—so don't."

Whenever I was allowed to help Helga in the kitchen, mixing in the pudding bowl, rolling out pastry and scattering raisins or slicing fruit and chopping carrots, she made me whistle to prevent me from eating the odd stolen cherry, nut, or, as then, the cheese I was grating.

"And whistle something more tuneful, otherwise you'll set that damned dog of yours howling."

"It's winter."

Helga, making a pancake of a damp cloth, turned in the doorway and her face, as large as the full moon, stared down on me from the night of her momentary blackness; softening.

"I'll get you an apple from the stables when I'm through. But only if you finish grating that cheese."

"And may Hubbard have a bone?"

"If he gnaws it in the yard."

"Out in the snow?"

"Yes. God willing, he may catch his death out there. Mightn't you? Eh, Hubbard? You damned dog you."

But she didn't pat him or scratch him behind his ear.

One lonely day, very like all others, I set off on a long journey, resolved to count the number of rooms in the house. Usually I was waylaid by my imagination but in this instance, by a bureau I had not noticed before. It had countless small drawers. On each were painted spindly-legged insects and exotic, brilliantly sheened butterflies which I first mistook to be real, so skilfully were they represented and their illusionary shadows painted. Compelled to stop and look and walk about the bureau, curious to discover if the artist had been forced to repeat any of the hundreds of insects and butterflies, my original intention of counting the number of rooms was soon forgotten.

My obsession with insects and spiders was probably due to the fact that in that silent house, these minute creatures moved, breathed and busied themselves with the complicated task of living and, but more important, did not involve me in their lives. True, they were occasionally squashed or swept up into dustpans, but they had an independence of which I was jealous. I did not have an insect as a pet, neither did I collect them in matchboxes as some boys do, for the truth was that I could not bring myself to touch them. If I was feeling very bold, I might prod a dead fly with a wisp of grass but beyond that I would not dare. A broad windowsill, onto which the sun would shine for most of the day in summer, became a paradise for about two months when one year a maid neglected to dust it so that it became littered with the husks of flies and other insects which had either died in a head-on collision with the windowpanes or fallen prey to the many spiders who spun their webs in the unlikeliest of places. I would watch for hours these scurrying spiders responding to the frantic buzzing of the flies stuck and struggling in their webs or the occasional wasp which, in its determination to escape, reduced to tatters the most beautiful of webs and, freeing itself, flew off angrily, trailing a wisp of the broken thread. I was dimly aware of the necessity and, indeed, the inevitability of this life and death struggle, but what I could not comprehend was the stupidity of the flies and insects which, for hours on end, would buzz the panes of glass instead of being elsewhere, eating and making little homes for themselves. All too soon, my paradise was wiped and polished, and made thoroughly disinfectant and I had to search elsewhere.

There were other reasons why my efforts were thwarted when I endeavoured to walk the length and breadth of the house and to climb to its heights, besides my interest in insects.

I could be halted abruptly by the fear of entering a room darkened by closed shutters and in which the carpets lay rolled and the dust sheets covering the furniture made me imagine the room was inhabited by ghostly, humpbacked dwarfs. I would retreat in fright, my mission forgotten, while I raced down the silent, narrow carpeted corridors reliving a terror of my nightmares. Nightmares which Gudrun had implanted with her stories of the grubs which formed in the rotting corpse of the Giant Ymir and which grew into dwarfs with human form. Understandably, whenever I did chance to come upon a grub, I squashed it underfoot, feeling I was helping to obliterate this race of dwarfs, and denying them the chance of ever outnumbering us, frail mortals.

Occasionally, very occasionally, I was forced to abandon my projected marathon when I found my way unexpectedly blocked by the exaggerated courtesy of an unknown guest who would inevitably pat my head and treat me to a prolonged assault of childishness and ply me with questions intended to underline their understanding of, and affinity with, small children. It was generally the male guest who surrendered his adult sovereignty in this manner, whereas the female guests were inclined to pet and fondle me in an unfamiliar way and, although I resisted, especially when they lifted up my little frock to see if I wore knickers, I secretly luxuriated in their seductive embraces and received their warm, scent-laden bussings with an almost erotic delight. That I was quickly put down or annoyance shown if I dogged their heels too frequently, I came to realise, at a very tender age, was proof of female fickleness. One aunt in particular revealed this vice. For some reason which was inexplicable to me, she regarded me as her pet and I was therefore stroked, bussed, whispered to, tickled and my flesh laved with eau-de-Cologne to make, as she said—and always with her lips pouted, "Boy-boy smell nice for Auntie Esta." She was particularly fond of baring my stomach and planting wet, noisy kisses in my navel when she wasn't otherwise massaging my lean belly with her greedy fingers. With me sat on her knee, she would embrace me tightly and hug me to her sparse breast—sucking in a hasty breath between her clenched teeth. On such days, a tear would escape from her eye and her slight frame tremble. Invariably, after this show of emotion, she kiss-kissed my ears and eyes, whispering absurdities while her too insistent hands goosed my flesh. Under such devotion, I would become rigid with excitement and would want, desperately, to urinate into her lap. That this never occurred was more luck than anything and also because, reminded of her "condition" by the elders, Aunt Estrild would set me down reluctantly, pat my bottom and tell me to run along. "There's my pet." At such moments, I could have bitten her breast. It wasn't until I deliberately laid my hand on her swelling stomach that she slapped me. Told she was expecting a baby and therefore inclined to be unpredictable, I nevertheless hoped the baby she was carrying would use its nails and scratch the inside of her belly. I said as much. For my indiscretion, my mother knocked me down with a blow round the head; for that and for many other smacks, I never forgave her. So, whilst other children of my age were making unreasonable demands and being thoroughly spoilt by doting parents, I was wandering the lonely house learning to discipline myself in the face of unreasonableness, to avoid contact with elders whenever possible and contenting myself with the briefest of capricious embraces in preparation for a whole life to be spent in a barren wilderness sustained only by sipping at occasional oases of affection which, as in deserts, stand in time and distance a very long way apart.

At other times my progress through the house might be terminated when, upon entering a room, I disturbed a dozing relative who, with grunts and snuffles, would rouse from the depths of an armchair and, refreshed after his catnap, become attentive, retrospective and thoroughly boring while he meandered through his life's history in which an incomprehensible subtlety and idiosyncratic concern for the trivial made me rigid with boredom so that I sat yawning, hypnotized by the monotonous drone. In such vacuums, I cannot recall a single thought ever entering my head but I was always brought back to cold reality by being scolded severely for my rude inattentiveness and reminded of my responsibility as the only surviving heir. This puzzled me for, dressed as a girl but not feeling I was of a particular gender, I could not understand why the elders always picked on me when my sister was that much older. I sensed during these harangues that I was despised—why I don't know, for I was not of an age when I could order my own destiny, but their disdain did not compare with my contempt for the heritage of a name which no one outside the grandeur of our house wished to have perpetuated if, that is, they could recall our illustrious name. For, the very elders who beseeched me to live up to the nobility of our past were the very same who outlined our decline and who went to great lengths to detail the contempt the peasants felt for us.

On other days when I set off, steeled with resolution to count the rooms, I might unexpectedly find myself in a room full of motionless adults, dotted about and isolated from each other in what I took to be the limp and introspective attitudes of mourners. On such occasions, retreat was essential but if an overheard phrase or remark arrested my attention, I would stand listening or, by sneaking into the room and hugging the walls closer than my shadow, become an unobserved witness to the most appalling of family intimacies which were quite inappropriate for the ears of a young, impressionable child who understood not a word but who, nevertheless, was moved by the drama to take sides and unwittingly share the vilification of a member of the family under attack who was being forced into the most shameful of confessions by a majority composed of old, head-shaking, cane-thumping adults who, like crows, squatted round their victim pecking at the rawness until, exposed and defenceless, the re-cusant fled weeping from the room, or, broken, was left to the isolation of an overwhelming humiliation in a room empty of all but me, hidden beneath a table, quaking from head to toe.

These, and many other diversions, prevented me from counting the rooms. After twenty years, I still do not know how many there are. I once heard my grandmother, Nanna Axell, say there were eighty-two. Certainly there are no fewer.

"Anything in the newspaper today, Knut?"
"I am not allowed to read it, Uncle."
"What did you say?"
"My mother has forbidden me to read the newspaper."
"Not allowed?"
"Yes."

It was a small, belittling annoyance at which I pretended concern by an avid curiosity in the paper whenever my mother chanced to pick it up, which was very seldom because she detested both politics and crime but tolerated its presence in the house on account of the daily court circular which was printed in it. Or, when one of my many relations sat reading it and my mother was present in the room, sewing or, as was more often the case, just sitting, gazing out of the window and giving expression to her languorous nature by her relaxed immobility and the occasional sigh of a person bored with life and the possibility that death might only be the beginning, at such times I would lean forward in my chair if a relative or guest sat opposite to me reading the paper and scrutinise the headlines I could focus upon. If this did not attract my mother's attention, I would sink down onto my hands and knees and, with all the cunning and skill of a stalking cat, slowly crawl towards the opened paper. Stealth was essential for I did not want my mother to think I was trying to attract her attention, yet my actions had to be such that they would not go unnoticed, for there was little fun in kneeling before a newspaper in which not one single word held my interest. With studied clumsiness, in order to be discovered doing what I was forbidden, I would chance to kick a table leg or break a pencil against the carpet which, in the silence, sounded like the sharp crack of a hunting rifle. Discovered, I saw my mother's watchfulness expressed in extreme annoyance and the snapped command to behave myself. I would pretend annoyance and bounce back onto my chair feigning the sulkiness and frustration of a spoilt child.

"As a boy, I found more pleasure in the things I was expressly forbidden to do than in all the permitted pastimes which boys indulge in."

"You have been round the world twice, Uncle Mungo."

"I have lived through two wars."

"Tell me about war, Uncle."

"Have you seen my spectacles?"

"You are sitting on them."

"What?"

"Behind you. On the chair."

"Thank you. Ah, good, they're not broken. You are a very perceptive lad."

"Everyone knows there is no glass in your spectacles."

"I am deaf."

"I know. It tires Mother to speak to you. She said so."

"It's becoming worse. That's why I wear these spectacles."

"But you don't need to hear to read; do you?"

"The organs of sight and sound are closely linked, young lad. Have you never seen Roderick open his mouth whenever he puts his monocle to his eye? Mmm? Or a person drop their jaw to stare? It's the same with these spectacles. They improve my hearing. It stands to reason. Now. Take this newspaper."

"I'm forbidden, Uncle."

"Very well. Don't. I shall read it to you. Or parts of it. But I should warn you, it's a paper I do not care for and, as a radical, think it fit only to be used to light domestic fires. Now, where's that editorial?"

"Tell me about war, Uncle."

"Not today. Today we begin your education. And God knows, it is about time someone took an interest in it."

"I'm to have a tutor."

"First I shall read and then we will discuss." Uncle Mungo sniffed, cleared his throat, beat out the wrinkles in the newspaper and settled his spectacles. Had I been more attentive to Mungo in those early years, I might have had the courage to flee. As it turned out, it was my sister who benefited from his surplus of affection, not I.

Winter was that time of year when my ageing relatives remained in their rooms, snug in bed, or, well-wrapped about by ancient rugs and smelling of urine, sat huddled up against the fire, slowly scorching. The delicate net curtains no longer billowed into gossamer crinolines, ballooning and expiring with puckish respiration, but hung limp and stagnant and the once bobbing tassels which danced an erratic jig at their edge remained strung in a dead straight line like a row of white corpses. The more active of the elders would congregate in the smallest of the drawing rooms. Called the pine room because of the honey-coloured panelling, it had a mellow atmosphere and was the only room downstairs with an open fire-place. Unfortunately the elders created an unbreathable fug when they crowded into the pine room to play chess, read, discuss or merely to sit about. More often than not, they quarrelled. If the protagonist did not storm out of the room in a temper but remained and sulked, the others wore thunderous frowns and sat in an impregnable silence. This would last for several weeks and the only sounds in the room would be an occa-sional cough, a hand-clapped yawn, the quiet purr of the patience cards being shuffled or the crackle of a glued book spine being broken slowly open. The alienated, if he or she chose to remain, retaliated by the unne-cessary rattling of the chess pieces when they were returned to the empty box or by the deliberate counting aloud of the number of stitches in her knitting, or some other childish irritation, such as the crumpling and straightening out of the newspaper which, in the quietened room, soun-ded like the destructive crackle of a log fire. Some gestures of defiance were so deliberate as to be offensive, as when my Uncle Godric, a master of such effrontery, would deliberately heap the blazing fire with coal so that the bright flames were smothered and the fire went cold and smoked. This done, he would leave the room and the more active of the remaining males would be forced to use the tongs and poker to restore the flames. And suddenly, everyone would be talking loudly, while Uncle Godric, a military man and a supreme tactician, would stalk, with ramrod back, up to his room, well satisfied by the confusion he had caused in the enemy camp below.

Winter was also that time of year when, because of my weak chest, I was forbidden to go outside. In many ways I was thankful, not only because my chilblains would split and become unbearably irritable when I returned to the heat of the house, but more especially because I was frightened of touching iron; having overheard Uncle Godric relate how a sick peasant girl had caught hold of a railing outside his town house to steady herself and, because it was many degrees below zero, the unfortunate girl had lost the skin of her palm, leaving it stuck to the railing when she had snatched her hand away. He had also begun to relate another tale about some troops under his command who had been ordered to drag a cannon across a frozen lake and of one damn fool of a soldier who had sat astride the muzzle but, seeing Aunt Beclier frown disapprovingly and, with a sidelong glance, indicate my presence, never finished the tale but shook his head from side to side, muttering, "It was unbelievable; unbelievable". But I had heard sufficient and being impressionable, and nervous to the point of timidity, it was understandable that during the winters which followed, when there was a sudden but brief change in the weather and I was forced for the sake of my lungs to go for a walk and fill them with the stinging, curative air, I insisted upon keeping my hands thrust deep into my pockets and prudently circumnavigated any metal which might be iron. So it was that when my mother, thinking me too weak to walk, insisted upon my riding in a pony and trap instead of the usual brisk turn about the house on foot, it led to the bizarre spectacle of a boy aged nearly ten, rigid with fear, being lifted bodily by a girl not much older than himself, into the back of a pony and trap. The reason for my fear was simple. The cart had iron guardrails round the sides and front as well as iron handles to help one mount the cart. It speaks well of Gudrun that on these occasions she never questioned nor thought my behaviour odd; neither did she scold me while she tucked the rugs about me nor raise her hand in anger. It was this quality of Gudrun's, of accepting me as I was, which drew me to her and gave me the necessary courage to struggle against the temptation of embracing death as an alternative to living out my wretchedness alone.

At the onset of my winter cough, my mother would make her rare but longed-for gesture of reconciliation and expressed what I hoped was love, by touching me. When I was naked and stood in front of her, she would bind a scratchy lint, thick with embrocation, onto my chest. While she passed the bandage round my hooped and starving ribs, I would stand with my eyes tight closed lest the fumes of the liniment scorched my eye-balls. When she had done, she would dress me in twice the number of underclothes I normally wore, then, picked up and sat on her knee, I was forced to drink down a thick syrup. Sweet and not unlike burnt toffee to which had been added the sharp tang of a citrus fruit, the mixture flamed my throat, making me gasp and cough more violently than before. My mother, stubborn in her belief that the concoction could only be beneficial, would insist upon dosing me with more of the wretched physic; forcing it between my compressed lips until my coughing ceased. If I did not vomit, the rack in my chest eventually subsided and my lungs became strangely calm and cool. This, I later learnt, was because the syrup contained chloroform which anaesthetised the nerve endings in my throat. When my mother was satisfied the emollient was easing the congestion, she would put me down with the order not to run about the house without my overcoat and to wear my woollen gloves. To protect my chilblains, she rubbed my fingers with a brown grease which stank and my woollen gloves became impregnated with the stuff, so much so, I left greasy marks on everything I touched. Scolded, I walked about like a zombie with my hands hanging by my side and having to kick a door to get someone to open it for me. Unfortunately, the daily administrations of the syrup, whether I coughed or not, made me listless and Mother, thinking I was about to succumb despite her efforts, would clasp me to her as if I was about to die. Sat in a chair, she would rock backwards and forwards, clutching me and moaning, "Poor child; poor child". Smothered by her sudden affection—although I was too young to know it was brought on by a feeling of guilt and that she was really easing her own conscience—I took advantage of her rare embrace whilst being slowly suffocated against her resilient bosom. Torn between a desire to absorb and enjoy the warmth of her embrace or be smothered, I chose the latter and endured the suffocation. But an instinctive desire to survive, to breathe, to fill my little lungs with the air I so desperately needed, would eventually force me to struggle against her compression. This was taken by my mother to be indicative of my wilful ungratefulness and I was hastily set down while, barely concealing her anger, she stood up and, with the palm of her hand, brushed away the invisible dust of contact I had left clinging to her skirts. It was a gesture I was to come to know very well. The most poignant time was when Gudrun, whom my mother was dismissing, took hold of my mother's arm, imploring her to reconsider her sudden decision. My mother would have none of it and Gudrun, shouting abuse, was pulled away from her. The only movement my mother made was to wipe clean her sleeve where Gudrun had taken hold. So, when I was set down, Mother, made irritable and the gamut of her affection exhausted by me, her ungrateful brat, relinquished me to the tender care of Gudrun to do what she could with me after first being instructed not to give in to my tantrums and to notify her immediately I looked like having a relapse.

Such a traumatic deterioration never occurred. Whereas I believed it was my determination to live, to outwit my mother, to spoil her pleasure of weeping tears into my small, satin-lined coffin, and took the necessary, extra precaution of going into dark, out-of-the-way corners to cough and spit into my handkerchiefs which, like sandwiches cut for a picnic, stood in piles upon my dresser, in all probability it was Gudrun's common sense which prevented a relapse and saved me from death. From the moment I was put into her care, my body was divested of all unnecessary undergarments, the chest protector removed and burnt and my mother's sovereign remedy left to deteriorate in the bottle and crust the friable cork stopper. Dragged from cupboards, where I went to conceal a momentary breathlessness, I was encouraged to run about the house without my overcoat, allowed to discard my woollen gloves, the heat and tickle of which tortured my fingers, and able to choose whether I stayed close to the stoves or not—all contributed to my partial recovery and underlined Gudrun's sense. Even so, I sometimes had to take to my bed and Doctor Borg was sent for. Dutifully he listened to my wheezing chest; tapping it with his hard, old knuckles while I gazed up his nostrils, troubled by the hairs which grew inside, imagining I was gazing into the burrows of a prickly hedgehog. Once when he was leaning over me, a gold ball which was suspended on his watch chain, broke open and fell into the form of a cross. Questioned, he quickly manipulated the segments to reform the ball which mysteriously held its shape and then slipped it back into his vest pocket. After his visits, during which my mother was never present, Gudrun, if Borg prescribed a pill or, as was more often the case, a bottle of tonic and a loathsome inhalant, would dutifully administer it to me until it was all used up and throw away the bottle without informing my mother that it was finished.

During these days and nights when I was ordered to keep to my bed, Gudrun became my little mother, teaching me the rudiments of reading and writing, which she herself had learnt from her grandmother but had never found any use for, and, but much more important, bestowing upon me the mysteries of affection.

And so a winter passed.

"If you insist upon playing in the conservatory, why don't you make yourself useful and pick off the dead leaves."

"As you wish."

A bucketful would satisfy her vindictiveness and be proof of my willingness to labour.

"It is not my wish."

"Then I will not do it."

"Don't be churlish, Knut!"

In my white apron, I felt particularly vulnerable.

"Shall I pick off the dead leaves?"

"Do what you like, but don't come whimpering to me if Gardol cuffs your ears. It's time you learnt self-discipline is achieved by denial; not indulgence."

I waited for her to elaborate or, as I hoped, explain what might be accomplished by disciplined indulgence; but she did not, so I went through, into the conservatory; passing very close to her skirts which she snatched away.

Closing the glass doors, I stood in the conservatory and looked back into the golden drawing room. My mother, still holding the bunched fold of her skirts, was turned towards me. I watched her mouth open and close, saw her head nod and shake, her eyebrows rise then bunch into a frown while she underlined her aggressiveness with a finger stabbed in my direction; but not a word did I hear. With her head on one side, she waited for my reply. Knowing my mother did not like to be crossed, I nodded. This seemed to satisfy her because she turned her back on me and swept out of the room. Left on my own, I turned to pick the yellowing leaves from the exhausted plants.

As an afterthought, but with imagination, the conservatory had been attached to the house and, like a natural ivy which twines about an old oak—one seemingly dependent upon the other, the house and the conservatory could not be imagined apart. Cast-iron pillars allowed for a large curving span, glass domes and tall, arched doorways which led out onto one of the terraces. I was told, probably by Uncle Mungo, that only in England did other, comparable, conservatories exist. It not only reflected and complemented the overall design of the ancient house and added to its dignity, but also brought into the golden drawing room, the leaves and abundant growth of the potted plants more effectively than the lawns, lake and mausoleum which the ballroom windows were purposely designed to embrace; even though the avenue of trees, planted to reinforce a false perspective, were one of the wonders of the district.

My Uncle Godric called the conservatory, "that damned glass house", and always added, "Why your father had to go to all that expense to put himself on view, I'll never know. And him a military man, too." Presumably, Uncle Godric, a colonel to whom every aspect of life was approached with the foresight of a gimlet-eyed, military strategist, deemed so much glass a hazard and liable to shatter and fragment with the first exploding enemy shell aimed towards our house. For a man who had lived most of his life dressed in military uniform but who had never had to face an enemy except across a sand table in theoretical exercises, his eccentricity was a subtle combination of frustration and grand illusion; the same marrying of faults which makes turkey-cocks of successful politicians. However, annoying as my uncle's attitude was towards my father, his veiled hints as to why he had caused the conservatory to be built, but which my uncle would not reveal, were irritable to a questioning child. With his hands behind his English tweed jacket, making him strangely foreign, his shoulders squared and the strong Strobl chin thrust out, he would say, "I warned them. I said he was unpredictable. Do you think they listened to me? No. You exaggerate, Godric, they said. Well, young man, I was right; wasn't I? Even before they puttied in the first pane of glass, I knew." I asked him to elaborate, but he cleared his throat and muttered, "Time enough before you shoulder responsibilities," and marched up and down, like a soldier on sentry duty, tight-lipped and guarding his secret. Perhaps I came to distrust him when, later, he knocked out his pipe on the heel of his riding-boot and, seemingly contradicting his knowledgeableness, said, "Of all the things your father could have built, he chose to build a glass house. Why?" and he clenched the stem of his old pipe between his yellowing teeth and, head erect, dismissed himself and marched from the room; arms swinging.

Whenever Uncle Godric's actions struck me as comical or pompous, I could never raise a conspiratorial smile in my Uncle Mungo who, on these occasions, would lower his eyes as if embarrassed, or if, with the callousness of youth, I attempted to deride Uncle Godric's ludicrous manner and dared mimic his walk, he would instantly, and with great dignity, pinch out my arrogance with as few unkind words as possible before walking from the room and closing the door quietly behind him. Given time and the solitude to reflect upon my rudeness, I still could not fathom Uncle Godric's contempt for my father's "glass house". It wasn't until I was much older, perhaps in my twenties, I was told by my sister that our father had the misfortune to be labelled a "ladies' man" and most of his amorous misadventures took place in the conservatory where, visible for all to see, he was compromised more than once. In the light of an incident which occurred shortly before his death, my sister and I reasoned Father was incapable of such behaviour, especially such blatant conduct, for the poor man suffered, to an unusual degree, the strictures of guilt and therefore would have been inhibited in a boudoir not to mention the exposed interior of the "glass house".

There were other "glass houses"—greenhouses—in the grounds. They had been built for the express purpose of growing out-of-season blooms to decorate the rooms or to house the tender bedding plants. These greenhouses were now totally derelict. The panes were broken and green with algae. The interiors bulged with weeds which sprouted, escaping and curling through the many gaps and holes in the leaning, unsafe frames and lopsided doors. One greenhouse, in which several vines had once grown, though jungled and left unpruned, did, only very occasionally, produce grapes which, though not fully ripe because the heating system had corroded and the furnace doors rusted solid, were edible but hard, with undeveloped pips and tasting bitter. Nevertheless, they were very tempting to a small boy. It was the one greenhouse I had the courage to enter and steal the fruit which, like the hard pears and inedible apples, my act of bravery made sweet when, hidden, I crouched in the ruins, a munching, happy savage whose inexplicable bellyache was thought to be colic and further evidence of general weakness.

The conservatory however, though neglected, had a certain ruinous charm. It was tended by my mother, but infrequently and only in spring when, under the influence of some mysterious urge, she would draw on her gardening gloves and, armed with a trowel, secateurs and a small watering can, tend the plants expressing surprise, not for the savagery of the blooms but that the plants had survived another year—seemingly forgetting that Gardol, when time allowed, loosened the earth and fed them water. But my mother grew quickly bored and the gloves were discarded, the earth left to dry on the trowel, the secateurs to rust in an out-of-the-way place whilst a spider, quick to seize the opportunity, illogically spun his web over the spout of the watering can. So, while Gardol, who had other, more important things to attend to, busied himself elsewhere, roots swelled and burst their confining pots to meander about the tiled floor seeking the darkness of the cracks and the damp earth below. Those plants lucky enough to have been planted directly into the islands of exposed earth flourished but, unpruned, destroyed themselves; flattening against the glass to be burnt in the summer, frozen in the winter or turning mouldy in the stagnant ground. Disease, I should think, was the only happily prolific and self-perpetuating growth which survived in the conservatory. And myself.

Warm in summer, the conservatory dripped from the rusting spans a condensation which smelt of green earth; reminding me of the liquidity and dankness of an old aquarium and filling the conservatory with a syncopated sound as it splashed onto the leaves and tiled floor. Why it did this, when the plants went unwatered, I did not understand, knowing nothing of the chemistry of plants. However, I enjoyed the humid atmosphere and it induced in me not only languidness, but an acute, sexual excitement.

This latter feeling and the first occasion—although I was well into my teens—when subjective fantasy superseded the then necessarily prolonged, unthinking agitation, to become a reckless and quickening image I used whilst crouched amongst the greenery, had its origin one afternoon, quite by chance, after Gudrun and I had walked to and fro amongst the forest of plants for some quite considerable time. I chanced to remark upon the humid atmosphere, adding that it was having a most disturbing effect upon me. "Don't you find it so, Gudrun? Aren't you in a sweat because of it?"

Gudrun regarded me with raised eyebrows while her pink tongue went searching and licking off the beads of perspiration glinting on her upper lip. "More than you might suppose, Knut." And she sat down heavily on the painted, white iron bench. "Much more."

To my surprise, she thrust out her legs in an undignified manner and hiked her skirt up over her knees. Unbuttoning three buttons on her blouse, she leaned back, broke a large green leaf off a monstera plant beside her and began farming herself vigorously. "It is such an atmosphere which gives Latins their temperament."

I said I knew nothing of that.

"The heat makes them indolent. You cannot feel voluptuous when your teeth chatter and your skin is rough with goosepimples. No. And you can bet it wasn't the Latins who invented cold linoleum."

"They provide us with a considerable quantity of oil."

I was walking away from her confused by her provocative pose and the necessity of continuing a normal conversation. At the back of my mind was the fact that linoleum had something in common with linseed oil.

"What's that got to do with it?" There was a rustling behind me. "I was talking of the sun. And the heat. This *glorious* heat."

"It certainly opens the pores." And I turned to walk back.

Lying along the bench, Gudrun, still fanning herself, lay with her knees drawn up. I saw between her legs—or rather I thought I saw—so many things within the dappled shadows beneath the hang of her skirt, that I quickly turned round, only to come face to face with the large shrub which had blocked my path originally. Gudrun, who had been watching me closely, gave a whoop of delight.

In panic, I made for the door leading down and out onto the lawn, but before I had succeeded in sliding the rusted bolt, she was by my side, breathing heavily and gripping my arm.

"Let go of me!"

"You're blushing."

"What if I am?"

A strong, acrid smell emanated from her and its pungency overlaid the soft green ozone of the conservatory. I was disturbed and not a little ashamed to discover that such a primitive odour, having its origin within the very pores and folds of her flesh, could, or should, hold out the promise of excitement. It did and I swallowed down an Adam's apple which had grown lumpy and unmanageable.

Gudrun moistened her lips. "Well?" She stood waiting, her head laid to one side and imperceptibly pressing closer. "It's not as if we were strangers."

I did not understand the sense off her remark but suspected the threat it implied.

The confirmation came when she slid her hand down and said, "In the past you never hid it from me."

In another desperate attempt to slide the bolt while she feverishly grappled with my clothing, the whole contraption came away in my hand and the glass door fell outwards, shattering.

We both ran in opposite directions; she to her room, I in circles until I came across Gardol and, having become calmer, explained untruthfully how the conservatory door came to be broken and would he fix it.

In retrospect, I was perhaps foolish not to allow myself to have been seduced by Gudrun who, unknown to me at the time, was pregnant, for she may have been able to divert the introversion of my sexuality—and, freed, my life been different. As it was, she was dismissed soon after when her condition became more apparent. Although no one was told who fathered the child, nor could it be wrung from her, my mother believed it was I, having long suspected Gudrun of seducing her son, if not in the bathroom, then certainly in the conservatory.

The only other female I used regularly to meet and talk with in the conservatory was my sister, but she had a happy knack of sublimating my desire into an energy of a different nature—drawing.

Somewhere or other, I had read that Da Vinci and other painters, when looking for a suitable landscape to include as background to their paintings, rather than return from the countryside with their sketchbooks filled with drawings, would bring back clods of earth, misshapen stones and lumps of rock and, seated in their studios with their noses pressed to these finds, see, as would an ant, landscapes of fantastic magnitude which they would painstakingly transpose to their finished paintings. That this is true, I have no doubt, if the eerie and unearthly quality of some early landscapes are to be explained.

So it was I, too, encouraged by my sister, and in my modest way, attempted to follow their example. Lying flat on my stomach with an eye pressed close to the rim of a pot, I journeyed in my imagination through the impenetrable jungle of lily stalks recording on my pad the fantastic landscapes and peopling them with dwarfs. My sister thought them very good. I was pleased to receive her praise but could not agree with her evaluation. To me, they were another way of passing time, and it was time which hung so heavily in that oppressive house.

Which is perhaps why I was glad to escape occasionally into the conservatory, for there, not only did I come to learn about nature and there stand in awe of it—unlike when I was dragged protesting on the innumerable walks about the house to clear my lungs—but I found happiness in my imagination.

It was in the conservatory I had my first bright orgasm, crouched amongst the greenery and journeying—toiling would be more apt—into Gudrun's imagined labyrinth in search of God knows what.

"**W**e shall have a birthday party."

"You're joking, Onan."

"No."

"But the children have never celebrated their birthdays."

"Then it's time we set a precedent."

"Knut is too young to sit down with the elders. Besides, they wouldn't tolerate a child at table."

My father and mother argued across my head. I was four; soon to be five.

"The Bruckstroems have bred like rabbits. The Soederbloms also. Hebbel has a son. Hofmannsthaal, two. You could also invite the Jungstillings' brats."

Apart from my sister, I had never seen another child. I knew there was a young girl in the kitchens but couldn't be sure I had glimpsed her or whether it was my sister's description of her long blonde hair which made me think I had. In those early days, the kitchens were out of bounds to me and likewise, the main body of the house to this blonde kitchen girl.

"But no mother in her right senses is going to allow her child to cross the valley in such deep snow."

"You will nevertheless send invitations."

"They'll think us mad. And what coachman is going to risk his horse when he knows there are drifts deep enough to bury them both?"

"It may have packed down by then."

"I'm told the sea is frozen over."

"All the more reason why the birthday should be turned into an occasion."

"I'm not having the house become a bedlam with hordes of screaming children. It will upset the elders."

"Then we will set aside the gymnasium for the party."

"Don't be so ridiculous."

"Madlin, whether you like it or not, we—are—going—to—have—a—party—to—celebrate—Knut's—birthday."

"Very well. If it is your wish. But the invitations will be in your name. Everyone shall know it is you, not I, who proposes to celebrate this midwinter madness."

The gymnasium, a very long, low-ceilinged room, was our playroom. The windows, which ran along one side, were a series of small, arched fanlights through which only the sky could be seen. Bleak and bare, the room had a curious, hollow echo which, in the days when the room was used for vaulting, must have vibrated with the sudden grunts of leapfrogging men exercising their bodies or improving their skills with the sabres and foils which still stood in the racks of a closed cupboard at the far end of the room. Monastic in its uncompromising bleakness, the room had the chill atmosphere of a catacomb in which an esoteric sect met to perform a manly ritual of bodily discipline, equating a godly morality with physical exhaustion. Unlike the library, which smelt of leather and pepper, or the gun room, which reeked of graphite and oil, our playroom had an odour of stale sweat which tinged the air with the pungency of chrysanthemums. There was ample space for my sister and me to run about in if we cared to and our shrieks and shouts could not impinge upon the still, quiet world of the adults up above us, so the room was eminently suitable for high-spirited children. But what had not been taken into account was that the room was ridiculously large for two small children and that it overwhelmed and dampened any enthusiasm we might have had. Lit by a single lamp throughout the winter months, as cold as the house's one, icy cellar, it was like a subterranean barrack room; was joyless and grim. Added to this was the indignity of being given toys to play with which had belonged to our father's father's children. Broken, dull with use, covered by unfamiliar scratches and the indentations of dead cousins' tiny teeth and the musty books scribbled over with unidentifiable graffiti, these toys were an affront. Isolated in our corner, my sister and I, with our little second-hand possessions, tried to amuse ourselves as best we could during the unending dark days of winter. What also kept us isolated in our corner was that any sudden shout of glee went skimming over the long, highly-polished plank flooring and returned from the darkness of the other, unexplored end, doubled in magnitude and with the hollow timbre of a black-tongued ogre who must surely have been squatting there, ogling us with his cluster of gooseberry eyes.

"You can help me blow up the balloons, Knut."

While my father, for once exuberant and his face flushed, blew the balloons up to bursting, I coughed my lungs into a bright red balloon which became wet and slippery with my spittle but stayed as limp and crinkled as a turkey's wattle.

A table had been set in the middle of the gymnasium, covered with a white tablecloth and a number of chairs placed round about. Cutlery laid and plates arranged, but as yet, no food. Set in the middle of the table were candelabra, the candles of which, though brightening the room, seemed to darken the corners; filling them with trembling shadows.

My sister, who was having more success with her balloon, suddenly took the wet nipple end out of her mouth and, with widening eyes, looked over my head into the shadows beyond.

Paler than a ghost, her unseen feet moving beneath a long white muslin party dress, came a bleached apparition with blonde hair, white-faced and unsmiling. Behind her, a woman of great bulk dressed in black, prodding the green-eyed apparition forward. While they moved towards us as silently as the flame of a burning candle, my sister tugged at my father's sleeve. Tying off a balloon, he turned and greeted the unlikely couple.

"Ah, Helga. Thank you."

The large woman went limp at the knees, straightened and withdrew silently into the darkness.

The pale child walked uncertainly towards me, approached too closely and, giving a clumsy curtsy, was forced to put out her hand to steady herself. Although she only held onto my satin blouse for a moment, I could feel a nervous tremble communicating itself to me through the fluttering material.

"Karen is your guest Knut. Your only one, I'm afraid."

My sister stared when Karen handed me a polished apple and, piqued, rudely turned her back and began chattering wildly to my father about anything and everything which entered her head. I do not think my father could have been paying much attention otherwise he would have scolded her for talking nonsense. Instead, with one finger, he tipped a balloon towards me.

Excited and discovering for the very first time the joy of patting a balloon which, unlike a ball, did not go rolling away demanding to be fetched, but remained inexplicably suspended, reluctant to be forcibly propelled in any one particular direction, apple lay forgotten on the floor at the feet of a silent, motionless I jumped and ran beneath it, showing while the present of an Karen.

Short of breath I stopped and, while the balloon floated to the floor, I turned towards Karen. For some reason, perhaps a splinter in the floor, when the balloon settled, it burst. Surprised myself, I saw Karen give a start and, fear enlarging her pale green eyes, glance nervously towards my father. Surprisingly, he laughed and, although my sister, who sat cross-legged on the floor with her back towards me, protested, my father tipped another balloon towards me. Overjoyed, I scooped it up and tapped it towards Karen to catch. The balloon bounced on her nose and slowly fell to the floor. She made no attempt to catch it or show that she wanted to play with me. Filled with contempt for this silent, skinny girl, I snatched the balloon from near her feet and, in a mad gallop, went biffing and walloping it up to the ceiling, taking not the slightest notice of my sister's warning that it would burst.

My sister's behaviour that afternoon was bewildering and curious. Generally passive, quiet, endearing and the one person whose emotional stability I could rely upon, even when she withdrew into herself and would not be roused, she had become, in the space of a few minutes, unnecessarily belligerent, talkative and spitefully assertive. It was as if she was making a determined effort to alienate me, to impress Father with her precociousness and Karen with her superiority. Because I was so young, I imagined she was being vindictive and tried hard to think back to what I had done or said which had been responsible for her dramatic change. At the back of my mind I feared that coupled with the loss of my mother's love and my father's uncertain regard, Katya's withdrawal of affection would isolate me in a dark world I already found intolerable. Wide-eyed and lost in thought, I stood squeaking the glutinous balloon with my sticky fingertips.

"Stop it, Knut! You'll burst it! Idiot."

At the very moment my sister spoke, the balloon my father had half-blown up left his lips and, with a "fluppering" sound, breezed erratically round the room. My sister and I went into hysterics of laughter whilst my father, a surprised look upon his face which had turned the colour of the purple balloon, slowly sank onto his knees and keeled over onto his side, emitting from his lips the hiss of escaping air in mimicry of the expiring balloon.

My sister ran from the room shouting at the top of her voice for Mother to come quickly.

Karen, not having been instructed how to behave in such circumstances, remained rooted to the spot whilst I ran to my father with a balloon the colour of raspberries for him to blow up and send winding about the room. But he was as black as an Indian and the balloon wouldn't stay between his wet lips.

Pulled away by my mother, I was taken upstairs, past curious relatives hastening to the gymnasium, where my last impression was of Karen, her spindly arms hanging by her sides, dressed in her thin muslin shroud; perfectly motionless; dwarfed by the size of the room and half-engulfed by shadows.

I did not understand that my father was dead but only that I was not to have a party. At this I burst into tears and was promptly slapped by my sister. Stunned, I sat on a bed for what seemed like an age while my sister, coldly silent, lay unmoving, flopped out in an armchair.

Long past our bedtime, unfed and our stomachs rumbling, we grew restless and disturbed by the constant passage and murmurings of people on the other side of the door. Their voices raised, they passed and re-passed the closed door until, unable to restrain herself, my sister, probably understanding more of what was going on than I, rushed to the door and out into the passage. Meekly, I followed.

Crowded in the passage were my relatives, included those who normally kept to their rooms, propped up on sticks with blankets about their shoulders and trembling from head to foot with rage. Amassed against my mother and sister they were trying to wrest a pair of my father's trousers from their grasp. My mother's arms were full of clothes, amongst which I caught a glimpse of my father's brilliant red dress uniform. I went to their aid, only to be pulled away. Whereupon my mother struck out so that I too became part of the tug of war. Distressed, uncomprehending—a disturbing but strong bond made me cling blindly to my mother's skirts in a determination to identify myself. So too my sister, and for the first and perhaps only time in our life, experienced the mysterious unification of a family bond. Impressed, but shaking their heads, the elders retreated; muttering and shaming us and filling me in particular with a foreboding of what was yet to come when daylight illuminated the satanic bedlam being played out on a precipice edged with banisters.

They regrouped outside their rooms and my sister and I, our arms piled high with Father's clothes ran the gauntlet of their tongues and grasping hands whilst my mother, carrying most, guided us out into the night air, towards the stables where a huge bonfire had been lit on the snow-covered yard.

So the night passed, journeying from my father's rooms to the bonfire and returning empty-handed. I would be given his portrait to throw onto the flames, gloves, his polished army belts, riding-boots, anything and everything which had once belonged to him, including shaving brushes and an odd sock. What I was doing, I did not know, but thought this is how it was. This was part of what was termed death. It was ritual which had to be gone through, a duty which I, as my father's daughter, was beholden to undertake; unquestioningly.

"Lindehost says all my front teeth must come out."

"What has it got to do with him?"

"He is a dentist."

"Is he? Then the man must be short of money if he suggested such a ridiculous thing."

"They say he is the best dentist in the district."

"'They'? Who are 'they'? And since when have we taken notice of what 'they' say?"

Nanna Axell, her frail bones thinly covered with a tissue of wrinkled skin, was as awesome as an Egyptian mummy exposed to the sunlight after a thousand years of incarceration. Imperious, she commanded authority and I went in awe of her because I thought she possessed the majesty of a Nile queen at the pinnacle of her gynarchy. To others, she may have resembled chopped firewood loosely bundled into a faded armchair and, like dried tinder, liable to spark and flame if the flint edge of reason was struck against the blunt stone of her cantankerousness. But to me she was Empress of all time, and absolute.

"Lindehost is an upstart. 'They' forget all too quickly that he once used to be a horse doctor and passed his time filing teeth and binding cannons. But if you must have your teeth extracted, although I cannot believe you do, consult Borg. He pulls teeth."

"Borg is old-fashioned. Besides, he refuses to administer gas."

"Gas! You'd allow Lindehost to render you insensible? A man whose reputation is questionable. Who is not qualified, and who has been divorced. I am shocked by your suggestion, Madlin."

"But if my health is not to suffer, my teeth must come out."

It pleased me when my mother and Nanna Axell wrangled. I hoped that my mother, whose every remark seemed calculated to draw a sob from my scarred breast, suffered equal torments when confronted by my intolerant grandmother. It pleased me even more to think that my mother might suffer pain if her teeth were not pulled.

Lying on my stomach, I began to draw a crocodile with a grinning mouth chock-full of gnashing teeth.

"I have had only one tooth drawn in the whole of my life. And has my health suffered? No."

"But Lindehost says . . ."

"Lindehost? Lindehost? Why all this talk of Lindehost? In the last few months, I have heard nothing but Lindehost. Why this interest in him all of a sudden? Good-looking he may be, but the man is common. And thoroughly dishonest. Yes. A cheat. So don't let me hear you have become infatuated and fallen under the spell of his charm. He's not to be trusted. Besides, he smiles too often. Too readily. You would disgrace the name of Strobl by such an indiscretion. And remember, Madlin—you are still in mourning."

Blackening the crocodile's teeth made me suddenly realise that my mother, without her teeth, would be a horrible sight. I scribbled over my drawing and wished her immediately better. Although I disliked her, I was not insensitive to her pretty face or so evil as to wish it spoiled by a hollow mouth full of blackness.

"They move. Look."

To my horror, Mother put her tongue behind her top teeth and pressed them forward, wobbling them.

"It's your gums. There's nothing wrong with your teeth. The family has always had receding gums. It's hereditary. Some would say we are too inbred."

"Onan was not my cousin."

Nervously, and very tentatively, I ran my tongue over my teeth, testing them. They were firm. I bit hard and ground my teeth together. To my great relief, my teeth, for the moment, were safe.

"True. True. Even so . . . I believe if we had bred occasionally from the servants, our stock would have been far healthier."

"Nanna!"

"Don't pretend indignity, Madlin. This family have farmed out their bastards instead of welcoming them into the house. You know that. Even Onan . . ."

"Knut! Go up to your room at once."

"Yes, Mother." And I left, happily clicking my teeth together.

"It is time for your bath, Herr Knut."

"Coming, Gudrun. One moment."

The Knight should have had silver armour but I only had yellow. Gudrun bowed her head and crossed her hands in front of her—the virgin downcast before her paramour.

The Knight was stiff with pride; with courage. His lips curled back over his teeth revealing his contempt and noble savagery. Mounted on a thunderous horse the colour of polished chestnuts, he was cleaving the head of a green dragon streaked red with its own gore. Before his timely intervention, the dragon had been about to gnash and gobble up in his monstrous flaming jaws, Fräulein Gudrun who was chained to a leafless tree which grew unexpectedly on an outcrop of rock washed by the spume of curling waves. It was all very real.

"What's this?"

The Knight, the dragon and Fräulein Gudrun vanished; up and away, with the suddenness of a roller blind.

"Get up off the floor this instant!"

While I scrambled to my feet, I prayed my drawing would combust and the flames go licking up my mother's pale arms, devouring and turning them crisp like streaky bacon so that when she sneezed, her arms would fall off and the air be filled with the wisps of tissued ash. That the flames would leap and sizzle into her eyes, burning out the soft orbs until the sockets were blackened and empty and only smoke curled out of the bone-hard holes where her eyes had been. But the Devil always seemed to busy himself with adults whilst I was left in the company of simpering angels who allowed my mother, standing above me, to tear my drawing to shreds.

"What rubbish you fill your head with, child."

A few months earlier, I would have kicked her shins.

"It was to be a present for Gudrun!"

"I'm not having you waste your time crayoning mythological nonsense. If you must colour, there are plenty of heraldic shields in the library which you can copy. And you would be learning something at the same time. Now off with you."

That evening, I took no pleasure in having my body bathed, even though Gudrun was especially nice to me and later, in defiance of my mother's explicit instructions, smuggled a hard, scraped carrot dipped in yeast for me to suck and gnaw on in bed.

Bored with the familiar rooms, I would sometimes venture into the service passages. Barely two feet wide, they were used by Gardol whose task it was to heap the coals and rake the cinders from the stoves which heated the house. The boxes of the stoves faced into these narrow passages, making it unnecessary for him to enter the rooms which they were intended to heat. This arrangement also meant there was no dust to settle on the furniture and, but more important, no one was disturbed by his passing in and out of the rooms, a coal bucket in each hand and the rakes and poker clamped awkwardly under one arm. When one sat in any of the rooms, Gardol's activity in the service passage was reduced to an indistinct scratching, like that of a mouse behind the wainscoting. Similarly, from the confines of the service passages, and depending how close to the stoves people were sat, their conversations were indistinct. However, if the fire was out and the flue open, by lying on the floor with my ear to the fire box I could distinctly hear what was being said. Many times I listened to scandalous gossip which a discreet adult would not have dared to repeat in my presence.

Warm though these passages were, they had a peculiar chemical odour, not unlike marsh gas which combusts with a weird blue flame and which Gudrun had pointed out to me one evening when we were returning late from an afternoon excursion in the trap and passed a marsh where the phenomenon of the blue-winged fairies dancing on the surface of the low-lying bog was explained to me. However, after being told by Gardol, who did not mind me entering the passages as long as he was with me, that the gas in the passages was poisonous and if I stayed too long I might be overcome by the fumes and die, I became too frightened to venture more than a few yards into the darkness on my own. Once, I stood just inside with the door closed to see how long it would take before I came near to fainting. After half an hour, becoming bored, I left and walked into the bright light and fresh air with only the faintest of headaches. Mild as the effect had been, it was enough to prove that Gardol, always blunt but fair, had not been lying; exaggerating, perhaps.

Liking to be confined in secret places but no longer daring to brave the service lanes, I took to going behind the tapestries. My sister shared my enthusiasm for this hiding game but she was too impatient and her fidgeting always led to our discovery. However, there was one tapestry in particular which offered an ideal hiding place for one.

This tapestry covered an entire wall in the blue room. It conveniently hid a recessed door which, had it not been locked, would have opened into the adjoining room. Stood in this shallow recess behind the tapestry, I was invisible. Hidden, it was often more than I could do to prevent myself giggling when my mother, worried it seemed but more often irritated by my disappearance, would ask of someone in the room, "Have you seen Knut?" or, "Where is that wretch?"

One day, concealed and my chest exploding with compressed mirth, I heard my mother enter the room. I recognised her step and could tell she was pacing to and fro because I could hear her feet click over the uncovered boards and then fall silent while she crossed the carpet only to become audible again when she stepped off it before turning near the window. Having listened to her pace backwards and forwards for several minutes, I heard her say to herself, and with anguish, "The disgrace of it!"

Naturally, I was very surprised when Nanna Axell, whom I had not heard enter, reply, "Doctor Borg is discreet."

"I don't trust that man." And Mother began her pacing again. "He and Onan are far too close for two men who have nothing in common."

"All men have one thing in common—sex."

"Onan's impotent."

"Nevertheless, it binds them closer than an oath. Like domesticated boars, they are quite content to grunt at the same trough. Even Onan would choose a drinking companion from the village rather than grace your table with refined conversation if given the chance. Perhaps then he wouldn't be, as you say, so impotent."

"I am partly to blame, I suppose, though God knows he's got a reputation I find hard to equate with the man as he presents himself to me."

"Joachim was no exception."

"I've never heard you speak ill of Joachim before."

"Oh, he too was a pig. Never once did he rouse me but from all the gossip you would have thought him Don Juan. But he could be trusted. As can Doctor Borg. Men do not understand our morality but have a conscience which they satisfy by a comradely discretion. The swine-herd will guard the secret of his master's infidelity knowing that his own bestiality will not be made known outside the manly circle. I tell you, Borg can be trusted. It will be the servants who will talk."

"Gardol found him."

"He will say nothing."

"Who then?"

"Helga could have seen. Tetty if she was out gathering sticks."

"Then we are ruined."

"Nonsense."

"When it becomes known what he has done we will never command respect from anyone ever again. If anyone does pay us call, it will be to come and view us as curiosities."

I did not understand what was being discussed, only that the family, because of something my father had done, was struggling with a crisis. Feeling certain my heartbeats could be heard, I dared not swallow but stood in the warmth of my own breath praying they would leave so I could crawl from my hiding place before I suffocated.

"Why, oh, why did he do such a thing?"

"You don't know?"

"I always suspected he was mad. Now I know."

"If that's what you believe, shouldn't you have more regard for Knut's sanity?"

"You think it infectious? That lunacy can be passed from father to son?"

"I did not say I thought Onan mad."

"His action was not that of a sane man. He's mad, I tell you."

"Oh no. No. Get rid of Anna."

In the room, while I stood behind the tapestry in the darkness breathing dust up my nose, there was complete silence. I strained to listen, hoping they might have left, but my mother must have walked to the speaking-tube for I heard her ask Karen to let Anna Frott know that Madam Strobl wished to see her in the blue room.

I straightened my back and opened my mouth wide. Breathing was becoming difficult and I feared I would betray myself because it was so laboured. To make matters worse, I had a sudden and urgent desire to urinate. I gave a jump when the whistle of the speaking-tube blew shrilly.

"What? Yes. I understand. Thank you."

"She is complaining of a headache and does not wish to be disturbed?"

"Yes."

"Yes. By this time tomorrow she will have left, having remembered a pressing engagement in the city which she wishes to keep. And that will be the last we see of her for some time. You hope."

"How long have you known about Anna and Onan?"

"I should imagine Onan became infatuated when she was here last summer. They spent a considerable time in each other's company—mostly in the conservatory."

"You think it no more than infatuation?"

"He may have given way to passion."

"Onan? Passionate? The man's a mouse!"

"A mouse with a conscience. Why else do you think he nailed his hand to a tree?"

Unable to contain myself any longer, I urinated into my knickers and stood there, panting but warm with relief.

"If thy eye offends thee, pluck it out. That would be Onan's attitude."

"I don't understand."

"Lurid and dramatic as his gesture was, I am convinced it was intended to be symbolic. A self-imposed punishment for the wrong he had done."

"But why his hand?"

"Oh come, Madlin, use your imagination."

"You mean he touched her?"

"Possibly. Although it's hardly likely that if he had penetrated her he would have nailed his member to a tree."

My mother let out a shriek of laughter.

"You should see it! A lepidopterist would be hard put to stick a pin in it! No. The man's mad!"

"Well, I would be generous enough to view his action as one of conscience and as such, forgive him."

"Never. He has humiliated me."

"Would you punish him further?"

"I must know what happened between them."

"My dear Madlin, if you start probing you may well start an avalanche of disclosures which will bare the very disgrace you wish kept hidden. And, but more important, knowing the details, suffer unnecessarily."

"Isn't doubt my worst enemy?"

"For you, Madlin, no. But the truth, maybe."

"Onan must be made to confess to Mogudo."

"Mogudo will not be persuaded to divulge Onan's sins."

"Our wretched little chapel is like Saint Peter's to Mogudo. Without our patronage, Mogudo would be a wandering priest. Can you imagine Mogudo dragging that fat carcass of his, braving the snow to beg at people's doors? Never. He will talk."

In the light which filtered under the bottom of the tapestry, I could see the glint of the pool I had made and in which I stood. I was not worried that my knickers and dress had turned chill, my socks and shoes uncomfortably wet, but that the puddle of urine would spread into the room and betray, not only my presence, but my shame.

"Mogudo is not so corrupt he will betray his order."

"Mogudo will see that the stability of this ancient family does not rest upon spiritual unity as much as upon the cohesion of separate personalities. He also has too much earthly pride to stand aside, to be spectator to the end of a dynasty to which his name is indelibly linked."

"Don't be absurd, Madlin. The frail and negligible remains of the house of Strobl are more likely to survive if you rid yourself of Mogudo. You are destroying the house from within by retaining him—more effectively than Jaroslav Hasek could have dreamed possible twelve years ago. The peasants may have forgotten us—abandoned us, if you prefer—but the State, never. Not until we have been effectively obliterated. Keeping that turncoat Mogudo, you are giving them every excuse to harass us. Get rid of him."

"Anna, yes. It will give me great pleasure and a deal of satisfaction to boot out that little tart. But Mogudo, never. He stays."

"I hope to God it is not because you need someone close to hand and to whom you can confess."

"What do you mean, Mother?"

"There is a viciousness in your caprices which I do not like. Especially not in my daughter."

Some fifteen minutes later, I was able to wriggle from behind the tapestry after Mother and Nanna Axell had left.

To lend proof to the lie I would tell my mother, I splashed my frock liberally with freezing water before I presented myself to her.

Her attention was elsewhere, for she did not listen to my explanation but changed my clothes hurriedly and without reproach.

That night, when my sister and I went to bid my father goodnight, his left hand was heavily bandaged and his face ashen.

"I was chopping wood. Chopping wood. Take care when you chop wood. The axe is liable to slip."

Every night was bath night. Water was poured into the cast-iron bath and the flames lit beneath it.

"Don't get in yet!"

"The flames are out."

"You will burn your feet and bottom. Wait for the heat to leave the metal."

I jumped about becoming colder and covered with more goosepimples every minute.

"I told you not to undress."

How could I tell Gudrun it was the one moment in the day I looked forward to? With the heat scoping into my bones and the steam opening my lungs, I would sit in a delicious coma while she soaped my back; creaming the lather until I could have swooned. To have the water scooped over me and to be lifted out into the enveloping warmth of a towel and to be shrugged dry, pressed close, breathing into her face, was my wicked paradise.

"There. You seemed to enjoy that."

Pleasantly exhausted, limp and sensuous, I stood while she rubbed talcum powder over me.

"Does anyone like you, Gudrun?"

"I would hope so."

"The way you would like to be liked?"

"I suppose you're going to tell me you do?"

"I love you."

"You'd better not let your mother hear you say that."

"I love you more than anyone."

"More than Katya?"

"She thinks I'm a sissy."

And for no reason I could think of, I suddenly burst into tears.

Standing there, naked, tears filling my eyes, I felt more exposed and vulnerable than if I had taken off my clothes and walked bare-skinned through a room full of strangers. I could not run towards Gudrun for the protection I needed so I waited, ashamed, for Gudrun to come to me. It seemed an age while her crystalled image turned, blushed, hesitated and then loomed into my vision with a monstrous hug. Calmed but still sobbing, I clung to her fiercely.

"Do you think I'm a sissy?"

"I'm not your sister, am I?"

One could not ignore the family mausoleum. Built of dark granite, it was a solid structure of such massive and heavy proportions that it seemed to be settling into the damp grass under its own weight. Because of its uncompromising, brutish design, morbid colour and positioning, the mausoleum dominated the landscape more than did the house. Foreboding, a continual reminder of the inevitability of death, its ominous, monolithic presence insinuated itself into one's guarded awareness. Envious of life, it absorbed the echo of spontaneous laughter and, like a bogeyman, crept up to the windowpanes of the safe house and gazed dumbly in, looming and frightening. Assertive, the mausoleum stubbornly impressed itself upon us: at night, with its grotesque silhouette; during the day, especially in summer, by darkening the lawns with its long shadow, whilst in winter, wet with rain, it glistened like a toad lumbering out of a swamp impatient to digest in its bronze jaws the frail relatives for whom the long winter was a disaster. Gapped or half buried in drifts of snow, the mausoleum seemed to contract, crushing its frozen victims in an iron-handed grip and reducing them to cubes of ice.

I had never been inside the building but had been told by my sister Katya that it was where the dead were buried. I was not impressed, having no understanding of death.

Because the mausoleum was windowless, the four walls presented me with a surface ideal for throwing a ball against. I would spend my time, when I was well enough in summer, improving my childish skill with a ball against the sunniest wall and inventing the most complicated games. My mother strongly disapproved of these and, with her hand in the small of my back, would move me away to play elsewhere. Only once did she lose her patience with me and raise her voice. It was after I had persistently disregarded her warnings. She lost her temper and clouted me round the head.

"For God's sake, child! Let them lie in peace! Do you want to anger them with your continuous bang-banging?"

Similar to other admonishments when, playing indoors, my ball went bouncing and rolling down a corridor to bump against the door of a dozing elder who, roused, would storm out into the passage, shake or thump a walking-stick and shout what business had I wakening him, my mother's outburst only succeeded in convincing me that the dead in the family mausoleum were only sleeping. Until my father's death, it never occurred to me that it could be otherwise.

"You're old enough to attend the funeral, Knut, but I don't want to be scolding you for fidgeting. So behave yourself. Stay close to your sister and do what she does."

The service in the private chapel was unimpressive and short. Although there were more people present than I had ever seen assembled before and all of whom were apparently related to me, it was the coffin which held my attention and the strange sight of all the women, including my sister, wearing black veils which completely covered their heads and faces. Their eyes moved behind them like fish beneath the dark surface of a pool; mysteriously and in another element. So completely did the veils obscure the women that had not my mother been standing next to me and warned me for "shuffling," I would not have known who she was amongst the many, similarly dressed, black-coated and veiled women.

"Father's in that coffin."

I had to ask my sister to repeat herself because she had spoken in a whisper.

"He's inside it. Screwed in."

My mother nudged me and I stared at the coffin.

I didn't believe my sister. It wasn't until later, when I entered the mausoleum for the first time in my life, I became suspicious and discovered dead people slept uneasily; screwed into boxes.

I did not know what to expect when I first entered the mausoleum, dutifully following the coffin at a boringly slow walking pace. I only recall that the interior was different from what I had imagined.

Leading down from the opened, bronze doors was a flight of stone steps; beyond, a very small, empty room; and very cold. And that was the mausoleum. Empty of everything except us. I noticed on the bare walls carved words and numbers, but nothing else. It was very disappointing. There were no coffins, no sleeping dead; nothing.

It was then my attention was directed to a large cavity in the wall into which my father's coffin was being manoeuvred. There then followed a short service at the end of which I was handed a small trowel heaped with a sweet-smelling earth which I was instructed to scatter over the coffin. This I did while being held up by my mother. The significance of my gesture was as curious as the burning of my father's clothes and possessions on the night he died but both rituals I dutifully carried out because I was under the domination and protection of adults, so being relieved of all responsibility for such peculiar conduct.

I waited about while people shuffled past, sniffed, paused and touched my mother on the arm sympathetically. When Mogudo moved towards the door, my mother, her hand in the middle of my back, guided me towards the daylight streaming in through the mausoleum door.

My sister was ahead of me and I ran to catch up with her.

"One moment, Knut. Come here, child. Do you see this?"

My mother indicated a dark hole in the wall with her black hand.

"One day you will be buried alongside your father. You will be the last member of the family to have the honour of being buried in here. This tomb has been reserved for you from the day you were born. It is yours. Try to live up to our trust because when you die you will be in the company of very many distinguished Strobls. Remember that, Knut."

I looked into the dark hole and quaked with terror. From that moment, unlike my aged relatives, I grew more and more frightened of the possibility of death. Worrying, death became an obsession and, like guilt, came upon me unexpectedly, when I least wanted to be reminded of it.

However, when the elders who had witnessed the interment and the priest Mogudo walked at a snail's pace towards the house, I hung back, waiting to see if the lights in the mausoleum were snuffed out and the bronze doors locked. With my head round the open door, I saw Gardol, and two other men who were strangers to me. Between them, grunting and sweating like demons, they lifted a very large slab of stone which exactly fitted the black hole in which my father's coffin rested. This in itself was sufficient to fill me with horror but when one of the men scooped a trowel full of cement from a bucket and began to seal my father into his tomb, the sudden understanding of what my own fate was to be so overwhelmed me I cried out in protest.

Gardol, turning, saw me. Shaking his head, he walked towards me and removed his hat.

"Run along, lad. Go look after your mother. She'll be needing you now your father's passed on."

I was too numb to move but at that moment my sister came up to me and, taking my hand, pulled me towards the house.

"What's being dead? Is it like being asleep?"

"No. You're dead. Your soul flies off to heaven. Or hell. Depending."

These were new words to puzzle me but I believed my sister.

"And is Father really in there? Screwed in?"

"Of course he is. He's dead, isn't he?"

"But when will they let him out?"

"Never."

"Ever?"

"Not ever."

I could not imagine such finality although the remembered sound of the trowel scraping along the cemented crack sealing my father into his grave should have convinced me. But two things disturbed me; how did you know you were dead and how could others be so sure? Often I had wanted to die, when my mother was especially intolerant or when I felt so ill I wished for everything to come to a stop, but I had not imagined such finality if in death I was to be boxed and sealed into granite. The death I sometimes longed for was a limbo in which, suspended, I could not be got at and was deaf to cruel words. It was not the death of blackness, of corruption and torment I wished for, but of peace and subliminal happiness.

"What will we do?"

"Do? We must stay together. Whatever happens, we must not be parted."

"From Mother?"

"No. From each other. We mustn't let the elders separate us."

It had never occurred to me that such a thing could happen.

"They can't!"

"They might. So we must stay close. We only have each other."

And my sister, older by two years, moved into my life with all the authority of an adult. Secure in the sudden glow of her affection, my admiration for her and my willingness to be dominated, expressed itself in a sudden flow of relieving tears.

"But you must be grown up."

She wiped away my tears and kissed me. I clung to her with an agonising hug, desperate for a love which would erase my previous loneliness. With the skill of an enchanted seductress, she held me long enough to convince me that I could depend upon her for the love I needed, before she took my hand and, with all the authority of an adult, walked me into the house.

Allowed a glass of wine, we stood amongst the black forest of our relatives, amongst the gnarled roots of their bunioned feet and clumpy shoes while we bit on hard biscuits and surreptitiously brushed off the falling crumbs. Our heads patted, our cheeks stroked, we shrank from the veined fingers scurrying like spiders over our shoulders, and sought the comfort of each other's hands. Clinging together, we made a pathetic picture and the maudlin elders huddled sympathetically round us, chucking our chins and trying to pinch colour and smiles into our cheeks. Only my mother, her veil flung back and her face tinged unordinarily red with the flush of wine, scowled at us; weighing up the newly-formed opposition.

Uncle Godric, smelling strongly of tobacco, grasped my wrist so tightly I yelped and tried to squirm out of his grip.

"I don't give a damn, Madlin. Summon Gort. Sue me. Do anything you like but I will have you certified. We'll have you committed."

Because I was biting and kicking, I could not be sure if my mother attacked him before the door slammed and I was hobbled, slung like a lamb for slaughter and carried down into the basement kitchens, a part of the house I was forbidden to enter.

Warm and smelling of cloves and hot bread and having an atmosphere spiced with cinnamon or pepper, the kitchens so surprised me, I ceased my yelling the instant my uncle set me down.

Approached by wooden steps which led directly down into them from the ground floor, the kitchens had barred windows high up in the walls through which could be seen the shrubs bordering the drive. In one kitchen all the washing-up was done, in another, all the baking and rolling-out of dough, and so on, each room having been laid out for a particular purpose, but everywhere there were chopping tables, innumerable pantry doors, nooks, grates for cooking on and shelves by the yard fixed at varying heights and on which were brightly polished pots and pans. All the rooms had the cluttered tidiness of a practical kitchen where everything either glistened with scouring or glowed white from the scrubbing and bleach. But what impressed me most upon that first visit, and which made the basement like no other floor or room in the house, was the warmth and smell; the two ingredients which other less fortunate children associate with the home from the moment they are born.

"Helga."

I saw a large woman wiping her hands on her apron walking towards me who appeared willing to please my uncle yet who held her head on one side as if she was distrustful of him. I did not recognise her as the wo-man who had escorted Karen upstairs to my birthday party.

"Yes, sir?"

"Get this boy's hair cut. Can you do it yourself? And for God's sake find him some trousers to wear. And get him a dog to play with. Or give him a gun."

Amazed, Helga gathered me to her and I disappeared into her monstrous hug and was lost amongst the strange smells of her warm bulk. Calmed by the strength of her gentleness, I could have swooned away.

"Try and undo the harm that's been done to him."

"With respect, sir, it would be more than my job is worth to go against Madam Strobl's wishes."

"Your mistress could forfeit all right to the child's affection if the family so wished it. Do I make myself understood?"

"Yes, sir. Poor boy."

"For God's sake, woman, don't sympathise with the lad! Be firm with him. And no spoiling. He has to be turned into a man!"

Left to the strangers in the kitchen, I was lifted, patted, kissed and hugged; sat on a high stool and an apron put round my neck.

"It seems a shame to have to cut off such pretty curls."

Afraid, I sat staring at Granoise, a very old woman with no teeth and a face like a crumpled sheet of paper who sat opposite me chopping carrots while she gnawed on her gums and stared fixedly at me with eyes which watered like crushed grapes. Somewhere behind me, a pair of scissors snipped. Frightened, I ducked but, warned that the points might stick into my eye or my ear be cut in two, I sat rigid with terror enduring a painless torture whilst my head became strangely cool and light. Into my watered vision, at the very moment I wanted to cry, walked Karen.

"What d'you think, Karen? He makes a good-looking boy, doesn't he?"

Karen just stood and stared at me with her pale green eyes, mute and open-mouthed.

After the ringlets had been admired, one kept, the rest burnt in the grate and my neck brushed and tidied, I was set down on my feet.

There was a moment's silence and then Old Granoise, thrusting her face close to mine, cackled. I was buffeted in the face by a gust of stale, warm breath and saw right into her dark, toothless mouth where a white muscle of a tongue lay twisting like a bleached and dying slug; frothing slightly. Helga too gave way to mirth and ruffled my shorn locks good humouredly. Even Karen smiled.

I burst into tears believing their laughter mockery because, although my hair was now short like a man's, I was still dressed in skirts and wore dainty plimsolls on my feet. Helga, to shield me from the derision, enfolded me and I was allowed to weep to my heart's content in her motherly cradle. When I had done, she dried my eyes on her apron and Karen offered me an apple.

"Well, young man, we will have to find you a pair of trousers from somewhere."

"Tetty is good with her needle."

"What is to be done until then?"

"Send Gardol with the Sledge."

"Yes. I'll go into Lindehult with him. Meanwhile, young man—off with that frock. And you, Karen, can get Gardol's jacket. The dark one which hangs on the back of the door in the passage."

Stripped to my underwear there was an uncomfortable silence while the women stared at me. Helga shook her head.

"What could she be thinking of?"

Old Granoise growled and chopped a carrot in half.

"I shall have to get you underclothes too."

Karen stood with the sleeve of Gardol's jacket to her mouth, staring.

"Come on, young madam. Let's have the jacket."

Under the watchful eye of a blushing Karen, I was buttoned into the too big coat and the sleeves rolled up. Completely enveloped I was sat next to the fire.

"I'll be gone three hours, Granoise. Less if the snow is packed. Meanwhile, Karen, you look after our young guest and make sure he doesn't catch cold."

Fed soup and hard toast, I eventually found sufficient courage to answer Karen's questions and, long before Helga returned from the village, was sat flicking dried beans across the table and knocking down Karen's towers of old corks while Granoise chopped and grated but never moving from her chair. It was Karen who fetched and carried; making herself useful in any number of ways.

Never considering ourselves to be part of Europe because we lived so far north—although our cultural heritage was, and is, distinctly European and civilised—nevertheless, when Norway was invaded by the Germans, the elders shook their heads, unable to decide what to do for the best.

"This house is not even strategically placed so we are hardly likely to be overrun."

"The house? The house? Who is worried about the house? Good grief, Godric, it is war which is the worry. War. To be occupied by those damned Germans. Those barbarians."

"They are not barbarians. They are soldiers. And damned fine ones too. But they won't invade. It would be a mistake. A tactical mistake. Besides, we will be useful to them—like the Swiss. They're no fools, the Germans. Believe me, they won't invade us."

"Is that why you are not in the reserve?"

"I haven't been notified as yet. Perhaps I am too old."

"Nonsense, Godric. You're not too old. Hojensen is in uniform. He's five years older than you. Not a colonel either. In any case, you could volunteer your services. After all, the Strobls have all been military men."

"Yes, Godric, why don't you volunteer? Would they have you, d'you think?"

Uncle Mungo's question infuriated Godric who stormed out of the room.

"What d'you mean—accept him? Of course they would. He's a soldier, isn't he? And very smart he looked too. Can't think why he never married."

I came to know very little about the war because the elders would not discuss it with me, so all I gleaned was what I overheard in conversations too abstruse to comprehend properly.

Several times, discreet military exercises were held in the district and on one occasion tanks and men were actually brought onto the estate.

"Does this mean they are anticipating an invasion, Godric?

"Don't know. Soon find out."

We all watched Uncle Godric in his military overcoat, which he had unearthed from some musty trunk, labour over the snow-covered lawns and skirt the frozen lake. A soldier, in white military camouflage—an officer presumably—detached himself from a group and walked to meet my uncle. They stood talking together for a long time. Occasionally my uncle pointed with his stick and we saw the officer nod, stamp his feet and, cupping his hands, blow into them. Eventually Godric, after having saluted and had his salute returned, walked back to the house.

"Well?"

"I've invited a few of the officers back to dinner. Hope you don't mind."

"But the invasion?"

"Eh? Oh, just manoeuvres."

"Was it wise to invite them back, Godric? Under the circumstances?"

"What circumstances? Don't know what you're talking about, Mungo. You're getting old—and insufferable."

But the officers never came to dinner. An orderly was dispatched to the house and a note handed in for Uncle Godric. When questioned about it he was taciturn. Mungo tried to goad him but Godric wouldn't be drawn.

It was assumed that the regiment, camped on our land, had other more important things to do, for the following morning when I looked out of my window, eager to glimpse them but forbidden to approach, the soldiers, tanks and guns had gone. I was very disappointed.

"Of course you realise the family has Jewish blood?"

"Nonsense. Sidony is the only one on that side of the family with any pretence to foreign blood—and she's childless. In any case, Madlin, we *look* more Aryan than the Germans themselves."

"Do I detect sarcasm in your voice or is it nostalgia for what you have never been?" Uncle Mungo looked over his lensless glasses. "Well? Is it?"

"I admire their ability to organise. Their confidence. Their determination to have things their own way. Their strength."

"Hear, hear." And Felix thumped his cane on the carpet.

"We could learn a lot from the Germans. This country wouldn't be so soft. Your socialism is a pap for layabouts to suck dry."

"You'd make an excellent Quisling, Felix."

"Mark my words, they will come to thank that man for saving their country. He's no turncoat, you know. Knew what he was about years ago. Laid his plans carefully. The man has vision. Vision. Who in this country can you say the same about? Eh? Name me one! One!"

Such arguments and depressing conversations raged across and above my head and were my total experience of that terrible war. That things changed, that times were made more difficult, I did not appreciate. However, the elders' anxiety was communicated to me but did not add to my experience, except for the knowledge that war was taken seriously by the adults and that women and children were the first and most honourable objects to be defended after one's country. No one mentioned ideals as worth saving; probably because ideals and security—the *status* quo if you are in an advantageous position—were one and the same thing in our house. Tales of the war did filter down to me, most were shushed, but I learnt children died in war and that women were brutalised. The men pretended distaste for these horrors but gave as their solution a perpetuation of the horror, envisaging slaughter on a massive scale to teach the Germans a lesson.

"I expect the stories are exaggerated. In my experience, they generally are."

"Your experience, Godric? When the devil have you ever been to war?"

"I know the extent to which propaganda can be used. In any case, in wars it is inevitable the odd battalion gets out of hand. The commander's to blame. Shoot him and you soon restore discipline. It's leadership which counts, every time."

I was twenty-one when the war in Europe ended and by that time the elders had dispersed. Even before they left, I detected an about-face by Godric although Felix remained adamant that Hitler was not being given a proper chance.

"He is being confused by the toadies. You always get toadies worming their way into office. Napoleon had them. So has Hitler. As for the concentration camps, it's untrue, and if it were, then serve the Jews right."

But no one listened to him.

During all the conversations, while I was still very young, no one expressed the opinion that wars were unjustifiable or that all might be saved by the assassination, the ritual assassination of the few invested with an authority they perversely flouted. The idea was not a new one but one which, as an adolescent, I could hardly be expected to put before my elders without being suppressed. The elders held to the old-fashioned view that power was glory, destiny divine and leadership the moral right of power—a singular and circular definition which justified an élite coterie. However, they readily agreed that there were obstacles. It was the populace, the easily led, whose fickleness made progress so difficult and which brought ignobly to their knees very many fine men of destiny. Only once did I argue with the elders but could not convince them that it was leaders who made wars, not the populace who were asked to fight them.

Long before the war in Europe ended, on a trip in the pony and trap with Gudrun, she pointed out several shallow holes and a splintered tree which, she said, had been caused by a German bomber, running out of fuel or lost, jettisoning its bombs. I had not heard the bombs explode nor had I heard any gossip connected with such a freak incident, but she swore it was true. I gazed at the holes, which even then were beginning to support new blades of grass, and saw how quickly they were becoming a natural part of the landscape. I was worried that I too would as quickly forget the horrors man could inflict upon his fellow men. But what did I care for the Roman wars, the barbarians of my textbooks? I remembered only the theatricality of their pompous gestures. But then, I was not a man of destiny, nor am; nor could I rip open the guts of any living thing.

"What *have* you done to yourself?"

The new pride with which Helga had bolstered my self-confidence evaporated and I shrank. Deflated, I went limp and my new clothes grew and enveloped me in absurdity.

"Where's all your beautiful hair?"

Although I was reaching an age when, on occasions, I could master the flow of tears, I could not yet control my face. Confronted by Katya I felt all my facial muscles bunch and my mouth contort. If she hadn't put her arm sympathetically round me and said, "Go on, blub if you must," I would have remained dry-eyed.

Later, sat on a window seat at the end of the corridor holding Katya's prize possession of a doll's teapot, I ventured to ask if she still liked me.

"I envied you your hair. Look at mine. It's like string."

"Oh no, Katya. It's beautiful."

"There's not a curl in it."

"But it's blonde."

"So is Karen's."

I am certain Katya had not intended to force me to choose between her and Karen. I liked both equally.

"You are my dearest sister."

"Has Karen seen you looking like that?"

"Yes."

"And did she laugh?"

"She gave me an apple."

"Why is she always giving you apples?"

"And she gave me a cork. Look."

"What an odd girl."

"She's going to become our companion and look after us."

"Who told you?"

"Helga. She said Karen's going to be a maid."

"She won't be able to play with us because maids make the beds and things."

"Do you think she'll serve at table?"

"Why?"

"It would be fun."

"I think I'm going to have my hair cut short like yours."

"But you're a girl. Girls have long hair."

"You've had yours cut."

"But I'm a boy!"

Katya gave me a look which stilled all talk. I had no idea what she was thinking or, in her steady gaze, whether she was trying to convey something to me. I was too disturbed by the look to ask. Often, Katya would withdraw into herself and, motionless, gaze into space. It was as if she left her physical body and went soaring up and away in spirit, leaving behind an empty shell. Sometimes, I would be halted in my chatter by her prolonged silence and turn to find her eyes fixed upon me, gazing into my very being; into my secret core and stripping me of all privacy. Exposed, I would blush with shame and, turning away, fall silent; praying she would never tell anyone what she had seen. Although these moments pained me, I was equally upset when, stilled and silent, she would drift away from me and, borne on her imagination, inhabit a private world of her own from which I, her loving brother, was totally excluded. Startled from these reveries she would smile and, calmed, continue with what she had been doing as if she had never been absent. But the sidelong, penetrating look she gave me while we sat upon the window seat was profound and was communicating a significance of which I was completely ignorant.

I grew embarrassed, blushed and rattled the lid of the teapot.

"Don't you break that, boy."

And the spell was broken.

"I don't want it."

I put it on the seat beside her and stood up.

"Where are you going?"

"I'm going to play with Karen. Helga said I could."

"Then I'll come with you."

I led Katya towards the kitchens. On the way she told me, much to my surprise, that she had been down to the kitchens before.

"You never told me."

"Mother caught me and forbade me to go down there again."

"Aren't you frightened then?"

"A little."

"There's no need to be. Uncle Godric said we could." I don't think Katya believed me but she followed. "And he's going to buy me a dog."

"Oh, Knut. Can I play with it too?"

"Maybe."

"Oh please, Knut. Please. I'll let you draw in my book and read to you in my room. Please."

"Very well."

Only Helga was in the kitchen and showed no surprise when we entered cautiously—our nerve having failed us on the bottom step so that we hung back.

"Come on. Come on in. Was it Karen you wanted? I think she's in her room. Go up those stairs to your right and keep on going until you reach the top. Karen's door is facing you. Be careful of the stairs. They're very steep."

We groped our way up the uncarpeted wooden steps which were narrow and filmed with dust. Standing in the gloom when we had turned the first rise, I asked Katya to precede me.

"How did she know we wanted to see Karen?"

I was far more concerned that Katya should be safely above me and the first to see the hunchbacked dwarf. She squeezed past and almost toppled me.

"Let go my skirt! You'll have me over backwards!"

Although the stairs were not spiral, they twisted and turned back on themselves so often that I became dizzy and completely disorientated. I could not believe the house was so high.

"Have we come to the end?"

"No."

And on we climbed; stumbling and using our hands.

"We must be there, Katya!"

"Stop tugging at me! It was you who wanted to see Karen, not me!"

On the way up we had passed two closed doors. I stopped when we came to a third.

"This might be her door, Katya."

"She said to climb to the top."

"Open it and see where we are."

"No. You."

"We only need peek."

We both grasped the handle and the door creaked open. A bewildering, dazzling light from a familiar corridor streamed into the cramped well of our little staircase.

"Mother's room! Shhh!"

We closed the door with the wariness and hushed giggles of naughty truants. My sister put her mouth to my ear.

"Come on. There's only one more flight."

"How d'you know?"

"The servants sleep in the attic, stupid!"

After several more twists about and getting our hands dirty, we climbed on all fours, like dogs, to emerge into the light of a bare passage.

The door of Karen's room opposite to us was ajar and we glimpsed her legs laying along a thin, white counterpane covering a bed. Tentatively, we pushed the door open wider and Karen's pale green, wide open eyes stared back at us. She didn't move but lay still, her thumb in her mouth; hunched into the warmth of her private world. I think my sister managed a weak "hello" while I stared round the smallest room I had ever seen.

There were no windows in the walls but a small skylight, over which the snow had fallen, darkening the room, was set into the sloping ceiling.

A bamboo table stood against one wall bearing a white basin and pitcher. On a rail, where the ceiling was highest, hung a few clothes. At the foot of the bed was an enamelled black tin trunk. The bed was unusual. It was iron and painted black and had brass knobs. The mattress, as I discovered when the three of us sat on it in a row facing the door, was very thin and most uncomfortable.

"Is this our room Karen?"

"Yes, Fräulein Strobl."

"Oh."

And we all three fell silent.

I swung my legs back and forth, hoping my sister would say something. She sighed and waited.

"I've still got the cork you gave me."

It was then that Katya noticed the thing tucked into the bed up by the pillow.

"What's that?"

"Gogo."

"What?"

"My doll. Gogo."

And Karen withdrew the most pathetic little rag of a doll I had ever seen; if indeed, it was a doll. To me it looked like a piece of very old, soiled cloth into which had been tied a ball of wool. It had no arms or legs, and there was no face but a tuft of carded wool for hair.

"Your doll?" Katya's disbelief was direct and innocent.

Karen, who I'm sure had been about to hand the doll to Katya, suddenly clasped it to herself, possessively. The child-mother was protecting her deformed baby from the scorn of her superiors.

"Yes, it is. My doll. Gogo."

Katya and I, both a nuisance because we were "getting under everyone's feet", were pushed unceremoniously into the gymnasium by Uncle Ira. I had not entered the room since my father's death two weeks previous. The table, at which I was to have had my birthday party, was no longer there; only the balloons remained to awaken a memory of that day.

Ordered to keep out of the way, we amused ourselves but without enthusiasm. With nothing better to do, Katya and I, a balloon apiece, began to pat them to and fro but, being cold and stiff, our actions reflected the utter boredom we felt and our play was lifeless. Perhaps for twenty minutes, repeatedly sighing and my sister tutting and becoming increasingly cross with her inability to control the balloons, we banged and patted. Whether it was because a storm was threatening or the hour was later than I imagined, I do not remember, but recall that it was dark. Not dark enough for us to call for a lamp to be lit, but so gloomy it was an effort to focus on a particular object; especially a moving, ethereal balloon. It was as if I had only one eye, which made everything flat, without dimensions or perspective, so I too repeatedly missed the balloons or misjudged their nearness.

Absorbed by this phenomenon, I jumped when, from the darkness, my mother's voice, gentle and untroubled but, because it was unexpected, startling, enquired what we were doing.

"Playing," I think we answered, and she left.

A moment later, for some inexplicable reason, Katya thrust a balloon from her and ran shrieking from the room.

I hung back, partly because I was so surprised and lacked the wits to follow her but because I sensed there was not a dreadful hobgoblin hovering behind my shoulder. However, frightened of being left on my own and Katya's fading footsteps reinforcing my isolation, I started after her, only to run slap into my mother who was walking down the passage.

She turned me back into the gymnasium and, after lighting the lamp, stood looking about her.

"Katya was quite right. Gather up the balloons, will you, Knut?"

Eagerly, for I liked to please my mother if I thought I could win her affection, I bent to the task of gathering up the balloons. When I had an armful the sudden bang of a bursting balloon made me turn. I saw my mother stoop, pick up another balloon and, squeezing, burst it against her chest.

"Oh no, Mother! No!"

"We must, Knut."

"No, Mother, you mustn't! Don't!"

I protested as well as I knew how; throwing the balloons from me and stamping my feet,

"It has to be done, Knut."

And she burst another.

"My dear boy, they are filled with your father's breath."

As I rushed towards my mother, ready to kick and scratch, to beat her with my fists and bite her if necessary, a balloon burst in my face and my father's spirit, moist and tactile, went rushing past me like a wind, fluttering my lashes.

Later that night, Katya crawled into my bed and cuddled me.

"Oh, Knut. Dear Knut."

I lay with my eyes wide open, unable to sleep, whilst the closeness and warmth of my sister stole over me, awakening a dream of violence and love while I struggled to forget the smell of my father's rancid breath which had been saved from the grave.

Our tutor, a young man by adult reckoning, was as pale as watered milk and with a mouth like the interior of a drawn turkey.

As we expectantly sat waiting his arrival in a room set aside for our studies, he appeared to us on that first morning to be clean and neatly suited. As the weeks passed and we became more familiar with his ways, we discovered he smelt, was shabbily dressed and had the loathsome habit of standing behind us if he wanted to pick his nose.

"You have made a very bad choice, Madlin."

"Nanna Axell, you know very well that the authorities disapprove of private education and put every conceivable obstacle in the way of a person wanting to be a tutor."

"I still think the man is unsuitable."

"He is qualified."

"How do you know his certificates are not forgeries?"

"I trust my intuition."

"Ha! A pretty dance your instincts have led you in the past. Get rid of him."

"No."

Lechner stayed.

In the beginning, perhaps because he was nervous or desiring to impress my mother if she should chance to look into our schoolroom, Herr Lechner sat behind the table provided for him with his books tidily stacked, his coloured pencils neatly in line and the inkwell full. From the moment he sat down and we began our first lesson, he picked up a ruler and did not lay it down until the day's work was finished. All day and every day, he toyed with this ruler. Unlike Mother's riding crop, I never went in fear of it except when he pointed it at me. It was not long before I realised that this ruler was an extension of one or either of his hands and, like a barometer, indicated his changing moods. Bridging it between his two hands, he was calm and desired silence. Tapped against his teeth, it showed that he was controlling his impatience, but, if he grasped it with both hands and, with his elbows resting on the table, leant his brow on the flat, cool side of the ruler, it meant that an answer was wrong and he despaired of us ever learning. When he slipped the ruler between his collar and neck and scratched his back, he was utterly bored and completely indifferent to his bad manners. Lost for words he made circular movements with the ruler; when tapped on his open palm with the precise beat of a metronome, it indicated he was about to lose his temper, which was not often. On the few occasions he did lose control, he struck the table with the edge of the ruler, momentarily frightening us. Our fear would change to sniggers because his voice became high-pitched and lacked the rumble of authority. When Herr Lechner put the ruler behind his head and held it with both hands like a milkmaid her yoke, we knew that the lesson was nearly over. Only when our books were closed and we stood waiting to be dismissed, did he lay the ruler down.

As lesson succeeded lesson, Herr Lechner's table became more and more untidy and, having set us to write in our copy books, he got into the habit of walking to the window to gaze and yawn. He yawned so often and stretched and sighed that Katya and I both became infected and would, in turn, yawn our heads off also. Noticing, he would rap the backs of our chairs with the ruler and we would bend our heads and look at our books with watery eyes. Time became a burden and Katya and I took to napping or, if Lechner roused himself, to looking him full in the face whilst fast asleep.

Slumped back in his chair one day, Herr Lechner, in a moment of thoughtlessness, put his feet on the table with the ruler held across his chest and deliberately closed his eyes. In the next instant he had jumped to his feet when Mother unexpectedly entered the room without knocking.

"How are the young students progressing, Herr Lechner?"

"They are very intelligent, Frau Strobl—as I would have expected."

Susceptible, my mother squirmed under such oily flattery and gave a pursed smile which made me shudder.

"They show promise?"

"I am not disappointed."

"They are inclined to be lazy."

"I am very watchful."

Had he not lied, I think Katya and I might have continued to work hard at our studies, despite his waning interest. As it was, we took advantage of his boredom by spending the hazy afternoons dozing.

In all probability, when first engaged to be our tutor, Herr Lechner had been overawed by the number and quality of the people with whom he sat down to dinner. Being a man who would advance his standing by toe-kissing rather than by application to hard work, he saw in the assembled household an opportunity for climbing the social ladder. Whether he imagined his transition would be from tutor to professor, I doubt. More likely, by association, he hoped something would rub off onto him which, though intangible, would mark him out as a man of some importance. I could only hazard a guess at the kind of person he wished to impress when his stay with us was over. He certainly did not impress any of my relations. Notwithstanding their rebuttal Herr Lechner, like so many of his kind, increased his efforts to insinuate himself but was promptly cut dead.

His isolation was further increased by the mass exodus of all the elders. This was a coincidence but no doubt Herr Lechner took it as a personal insult. The reason for their departure was my mother's behaviour. Increasingly intolerant, erratic and insulting, she had unwittingly welded them into a formidable opposition. Their going was intended to show their disapproval of everything my mother did. Unfortunately, she saw their departure as a triumph and became more arrogant and domineering than before. Not for several years did I see my relatives again, when, still bitter with enmity they returned like jackals to pick at the remains of the Strobl estate. However, Herr Lechner, finding himself alone in so large a house with only my mother and Nanna Axell for company, reverted to his natural state. Unable to ingratiate himself with my grandmother who would leave the instant he entered the room, or find a foothold in my mother's unpredictable and shrill relationship, he withdrew into his thin shell. Bored, he was no longer interested in our acquiring knowledge. As long as Katya and I kept our heads bent over our copy books and held our pencils poised, he did not trouble us; demanding little and expecting even less.

About this time my mother apparently gave Herr Lechner permission to borrow books from the library. This he did, and would spend the whole of our lesson reading, taking particular care we should not see the titles. Reading the books he became agitated beneath the table and would sweat whilst growing red in the face and gasping. Once, my mother, thinking the weather suitable for us to go outside, unexpectedly entered the classroom to ask Herr Lechner if he would accompany us on a nature walk. He closed the book hurriedly, slipped it beneath some exercise books and stood up, rubbing his damp palms on his trouser legs as if embarrassed. Agreeing readily to her suggestion, he walked us beyond the house and when we were not overlooked from any of the windows, Herr Lechner withdrew the book from his overcoat pocket and, after telling us to "go and look for squirrels", propped himself up against a tree and began to read.

"What do you read, Herr Lechner?"

I was not as brave as my sister and could not have stood so brazenly in front of him demanding an answer.

"It is a book, my dear Katya, which you would do well to read, but I doubt if your mother would approve. Now look for squirrels."

We saw no squirrels, only fallen acorns, which we stuffed into our pockets.

When it seemed that our relationship with Herr Lechner had deteriorated so much that there seemed little point in continuing our lessons with him, he suddenly roused himself and took an unusual and keen interest in us. In retrospect, his zeal was prompted by the intimacy created, and which Lechner could not ignore, when the three of us were compelled, because of the increasing gloom of winter days, to sit, knees and elbows touching, within the small circle of light cast by the one lamp Mother grudgingly allowed us.

To our astonishment, Lechner proved quite amusing and would talk at great length on any number of interesting subjects, including biology, prisons, torture and religion. However, because he questioned us closely about trivial, personal happenings I became puzzled and did not feel at ease—thinking some of his questioning to be improper. We played games too but I was reluctant to be caught in the darker parts of the room or behind the screen because he tickled me. Katya, too. However, although she enjoyed the excitement, she always returned to her seat red-faced and out of breath, pleading for an end to it.

"He's really quite jolly."

"I wish he wouldn't put his arm round me."

"It's better than French grammar."

Which of course was true.

"Did you know we are to have uniforms?"

"With buttons down the front?"

"I don't know. Herr Lechner's been measuring me for one."

In the morning, I asked Herr Lechner if I too was to have a school uniform. He seemed embarrassed and looked at Katya with his head on one side questioningly and frowning.

"I told Knut it was to be a surprise for our mother, Herr Lechner."

"I'm glad you remembered. Yes. We must keep it a secret. I will measure you after class, Knut. You too, Katya."

"Again?"

"I've mislaid the measurements I wrote down."

After the lessons were over in the afternoon, I went behind the screen to be measured for my uniform. Using a tape measure, Herr Lechner carefully noted down the length of my sleeves, the width of my shoulders and the narrowness of my chest. I was puzzled when he made me undo my trousers and looked down inside. His hand was cold on my flesh and I started involuntarily. After he had fondled me, he withdrew his hand and measured the leg of my trouser. While I was buttoning myself up, he squeezed me to him and extracted the promise not to tell Mother about the school uniform.

When I left, Katya went behind the screen.

The following morning, Katya was not sat down to table when I entered the breakfast room. This was not unusual but when she had not put in an appearance by the time our lessons were due to start, I went looking for her.

She was in bed and when I entered, she threw the bedclothes over her head and shouted for me to go away.

"You'll be late for Herr Lechner, Katya. It's gone nine."

Katya sat up. Her eyes were red from crying and her face white.

"He's gone, you fool. Gone!"

Katya disappeared under the bedclothes again. Bewildered, I stood picking at some fluff on her counterpane.

"Where to?"

"How do I know. Gardol took him in the Sledge."

"When?"

"Last night. I can see the drive from my window."

The second surprise of the day was my mother's illness. Nanna Axell supervised us. Always tender and most considerate, she was especially gentle with us, reading us stories and letting me draw. Even Katya became less moody and climbed from Nanna's lap to play with me.

"Do you think Mother will still let us have a school uniform?"

Katya pushed me in the face and fled from the room.

"She loves you, Knut. Don't be disheartened."

Our next tutor was a very old man with palsied hands who lived and ate in Tetty's lodge. Mother sat in the room while we were instructed. She tried to apply herself to embroidery but whether it was because of the tick-tock of the ormolu clock or that her threads were too thin and constantly broke, I do not know, but she pricked herself with the needle repeatedly and swore and fumed under her breath.

My mother, who was overfond of horses, or so it seemed to me when I watched her nuzzle their soft lips, talking to them and lovingly smoothing her hand over their flanks, took to riding more often after my father had died.

In the first weeks she went for the odd gallop and from an upstairs window could be seen thundering across the meadows, but as the days went by she took to going further afield and did not return until well after lunchtime. Wild-eyed, blanched by the cold winds and wet, she would sit sprawled out in a chair while Nanna Axell thumped the ferrule of her walking stick on the carpet.

"You're totally lacking in responsibility, Madlin. Besides which, it cannot be doing a woman of your age any good to be shaken about so much. In my day a gal only rode day-in and day-out if she thought it would bring on a miscarriage. At your age it's absurd. Think of the gossip. And why have you discarded your proper saddle?"

My mother normally rode side-saddle and my grandmother thought it most improper of Madlin to sit astride. But my mother's grand passion was brought to a sudden end, not by Nanna Axell's constant reproach or Gardol's mute disapproval of the way my mother overrode her horse, but by an accident.

Unknown to any but Gardol, she had taken to riding at night. Two miles south of Lindehult the horse had fallen and Mother was badly bruised. Brought back in the early morning by a labourer in his cart, Madlin had been carried upstairs like a bedraggled crow. My mother had insisted that the labourer be made to sit down with us at breakfast but Nanna Axell wisely gave the man money and he departed scratching his beard and sniffing his finger ends.

Although she never rode again, my mother dressed herself in hunting clothes and went about the house carrying a crop. Dressed in this absurd and manly attire, she would admonish me by tapping my skull with the tip of her riding crop, but later, a stinging blow across my thigh became a punishment. Naturally, I did my best to avoid her. This was difficult because she had also taken to striding about the house armed with ledgers from which stuck innumerable, dog-eared papers, and would come upon me in out-of-the-way places where, normally, I never expected to meet her. Like a rabbit, I depended upon my bolt holes being secure and I would scurry off towards them when I heard my mother walking the corridors thwacking her thigh or boot with the riding crop. But with the cunning of a poacher she allowed me to escape, knowing I would lead her directly to my lair. Made nervous in expectation of her footfall, I became jumpy and would start at the slightest sound. My sister suffered too and confessed that she slept badly and was experiencing nightmares. Like me, she had weals on her upper thigh. Comforted by each other, we stayed together and, when either of us heard the steady tread and thwack of Mother's approach, one of us would cry "wolf" and, hand in hand, dart off in the opposite direction. Even the kitchens were not safe. Although, and grudgingly, we were allowed to go down there, it seemed my mother resented Helga's maternal goodwill. Shewn the marks of the riding crop, Helga scratched under her bun, shook her head but did not comment. "Let's bake something. What about making a ginger man, Knut? With buttons down his middle." But whenever we were happily busy Mother invariably found an excuse to make our presence in one of the upstairs rooms imperative. Thoroughly bewildered, my sister and I would wander the house sniffing the air for the smell of the cigars Mother had taken to smoking. In this way we could tell where she had been and judged it unlikely that she would not return. As gamblers, we were very unlucky losers.

One day, Katya and I, for want of anything better to do, were avoiding all the cracks in the marble floor of the entrance hall, when Mother's voice cut the air above us.

"Katya! Come here, child!"

There were several ways of escape but my mother, holding herself like the bow of a ship breasting the waves, bore down upon us before we could scatter. In front of her walked Karen, being poked in the back by the tip of Mother's riding crop. She was white-faced, her eyes downcast and too frightened to cry.

"This wretched child has been stealing from us. Haven't you? Eh? Follow me, Katya."

Although not included, I followed at a distance, hugging the wall, and saw them enter the study.

Before my father's death the room had been a study-cum-office and into which Katya and I would troop to wish him goodnight. It was, perhaps, the only time of the day we would see him and therefore in our minds, the study had become strongly associated with our father. Now that he was dead, my mother regarded it as her room and forbade either Katya or myself to enter.

Intrigued but apprehensive, I edged towards the open door and looked round the jamb to see my mother sit down heavily in the swivel chair in front of the desk and cross her legs like a man. Katya and Karen stood side by side in front of her with their arms behind their backs.

"This, this little so-and-so has been stealing from us. Haven't you? Eh?" And she rattled the riding crop between Karen's parted legs. "Haven't you?"

"No, Frau Strobl!"

"Liar!"

"I am not a liar!"

"How do you explain you came by this, then?" shouted my mother, jabbing her crop into Karen.

My father had managed the task of administering the large household and estate very successfully when he retired from the army—even after dispensing with the services of a secretary—but my mother, or so it appeared as I peeked round the door of the study, had crumpled under the strain, allowing eccentricity and violence—a violence which had sexual overtones—to destroy and unbalance her reason. Which was not surprising. Given a temperament unsuitable for painstaking and repetitive administration, how else could she have reacted to a situation in which the only excitement to be had was in an outpouring of ungovernable temper? It made her widow's dull pulse race and brightened her eyes whenever she slashed out with her crop. So, armed with her untidy ledgers and pencil in hand, she made the outward gesture of administration but left bare the accountancy of her books while, like a mad priestess with her hair frizzed, she stalked from room to room, shouting, flaying, and demanding money be saved but unaware how it was being wasted. With this fixation she had evidently gone up into the servants' quarters to wrest from them a kronen of cheese-paring whilst below, in the body of the house, our relatives gorged themselves full.

"Well?" and again she rattled the crop between Karen's legs which drew a gasp and bent Karen double. "Answer me, you little slut!"

"Mother, I gave it to Karen!"

"You *what*? Gave it? Who gave you permission to give away your doll?"

Reasonably, my sister argued that as the doll was hers she could do with it what she liked. Give it away if she so wished.

Mother snatched up the doll which had been sat on top of the roll-topped desk and thrust it into Katya's arms.

"I bought you this doll."

"But I don't want it, Mother."

Incensed, my mother struck at my sister with the riding crop, and with all her maniacal force. Terrified, I turned and ran while Katya's and Karen's screams bored into my hand-clapped ears.

I think I hid behind a sofa; I remember weeping.

That same day or later, I was moving stealthily about searching for my sister when I came across both Karen and Katya standing ankle deep in the straw littering the floor of the far stable. They were using their fingers to draw in the dust which lay thick on a coffin propped against the wall. It was the casket which had been ordered for Nanna Axell years before but who, to spite the elders, had stubbornly refused to die.

"You won't tell Mother, will you? I mean, us being out here."

"No, of course not."

"She's forbidden Karen and me to speak to one another."

"She's mad."

"Cruel. Look what she's done to poor Karen."

Karen lifted her dress and showed me the marks of her beating. I was horrified to see how purple and black skin could become and was thankful my own welts were insignificant.

"Me too," said Katya, turning and showing. "Karen's got hold of some goose fat. Show Knut."

The slippery jar was full of a pale lard which smelt edible. I put my finger in to taste.

"Don't eat it! We're going to rub it on our bottoms!"

The girls struggled out of their pants and helped each other smear the greasy lard onto welts which extended from the middle of their backs to just above the back of their legs. Their skin was very tender and dabbing it on to the accompaniments of "oohs" and "aahs" and "ouch, that hurts", they smeared themselves liberally.

Seen naked from the waist down, the girls, under their protruding tummies, in no way resembled my own physiology. This was a great shock to me and I was filled with dread at the thought that I too, in my turn, would have to undergo the terrible surgery of having my what's-it cut off like them. Although dressed as a girl but sometimes called boy by the elders, regarded by Katya and Karen as neither one thing nor the other, I was none too certain of my sex and had experienced confusion when my natural instincts led me to do one thing while being ordered by my elders that such behaviour was improper.

When it came to my turn to have my slight bruises smeared with the grease, I resisted.

"Oh, don't be so silly, Knut. And take your knickers off. We can't do it like that!"

It was impossible to struggle so when I was eventually revealed in my complete and natural state, I stood pouring and on the verge of tears, while they held up my dress. My confidence returned—and so too pride—when I discerned in their astonished gaze what I thought was envy. Curiosity overcame their timidity and they examined me minutely, drawing from me giggles as their ticklish fingering explored the appendage I had but which they lacked. Told that it was through this I piddled, they shook their heads in disbelief until straining, and my stomach bulging, I succeeded in making a minimum of water into the straw to convince them.

"How very odd. Why?"

"How else?" But neither girl, and in the curious squatting position they adopted, was able to convince me there were other ways.

After this, our bruises forgotten and while we sat huddled on the straw, there followed a lengthy and absurd discussion in which ignorance and imagination helped compile a dictionary of misinformation for reference at a later date when fear would thumb its pages and guilt would tear them out.

The immediate consequences of this discussion were various. One result however was that for the next month or so, I sat down to urinate; being unable to make up my mind whether I was a boy or enjoyed being a girl more. It was only later, dressed like a boy, I infuriated my sister by piddling in any direction I chose.

Although spring is a time of year when the thunderous pall of winter's depression thins and lifts, when the body creaks to be active, when glands give sudden and alarming twists and turns, filling with juices of painful abundance, when dreams become warmer and bulge with erotic fantasies of familiars in the focused colours of brilliant indecency, it is also a time when there occurs that disturbing phenomenon which denudes the familiar and strips it to the unquiet and embarrassing awareness of time passing. Like the trip which catches and slows the perambulation for just long enough to print indelibly the gulf already jumped, there is a pause in the headlong rush towards death, enabling one to catch sight of the warning glint highlighting the rapidly emptying hourglass. At such a moment, when the circuit is shorted, the cycle arrested, a well-loved room can become unbearably shabby and lusty. Comforting books which one had hugged and nosed like a surrendering mistress in the delicious intimacy of the long and pleasurable winter months appear soiled and greasy like an ill and much used and abused skivvy, and the bed, a disordered womb in which biscuits were nibbled and scalding tea drunk, becomes a pit littered with black crumbs, odd hair and creased with midden stinks; even one's own skin is found to be filled with a fine, black dust and, standing denuded in front of a mirror, one's carcass is suddenly all the more vulnerable and mortal, pale and white, unhealthy and like the underside of a garden slug. Even the taint of urine which had lain like a winter's scent upon one's damp skin, becomes, on an instant, the pungent odour of harlot death.

These moments of discovery—when the familier ages, scours, and the loss of unrecorded time, like a stopped clock accentuates the gap—open up the past like one vast regret. Having read a few of the romantic novels with which my mother surrounded herself, like some women insist upon boxed chocolates to satiate their morbid gluttony, I imagine the regret for time passing is all the more poignant when ageing lovers turn on their soiled pillows and gaze at the other's tufted skull and the loose skin hanging from the hard bones and, giving each other a reassuring, toothless smile, betray the delusion and, made mad, prepare for limbo.

Perhaps my mother had seen the unfamiliar image in her mirror. An image which condensed the whole of her life and displayed it with all the panache of a contracting feather fan behind which, slowly revealed, lurked not the blushing, excited child of innocence but the bald death's-head in which rattled a few remaining, decaying teeth.

Spurred, made frantic and, like the mad harvester who winnows in a gale, throwing reason into the teeth of despair, my mother unlocked her boxed inhibitions releasing the glaireous vice which youthful modesty, adult morality and Christian fear had kept dryly embalmed waiting for the ringmaster's whip and the circus of a satanic resurrection. Wide-eyed, wet-lipped, her hair puffed like the grotesque head of a seeding dandelion, she rouged her wintered skin, clothed it in the clicking beads and sequins of an earthly wickedness and, as the crazed hermaphroditical clown, ordered a diversion; an entertainment: a mass to celebrate the death of winter.

Summoned from the misty forests around us, a thin troupe squeezed between the tall, dripping trees and, on tiptoe, ventured down into the mists of the valley, fingering their tambourines and dampening the splash of their whispering cymbals against buttoned costumes. Seen as vaporous shapes dancing in and out of the mists, descending, they came like sprites with tiny bells atip their liripipes to pirouette about the snail of their caravan where attendant, albino butterflies trembled their wings to a thin sounding reed flute. Whispering footfalls through the wet grass and fairy chatter barely disturbed the absolute stillness of the valley. Transformed, their gossip became subtle, mysterious echoes which chased each other with the delicacy of fireflies amongst the lost, fog-drenched hills. But as the troupe, swaying in their caravan, emerged from the haze to see my mother's handkerchief fluttering from an upper oriel window, they shattered the stillness with an unreasonable blast upon their trumpet and followed it up with hair-straightening shrieks, the clashing of cymbals, the rattle-cum-splash-pocking of excited tambourines while the booming *trommelschlag* of their bass drum rolled back the mists.

The din and racket scattered the inquisitive like rabbits, turned us children leaning out of upstairs windows into stone-eyed gargoyles and transformed the adults, quivering beneath the bedclothes biting their beads, into gibbering apostates.

Drawn by their pale, luminous horse, the troupe banged the sides of their caravan and caterwauled while the groaning cart turned a complete circle on the lawns in front of the house. Disgorged onto the grass, they ran whooping, gambolling and turning cartwheels up the gravel drive towards the opened doors. They came with the fecundity of rabbits jack-jumping out of a magician's hat; confusing visual reality and sensibility. The caravan which could only contain ten spawned thirty, all of whom met in a crush at the door and burst in upon us.

There were the inevitable dwarfs with phallic cucumbers who chased each other, dinning the empty corridors with their ribaldry; good-humoured clowns full of tease and devilment; a drunken Columbine, her corsets agape, her ribbons undone, her wig askew and all her beauty spots loose, whose bared milk breast hung out of her coat-hardie and at which the baby slung on her hip made frequent but unsuccessful attempts to grasp and suckle; Pantaloon, an old fool of a man, as thin as his bow, proud that at his age he had fathered a babe, hopped and jigged and worked his fiddle like a cricket; Pulcinella, doubling as drummer, humpbacked, bent over the bass drum, his member like a drum stick, excited by the image of Harlequin's bottom which, encased in mauve hose, looked like and as soft as two powder-puffs; Harlequin himself whose gestures, had his arms not been hairy, were womanly and endearing and thoroughly confusing yet who, behind his pale makeup and painted, dimpled smile and despite his silver wig, appraised with his black eyes, sought opportunities, an advantage and, occasionally, the satisfaction of his particular vice. Besides these and many others, the musicians, accompanying the revellers like noisy shadows, blew, fiddled, clashed and thumped suitable tarantellas to accompany the mad romp when the troupe mangled their flesh in a gigantic, giggling, rib-tickling pile; squeezing out cries with grabbing hands or inserted fingers, creating astonished gasps and moans.

Buried at the bottom of this writhing heap was my garishly rouged mother, her cigar drawing outraged cries from the burnt.

All this vicious foolery was the conclusion to an indifferent pantomime we children were allowed to watch. A pantomime which the patched and dusty clothes of the actors and actresses, the egg stains, the crutch-soiled hose, the wrinkled scenery which billowed like a ship's sail whenever a door was opened, the loose floorboard and, but above all, the bad acting, made painfully ludicrous. Of the saturnalia which followed, we saw little. Chased by dwarfs and clouted about the head with their giant rubber members, we fled the corridors, gladly leaving the battlefield to the grubs of Ymir. My sister and Karen, wedged into a secret cranny, sniffed and shuddered in each other's arms while the bedlam reigned. I tried to crawl into their snuggery to commiserate with them but for some mysterious and feminine reason, despising me, they hissed their disapproval and shut me out.

Left to my own devices, I became involved in a nightmare game of hide-and-seek during which I surprised dwarfs piddling into upholstered chairs or, with an accuracy of which a mathematician would have been proud, excreting in the very centre of a vast carpet in some deserted room. Made frightened, I circumnavigated dark corners where lubricious whispers coiled about each other and ran past alcoves in which fevered jockeys on combined, odd-sized mounts made panting configurations which lay outside my total experience and, fortunately, because everywhere was so shadowed and dark, added little to it save for the sounds of lechery which, as I grew, I came to associate only with dwarfs and darkness.

However, there was one scene which met my eyes and which caused my heart to burn. In the small, blue retiring room, the shallow recesses lit by sparkling wall brackets, was a romantic tableau which had the delicacy of a Meissen porcelain group but lacked the deft touch which would have given the idyllic charm this scene totally lacked because of its impropriety. In this momentary composition, Columbine, speechless with drink, her pannier broken and drooping, bore her weight down upon an uncomplaining Gudrun who Columbine had underpinned to the cramped chaise longue and was kissing with the passion of a man. Filled with a sudden shame, the experiment discovered, Gudrun threw aside Columbine and stood before me trembling. Speechless and red-faced, she picked up and threw down a bottle, shattering it, and ran from the room. I followed but in the confusion and the darkness she disappeared. I had wanted to tell her where Karen and Katya were hiding and maybe I would have hunted for her had it not been that I accidentally bumped into Helga. Arm in arm with a musician and talking earnestly, she was surprised to see me. Taking hold of my ear, she hurried me up to my room and, because she didn't trust me, locked the door, promising to let me out in the morning. Frustrated, there was nothing I could do but throw myself on the bed, listening to the occasional gusts of revelry which swept up the broad stairs.

It ended at dawn after a sudden scream and a long, long silence. Ghostly figures, like powdered and dusty goblins, slipped one by one across the acres of lawn and climbed silently into the waiting caravan which stood with its wheels deep in mist. While they waited for the rest to join them, they drew their cloaks or took old blankets and wrapped them about their heads to keep out the frosted dew. Time passed and after heads had been counted for the third time a last blast on the trumpet was given. The old horse tossed his white mane and the cart moved. The sound of the trumpet, besides disturbing the roosting birds, roused a sleeping goblin who rushed from the house somersaulting and cartwheeling in a mad pursuit of the retreating, creaking cart. As the mists swallowed them up, all that could be heard was the tinkle of the odds and ends roped onto the outside of the caravan and the creak and groan of an unoiled wheel. Soon there was silence. Complete and utter silence. It was all over. Almost. About midday, long after I had been let out of my room, Gardol drove Helga in search of the troupe and of Columbine in particular, who had left behind her baby which Gudrun had found fast asleep in an empty soup tureen beneath a table.

My mother kept to her room for over a week; not showing herself or stirring until Nanna Axell returned unexpectedly from Haggstianstad. Unlike a butterfly which emerges from its chrysalis and hardens and becomes bright and colourful in the warmth, my mother, after her sojourn, creaked through the door of her room to face the summer with skin like grey tissue which crinkled and shrank in the unexpected sunlight.

"**K**nut? Come, child."

I closed my fist round the medallion in my pocket.

"In here."

Earlier in the day, poking about beneath a bureau to retrieve a knuckle bone, I had found a gold medallion. On one side was the figure of a helmeted soldier on horseback who, with his long lance, was killing a dragon which lay coiled beneath his horse. There was a Maltese cross on the soldier's breastplate and in his helmet was stuck a plume of feathers. Surrounded by laurel leaves on the obverse side, was engraved my father's full name, *Jan Onan Norshinkaal Strobl*, and the date *1898*. There was nothing to indicate why he had been awarded the medal. I did not think for one moment that he had been decorated for slaying a dragon but imagined it must have been for some act of bravery or for his skill at arms. I preferred to think he had been singled out for his courage, and slipped the medal into my pocket.

Treasuring the medallion, feeling it was a talisman and, having magical properties which would raise me to the rank of hero, I had gone about the house puffed with a new pride; immune from the more common assaults on my sensitivity. But when my mother had unexpectedly summoned me to follow her, my new courage emptied out of me like slops from a bucket.

Gripped firmly in my hand, the medallion drew the heat from my palm in the secrecy of my pocket as I followed her.

"Your Uncle Janefi wants to talk with you, Knut."

I was taken aback for I had not reckoned my mother enlisting support to wrest the medallion from me.

"Your mother tells me you have my old microscope."

My uncle was cunning. Knowing I could not be bullied into parting with the medallion, he was going to bargain it for the microscope. What he did not know was that I now preferred the medallion.

"If you are so interested, I will let you have some slides from the Institute. Hundreds are discarded each year. And I don't see why they should be wasted, do you?

I was not going to be enticed out of my protective shell and into a trap.

"Well?"

"There is no need to be frightened, Knut."

Standing side by side, my mother and Uncle Janeff looked down from their Olympian heights threateningly; disguising their malice with broad smiles. Faced with such formidable opposition and detecting the smell of treachery, I turned and bolted for the door but my mother had hold of me before I reached it.

"Oh no you don't. Back you come. Uncle Janeff only wants to examine you."

He laid his large hand on my shoulder and I sensed his strength through the material. He increased the pressure and I rocked on my heels.

"If you're good, Knut, Janeff will let you have those slides."

"I will have them boxed, labelled and sent the day I return. I promise. Now, will you let me examine you?"

I kept a grip on the medallion.

Uncle Janeff, I knew, was a doctor, but what I couldn't understand was why my mother was getting him to examine me when I hadn't complained about my chest nor been taken ill since the previous autumn. Why Uncle Janeff and not old Borg?

"Just let your trousers down."

It was all so simple! With my trousers off, Uncle Janeff would hold me down while Mother went through my pockets.

"Now don't be silly, Knut! Uncle Janeff only wants to look."

My mother had already started to undo the button at my waist.

"Knut! I insist!"

And she smacked my calf with the flat of her hand.

"And take your hand out of your pocket. How can I get your trousers down!"

Powerless but not defeated, I withdrew my hand and, with the medallion concealed, put it behind my back. Uncle Janeff sank down onto his heels and looked at me.

"Better have him on the bed."

With my trousers and underwear round my ankles, Uncle Janeff lifted me bodily and sat me on the bed.

Unbelievably soft, the bed embraced my bottom and I sank into the down, releasing the pungent scents of powdered lilac, my mother's favourite perfume.

"You'll have to lie back, Knut."

And I was pushed gently but firmly onto my back.

Staring at the ceiling, I lay on my back, my fist beneath me, knuckling my spine, and within it, the medallion safely concealed. They would never find it.

"Spread your legs apart."

I moved them perhaps an inch and gave an involuntary shudder.

"How old is he?"

"Thirteen."

"I won't hurt you, Knut."

He put his warm hands between my legs and felt me.

Whether it was embarrassment at the way he spread my legs or the shame of being so exposed before my mother, I began to wriggle and to draw away from his kneading fingers. I wanted to giggle with ticklishness and yet also shout my protest at Janeff's indecent assault of my person; I succeeded only in snorting down my nose while I tried to squirm away from his insistent fingering.

"One moment longer, Knut."

And still he fingered me with one hand whilst holding me down with the other. I went rigid and began to tremble because of the shaming polarisation of his violation. At the very moment when the facility of his manipulation began to awaken a dormant eroticism, he released me and I doubled up with shame, but not before I had glimpsed an indelicate smirk upon my mother's face.

"All over, Knut."

And Uncle Janeff tousled my bowed head.

"I don't think you have need for concern, Madlin. They are both there but held by the external ring. Have Borg look at him in a year's time if you're still worried."

I was having difficulty buttoning up my trousers because I still gripped the medallion in my fist.

"What have you got there?"

I opened my sweating palm.

"Well, well. One of my brother's medals. Like other boys amassed pimples, your father acquired a rash of medals. I used to envy him. I was hopelessly bad at any form of athletics."

Uncle Janeff handed the coin back to me but I turned and ran out of the room, my trousers still undone.

"I won't forget to send you those slides!"

That evening, Gudrun did not try to force the bathroom door when I locked it against her.

"Soap round the corners. And make sure you dry yourself *properly*," she shouted through the door.

Afterwards, when I was safely in my nightshirt, she inspected behind my ears and dried my hair.

"The mess you've made. There's enough water on the floor to float a boat. Now into bed. Quickly."

"Uncle Janeff said I was all right."

"Did he now."

"What did you think was wrong with me?"

"Are you going to read or shall I turn off the light?"

"Tell me, Gudrun!"

She plumped up my pillows, straightened the sheets and altogether busied herself too much.

"Gudrun! I want to know! What did you tell Mother?"

She stood by the open door, her hand on the knob.

"I told her that I thought you ought to be more of a boy than you are. I was wrong, wasn't I? So we have nothing to worry about. Have we? Good-night."

Klmit, as fiery as his red hair, made the house reel with his loud voice and extravagant gestures.

"You should be stood against the wall and shot! Or else made to work down the mines!"

"The key to the gunroom hangs above the desk, Herr Klmit. Third from the left. Second row. The label will tell you if it is the right key."

Matched in temperament, my mother, far from throwing Herr Klmit out on his ear, fell under the spell of his audacity and, fascinated, warmed to his youth and vitality.

"When the time comes, Frau Strobl, I will run you through with a bayonet. Clean through your aristocratic navel. It will be like skewering a rotten tomato."

"Presumably, this will be after I have exhausted my body in the mines."

"You and your children."

My mother, tolerant of our presence at table, would not allow Klmit to include us in his grand scheme for revenge.

"Oh no, Herr Klmit. No. No. Not even in jest."

"I am in deadly earnest, Frau Strobl."

"Then you do not understand, nor could have witnessed, the instinctive savagery of a mother defending her children's innocence. I would readily—greedily—spoon out your eye with my fork if you so much as spat upon them."

"You may whip your horses, Frau Strobl, to instil obedience, and prove who is mistress by beating your servants, but I imagine in defence of your children you would prove to be a rotten mother."

My mother stabbed the fork she was holding into Klmit's hand. He flinched, but I think more with surprise than pain.

The blood oozed out of the pronged wound and dribbled onto the damask tablecloth. Klmit lifted his hand to his mouth and sucked.

"That proved—nothing."

Katya and I, uneasy on our seats, looked at one another and wondered if we should leave.

"Stay where you are, children. In defiance of his true nature, Herr Klmit is demonstrating the stoicism of the very class, the ruling class, whom he despises; envies would perhaps be a better word. More accurate. Whereas Herr Klmit has controlled his passions, a true peasant would have attacked me with the carving knife. Am I right?"

Her question was directed to Herr Klmit, for which I was grateful. Not having the remotest idea what she was talking about, I would have been too frightened to answer in case it revealed my foolishness.

"Frau Strobl. When the time comes for you to assess my ability as a teacher, you may find the standard of your children's French or Maths, or whatever, to be extremely low. But one thing I think you will discover is that I have taught them the truth."

"How very dangerous."

She dipped her serviette into a glass of water and dabbed Klmit's hand.

"Especially as there is no such thing. The Church, the Government, you and I, create the truth we need in order to give credence to our particular philosophy. There is no such thing as truth—*per se*."

Klmit wound the serviette round his hand.

"What truth would you use to explain injustice?"

"Injustice is a comparative term. For this very reason, in your socialist state, equality will remain an ideological albatross. You may make the peasant or the industrial worker more content by improving his standard of living, but when he compares his crumb of comfort with that of, let's say, a party official, he will see that he is still an agricultural or industrial worker.

"The only equality you will achieve is the right of every person to work solely for the state. When this happens the majority of citizens will become the serfs of the minority party. A supra-nationalism will be urged upon the majority to wield them into a 'governable' community. And it is this very nationalism which will work against the majority. Nationalism, in any guise, is a disease of man because the minority, the governing clique have a sensitive pride or, to put it more bluntly, a determination to hold on to power at all cost. But worse, is that if one pricks or challenges the pride of this tiny minority who boastfully—and quite untruthfully, claim they speak for us all—the result is inevitably war and which we, the majority, have to fight for them. It has always been the case."

"You have described the capitalist system exactly, Frau Strobl."

"That is Eastern terminology."

"It is the intention that it will not be a monopoly of the East."

"I am a romantic, Herr Klmit. Until the day dawns when all men are paid and housed—and I emphasise—*all* men, no matter their capacity to work either with brain or muscle, are paid the same wages, live in the same houses and have the same advantages, I see no point in living under any system which bends truth for the sake of power. Death would be preferable."

More and more uneasy, I glanced towards Katya hoping she was as bewildered as I. Katya turned her eyes to heaven, let out a bored sigh and returned to playing with some gristle on the side of her plate.

"I do believe, Frau Strobl, you would go to your death still as arrogant and proud as you have always been believing yourself to be the victim of injustice."

"On the contrary, Herr Klmit. I would face my execution knowing I was the victim of intolerance."

Katya, with her hand partially covering her mouth, kicked my shin beneath the table.

"Ask to get down. Go on."

"You!"

Katya, her mouth shielded, poked out her tongue, wrinkling her nose. I slid my hand beneath the cloth and tweaked her thigh.

". . . by erasing this structure, reducing the churches to rubble, the palaces or any other monuments or buildings of a previous epoch or culture, how can the citizens identify themselves with a heritage?"

"Mother?"

"How can they be proud, their inner, perhaps spiritual, being roused if you only offer them tractors to look at?"

"Mother!"

"Show them a chased gold cup which has no use, and they will marvel at man's inspiration and dexterity and will take pride in their heritage and . . ."

"May we be excused?"

"I haven't taken into account that you might be intending to organise their culture and leisure, hoping to stupefy them . . . What is it, Katya!"

"May we be excused?"

"You may. Now where was I?"

Katya took hold of my hand and dragged me from the room.

"How they do talk," groaned Katya, when we groped our way upstairs.

I agreed but secretly was full of admiration for my mother and wished I was older so I might understand and be able to join in the conversation.

"I expect Klmit will blast off again tomorrow. He always does after an argument with Mother."

I fell about giggling at Katya's use of rude words so that she had to twist my arm to get me up the stairs.

Klmit was our third and, as it turned out, our last tutor. His enthusiasm was infectious and he inspired us to work. Learning was no longer a drudge and the schoolroom a place we looked forward to entering. Always untidy—chaotic, my mother said, holding her head in her hands while she looked round the muddle—the schoolroom had a relaxed but studious atmosphere.

"You'll poison them, Conrad. And think of poor Knut's chest."

My mother was referring to the fog of smoke from Herr Klmit's fat pipe which filled the classroom.

"Nonsense. It will kill the germs harbouring there. Look at the insects I have already slaughtered."

And there, on the windowsill, some pedalling their legs in the air, were dead and dying flies.

My mother tossed her head. "Peasant!" and swept out into the corridor, slamming the door.

In conversation with Karen, we were surprised to learn that she too was receiving tuition from Klmit. Excited, we asked Mother if Karen could join us in the classroom.

"Certainly not. In deference to Herr Klmit's wishes I have allowed this most unusual arrangement. And only if she shows promise and does not neglect her work on account of it."

We argued but she was adamant, so we took the unprecedented step of siding with Herr Klmit when the occasion presented itself. Mother bared her ugly authority and, humiliated, we crept from the room, surprised that Herr Klmit was so timid in his acceptance of Mother's domination.

"I think Mother's in love with Herr Klmit."

Such an absurd possibility was unthinkable.

"Don't be so soft, Katya!"

"Katya may be right, Knut. Herr Klmit is gone on your mother."

"What do *you* know about it, stupid!"

For the first and only time in my life, I dissociated myself from Karen's blossoming friendship by the objectionable relegation of her status to that of maid. Fortunately, Karen mistook my momentary antipathy for an instinctive desire to defend my mother.

"They've been talking in the kitchen."

"What have they been saying, Karen? Do tell."

My sister was agitated with excitement.

"Only that Frau Strobl's gone soft on Herr Klmit. Again."

"Again? Was she before?"

All three of us were sat in a darkened room on the second floor. It was a bedroom which was never used and the mattress normally lay rolled at the end of the bed. When we met to discuss, we unrolled the mattress and sat facing each other on the bed with our legs tucked under us.

"She hates him!"

"Oh, do shut up, Knut. What's this about being in love with him *again?*"

Karen was not certain and could only repeat the gossip she had over-heard in the kitchens.

The full significance of all she was able to relate was lost upon us. It was only in later years we came to the conclusion Mother had an unpredictable but positive yen for men of all types. Possibly, it was her way of showing her dislike of males because her affairs were inexplicable, panic-stricken and always ended with the total rejection of the man concerned. Invariably, she despised them for having succumbed to her charms but this very surrendering was a necessary part of her triumph over them. It was as if she had to test her domination repeatedly in order to convince herself that masculinity was a state to be despised. Of the details of her affairs, we never learnt; only from casual remarks and her skittish behaviour could we conclude that something was going on. Even though in later years Karen dressed Mother's hair and acted as personal maid, the two were antagonised and no confidences were exchanged and so we learnt very little. Of all her affairs, the one which she most undoubtedly had with Marcel, a butler who was yet to be employed, was the most secretive and possibly the most vicious. The two were admirably suited but it would be sheer speculation to guess at what they got up to together.

Made aware by Karen's repeated gossip, we looked upon Klmit with refreshed interest and tried to detect from his and Mother's looks, if there was anything "going on" between them. I had no idea what to look for and when Katya, groaning with adolescent jealousy, remarked she would just die if Mother married Klmit, our childish game of guessing took on a sinister aspect.

The idea that Mother might marry filled me with a frustrating hatred. I felt impotent to prevent such a humiliating disaster. Which was odd because hating my mother as I did, I could not see why it should effect me one way or the other. It is only since I have realised that, denied love, I was petulant because it was being granted to another and secondly, having taken the place of my father, I was indignant to be ousted and have my ineffectiveness demonstrably underscored.

Now that we took our luncheon with the elders regularly, having proved to Mother we were grown up by behaving ourselves, the luncheons became the high spot of the day. However, Mother, never generous, could not give without taking. We had to bargain for her love and the exchange was invariably humiliating because we had to pay far too high a price for a love which was as false as paper flowers. Seeing Klmit supping what should have been our love, Katya and I both became less and less attracted to him.

"I asked if you wanted more wine, Herr Klmit?"

"Thank you, no, Frau Strobl. I am not used, nor want to become accustomed to such a decadent style of living."

Nanna Axell's knife and fork clattered onto her plate.

"Don't be such a humbug, little man. Your peasants quaff a litre of wine a day without giving it a thought."

"On the contrary, Frau Axell, they pay a great deal of attention to the wine they drink. And it requires a strong wine to swill away the taste of the offal they are forced to eat. Wine also gives them the illusion their bellies are full and that the society in which they live is not, after all, exploiting them."

"Don't talk drivel! They eat better than they have ever done and luxuriate on fat pork. They wouldn't give a damn for this fiddling little widgeon unless it was in a pie along with twelve others."

She poked the remains of her meal with her knife.

"Show me a peasant whose stomach is glued to the back of his spine through hunger and I will take a pick and work in the fields alongside your underprivileged."

I burst out laughing at the thought of Nanna Axell, her skirts tucked up into her waistband and a kerchief round her head, stood in a field picking at the frozen earth.

"Knut! Behave yourself."

"If it weren't for the fact, Frau Axell, that you would be pelted with stones—and all else besides—I would gladly accompany you on a visit to the homes of peasants who are too weak to work through lack of food."

He could not outstare Nanna Axell and began drawing on the table-cloth with the points of his fork.

"Young man. I was alive when your peasants—and I wish you wouldn't keep referring to them as *your* peasants—joined in with us at thanksgiving and afterwards invited us to share *their* meal. It was no cap-in-hand affair. There was respect on both sides. We were a large family and each was dependent upon the other because it was the success of the harvest which dominated our lives. Your city workers changed all that. You took our men and women, ill-used them and, discontent, they rebelled. You undermined our structure and now have the audacity to lay the blame at our feet!"

Mother tried to ease Nanna Axell and Herr Klmit gently apart by asking Nanna if she wanted pudding. Nanna Axell brushed aside the suggestion with an impatient gesture of her jewelled hand. Her attention was not going to be diverted while she was doing battle with the most hated of her antagonists.

"I bow to your age, Frau Axell, but not to your wisdom."

He was about to add that some believed the two synonymous, when Nanna Axell interrupted him.

"Then you are a fool. A man bows to no one except his God and for no other reason that he is acknowledging his own insignificance. Excuse me."

She laid down her napkin and moved towards the door with the dignity of an empress. She paused at the door.

"You would be correct in thinking I cannot stomach your company, Herr Klmit, but you would be wrong if you thought that is why I am withdrawing. The truth is I have a very important letter to write to Hans Vetch."

Herr Klmit started out of his seat but sat back, a surprised look on his face. Scowling, he began to twist the stem of his wine glass.

Katya nudged me under the table when Mother laid her hand upon Klmit's.

"Frau Axell is teasing you, Klmit. She's of another age. And not always truthful. Have some wine."

Klmit refused and hung his head, remaining sullen.

Our spirits dampened, the luncheon became boring and Katya and I disinterestedly finished up our food so we could be excused the sooner. Especially as Mother, seeming to regret the amount of wine she had drunk, had become irritable.

While my mother slept in her room that afternoon, Herr Klmit, after setting us some work to do, left us on our own. When he did not return after an hour had passed, Katya fell asleep while I, not wanting to be caught napping, stayed awake, ready in an instant to rouse a lightly snoring Katya.

But it was not from her afternoon nap Katya was aroused, but from her sleep in the early hours of the following morning when both of us, unknown to anyone, were fast asleep in my bed.

Mother's screams had us quickly out of bed. Guiltily opening the door of my room, we saw Mother in her nightdress walking, drunkenly as we thought, down the corridor, staggering from side to side. She must have heard us for she turned. From somewhere below her waist, blood was pouring down, wetting her nightdress. Katya cried out and ran towards her. I hung back, ready to sob.

"Fetch Helga. The doctor. Quickly!"

Katya sped silently away down the long corridor, her thin nightdress breezing out behind her. Mother straightened and beckoned to me.

"Here, boy. Help me."

I was almost too scared to approach but when I did, she rested heavily on my shoulder.

"Get me back to my room."

She collapsed before we reached the door and, thankfully, Helga came panting down the corridor with Katya tugging her by the hand. One look at Mother was sufficient for Helga to tell Katya to ring for the doctor. While Helga fetched blankets off Mother's bed and ripped a sheet, she ordered me to go to my room. Willingly, I left and, like a coward, closed the door quietly.

But was I really a coward? Had I not seen with my own eyes the knife which stuck out of Mother's groin? Even as I crawled under the bedclothes to hide, I was not convinced the whole incident was not a nightmare and from which I would surely wake.

After Borg had attended to Mother, he questioned Katya and me while we sat huddled together on my bed. We told him, truthfully, we had not seen how the accident had occurred. He was content and kept repeating that it was an accident.

"That's all you need remember. It was an accident. Your mother had an accident with a knife. Just an unfortunate accident."

Afterwards, sitting on the bed, Katya and I, having been assured Mother would live, talked of other things until near midday when Helga came in search of us and scolded Katya and me for not having dressed.

We never learnt the reason why Mother was stabbed although we automatically linked the incident with Klmit, for he left mysteriously the same night she was wounded. It seemed to both Katya and me, a logical explanation; the only one. Mother never referred to the incident although she was to walk with a limp for the rest of her life. But she was not embittered, on the contrary; although subdued, she was altogether more considerate, only occasionally shewing the malice which she seemed to reserve especially for me.

Gathered round the kitchen table, the staff generally ate the same food as we did but, with the household so depleted, Helga found more time to cook the foods they preferred. And it was Gardol, his bulk towering above the others, who insisted upon more substantial meals.

"Can't keep a man's body covered in hair on sparrow's millet. That's ladies' food you eat, lad. Have some of this."

For the first time in my life, a place was made for me at their table and, sitting next to Gardol who, stripped of his jacket and his shirt sleeves rolled up, smelt of horse dung and soot, I tasted and relished the heart-warming, substantial meal of turnip tops and pickled pork.

"Wouldn't have that chest of yours if you ate this every day."

I cast a secret admiring glance at his hairy arms and hoped that someday mine would look the same.

"Be a poor look out for us girls if all the men turned into hairy apes like you."

Helga tapped Gudrun's arm with her knife.

"A little more respect, young madam—if you please."

Gudrun blushed, looked across to me and then down at her plate.

"The girl's nearly a woman, Helga, leave her be. Besides, I don't take offence. A young filly kicks out to measure her worth. Hobble her too soon and you'll break her spirit."

Gudrun blushed bright red.

"So you speak up, girl, if you've a mind to. I won't object. How's the pork, Knut? D'you like the turnips?"

I smiled and nodded, my mouth being full of juiciness and meat.

"If you called at a dozen houses right this minute, the chances are you'd find them all sat down to this very meal."

Gardol sopped up the juice with a wedge of thick, rough bread; a dark bread which Helga especially baked for the house staff.

"Help yourself and pass the wine, young man."

While the wine travelled round the table, I looked across to Karen, whose large head on her spindly neck was bent over her plate. Her cheeks bulging, she was devouring hungrily the piled food on her rapidly emptying plate, cutting and forking noisily.

"Heavens, child, you'll explode!"

Karen swallowed with difficulty, blushed and restrained herself, her pale green eyes wide with frustration while she sat gripping her knife and fork, thwarted midway in her ecstatic gluttony.

"You'll soon learn manners upstairs. Won't she, Knut? Did you know Frau Strobl says she can begin next week? Aside from the bedrooms, she's going to help serve at table. God willing and with luck, we'll make a lady of her yet. You young tomboy you."

Old Granoise snarled and, minus teeth, went on chomping the pork between her gums.

The meal continued in silence until the sound of footsteps on the gravel driveway above us carried quite clearly down into the kitchen. Everyone turned and looked up at the high barred windows above us.

"Heavens. Who could it be? You'd better get your coat on, Gardol."

"Time enough."

Helga rose and carried the chair to the window. Standing on tiptoe on the chair, she rubbed a small hole in the condensation and looked out.

"Who is it, Helga?"

"I don't recognise him."

"A man, is it? Borg perhaps?"

"I know Borg, silly. This man has his back to us. God Almighty!"

She turned on the chair with her hand to her mouth.

"It's Vetch!"

Gardol, half out of his chair, froze.

"Hurry, Gardol. Quickly, man. They do say he keeps a list. Don't cross him, for goodness' sake!"

Grabbing his coat, Gardol moved swiftly for a man of his size and was already halfway up the stairs before the bell jangled violently on its spring.

Helga carried her chair back to the table and sat down; pushing her plate away.

"Who's Vetch?"

"You'll know one day. There's no need to worry your head about him 'til then. By then he might be dead."

We sat in silence until Gardol returned. He slid into his chair and, picking up his knife and fork, sniffed.

"Well? Who did he want?"

Old Granoise leant towards Gardel and slid her hand along the table.

"He was most civil."

"But who did he want?"

"Frau Axell."

Helga sat back in her chair relieved, and Old Granoise withdrew her hand.

"Close to, he's much smaller than I expected. There's nothing to him. I'd have judged him a weak man."

"Have you never seen a ferret?"

"That was my opinion exactly. Pass the wine."

"I wonder what he could be wanting?"

Unanswered, the question blanketed the room in silence. After several minutes had passed, Helga stood up and began to gather the empty plates.

"I wouldn't have expected him to walk."

"Probably only from the lodge. Tetty may have been in one of her more obstinate moods and refused to open the gates."

"You'd have thought she'd have rung through and warned us."

"Don't go ringing her until he's left."

I sat up to the bare table swinging my legs, waiting for Gardol to finish. Finally he put his knife and fork together and drained his glass of wine.

"When's this, this man—what's his name? Marcel. When's he due?"

"Sunday to start work Monday."

Gardol picked between his teeth with his fingernail, and sucked.

"I'll move out to the stables Saturday, then."

"Now don't be so silly, Gardol. Nothing's going to change."

But it did. For all of us, now that Karen, Marcel, Katya and I were under the same roof together.

Returning from a very short morning walk before the household stirred itself, I was surprised by a dark-skinned man who passed me at the foot of the staircase, walking silently across the marble hall.

"Good morning, Herr Knut."

He had spoken without glancing at me with his chin held high as if he was stretching his neck. The tone of his greeting was respectful yet authoritative; his voice rich and deep but with the unmistakable clipped quality I associated with townspeople. I stared after him.

"What an odd fellow that Marcel is, Katya."

"You think so?"

"One could easily mistake him for. . . . He's not like I imagine a servant."

"Don't you like him? I think he's very attractive."

Dark, curly hair, black eyes and a skin the colour of dried figs, Marcel looked as I imagined foreigners to be.

"An Italian boat must have docked the day his mother conceived."

"Don't be so unkind, Nanna."

"He's too handsome, Madlin."

"Can a man be too handsome?"

"If he is a servant, yes."

Personally, although I grudgingly agreed he was handsome, I thought his features coarse and large, covering too much of his face. His forehead was too shallow and his crinkled hair too near to his bushy black eyebrows to inspire confidence in his intelligence; his eyes too large and moist, too heavily lidded, concealed the emptiness of his fleeting thoughts but, together with his thick lips, betrayed his sensuality. His lips which, when I first saw them, I mistakenly believed chapped because they appeared swollen and puffed and unnaturally pink as if he had applied lipstick, were used, and all too often, to give a disarming smile. It came too readily, was too exaggerated and, although the smile dazzled, it was visibly insincere. Unfortunately, he knew his exceptionally white teeth and his broad smile could be used to advantage and, like a virtuoso, never let a moment pass without showing off his skill to impress us with his wicked charm.

"But he's so goodlooking, Knut."

"Don't say you've fallen under his spell too, Katya?"

"I think he's gorgeous."

"Mother has a rival then."

Katya's moods were undergoing a change. Normally passive, she now appeared brittle but I put it down to her advancing adolescence, though at times my patience was stretched by the reversal of effervescence into tragic gloom at the blink of an eye. Unable to control her moods, I, more than others, was subjected to her exasperating changes and could do nothing to combat them. Before my cynical remark about Mother and Marcel, which had been deliberately calculated to sting her into a rational assessment of Marcel, she had been moving about the room with all the ethereal grace of a romantic who feels love lightening her feet and giving new significance to common objects quite out of proportion to the praise or attention they merited; as when a loved one's handkerchief which has been deliberately dropped or accidentally discarded, stolen, even, takes on a fetish significance because of its association with the loved one. But suggest to the lovesick a similar reverence be paid to a boot belonging to a tramp or to a handkerchief found on the street and well coloured with green snot and they will grow faint at the thought of fondling, kissing or sniffing the object. And my sister reacted to my remark as if I had made such a suggestion. Her limbs became heavy, her bright eyes dulled and her shoulders drooped. Even her skin paled and her hair seemed to hang limp and lifeless.

"How can you be so unkind?"

"Be sensible, Katya."

"Idiot suggesting Mother. . . . How would you like it if I told you

Gudrun had kissed Marcel?"

"But she hasn't."

"That's all you know!"

She poked out her tongue and marched away with her head held high.

"I? Kissed Marcel? I'll rub soap into her eyes when I next wash her hair."

"No, Gudrun! Don't. She was only trying to hurt me."

"Hurt you? Have I not feelings?"

"But she knows I love you."

It was extraordinary the effect Marcel was having on us all without as yet exchanging more than a few polite words with any of us.

That same evening, Katya, in her nightdress, confronted me while I sat in bed. Her manner was not that of an outraged girl stamping her foot and gobbing words like an idiotic turkey, but of an unruffled young woman whose new sophistication was worn with an adolescent confidence and embarrassing exaggeration.

"Knut, darling . . . if Gudrun becomes pregnant by Marcel, you won't be so stupid as to tell Mother you were responsible, will you?"

It was uncanny how my sister knew me better than myself and it was only after remarks like these I came, or thought I came, to realise how transparent I was to others whilst to myself remained a perpetual enigma.

I did not for one moment believe Gudrun would be so foolish as to associate with Marcel. As it turned out, Katya's snide remark proved to be prophetic but I was too downcast to confront Mother with a lie and take upon myself the parentage of the child Gudrun had conceived even though convinced my timidity and Gudrun's inhibiting position of trust had driven her into the arms of Marcel who had taken unfair advantage of her sexual frustration. In retrospect this is probably true although I must admit Marcel's devilish good looks and manner corrupted most of the household, Katya and Karen included; but these he polluted and in a way which not only proved disastrous but showed that, for all his manliness, Marcel, in reality, was as perverted as his depraved smile.

"Do you like me, Gudrun?"

"You're the horriblest boy I know."

I stood up for the water to be ladelled over me from a small enamel bowl.

"Horrible, horrible?"

"Horrible."

Unlike the redeeming ecstasy of baptism, my evening and ritual douche was entirely sensual and while the water flowed over my body I prickled with eroticism.

"But do you still like me?"

Gudrun gave my bottom a playful flick.

"Out!"

"Oh, answer me, Gudrun! Do you like me?"

"No. Out."

Gudrun bent down and, using her hand, swilled the lather off my legs.

"Is that why you want to gobble me up?"

"Every last bit of you."

The familiar way Gudrun manipulated my limbs to soap me, the thoroughness with which she rinsed off the lather, or perhaps the sensuousness of the water—even the sound of the water, slopping over me and dribbling into the bath—all contributed to the erection of my penis. I did not associate Gudrun's turning of her back with her embarrassment at this phenomenon. While I stood waiting to be wrapped in the turkish towel, my own feeling, if any, was one of pride.

"Do you love me, Gudrun?"

"Get out and dry yourself."

"But I want to know!"

Without turning, Gudrun passed me the towel and I clambered out of the bath. Jumping up and down, and shivering, I asked her to tell me but she ordered me to dry myself and busied herself over the bathtub, wiping the sides while the water gurgled down the waste pipe.

Having finished drying myself, I held out a large crock bowl filled with talcum powder.

"Rub it in yourself."

Vexed, I took a handful and began to pat myself, creating a cloud in which I sneezed.

"Not that way! You'll have your mother after me for wasting it! Give it here." And Gudrun, muttering to herself, rubbed the talcum onto my body until my skin was smooth and silky and her hand slid over me with the sensuousness of nuzzled fur.

"You must learn to do it yourself, Knut. You're old enough. Now duck into your nightshirt and into bed with you. Go on. Hurry."

Almost as if she dared not, Gudrun, when I was dressed, gave my arm a gentle slap. But it was the look in her eye which made me think I was lost to her for ever. I had seen the same look when Gardol, instructed to turn the horses loose for the spring mating up in the hills, had slapped their rumps and stood looking before the horses, slow to sense their freedom at first, eventually picked up their feet and trotted away.

I lay in bed sullen and long-faced with only my eyes showing above the sheet. Gudrun leaned over me and, suspecting I was near to tears, pulled down the sheet a little way to look at my tell-tale mouth, turned down at the comers and quivering slightly.

"I have my feelings too, Knut. But I have responsibilities. If you were older . . . Now don't fret. I won't leave you. I promise."

She tucked in the blankets. Satisfied I was cocooned for the night, she unexpectedly kissed my mouth.

I lay for a long time tasting and relishing the kiss her lips had left on mine while the juices of desire flushed my cheeks.

Falling asleep, I dreamt my mother entered my bed, took me in her arms and, before kissing me with her talcumed lips, looked down at me with the face of Gudrun.

The next morning, Gudrun, more than usually bustling and efficient, swept and tidied without once pausing to interest herself in me; not asking how I felt or how I intended to pass the day. Without being told, I knew there was to be no more tickling, no more laughing until I was nearly sick and, but more devastating to my morale, for I desired above all else to be able to cling to someone warm and loving, there were to be no more unsolicited embraces.

And that is how it was.

Instead of patting my bottom with an "into bed", Gudrun clapped her hands and, in a toneless voice told me to hurry along, addressing me as "boy". Instead of shrugging me to her whenever I put my arm around her, she pushed me away. Instead of her untiring concern and efforts to make me happy, I became the butt of her irritability and was told I was a nuisance.

"Off with you. I've got things to do."

If I became stubborn and resisted, she would say, "Shoo! Off with you. You're like Dandy the way you follow me about."

Dandy was Aunt Beclier's French poodle. Detested by the family, Dandy had the embarrassing habit of embracing my leg with his two front paws and jerking himself against my woollen sock. I had no idea what he was doing or why, but from the reaction of various elders who pulled him away and bundled him out of the room with a sound slap, I knew it was something to be disapproved of. To be compared by Gudrun to this disgusting dog was an insult and one which rankled.

So too was the instruction to "go find Katya" if I attempted the slightest intimacy such as putting my arm about her neck and reading over her shoulder.

Gudrun's rejection was humiliating. I looked in the mirror hoping to find the reason. To me, I was still the me I had always been and while I stood gazing back at myself trying to imagine how I appeared to Gudrun, I found one spot which had not been there before; otherwise I had not altered.

I took to avoiding Gudrun on every possible occasion and was gratified to see that it had an effect upon her. Called for, looked for and chased after, I stretched her patience to the limit. But, even while she stood scolding me, threatening to report my wilful misbehaviour to my mother, I sensed the artificiality of her mock temper. I took great satisfaction in this discovery and carefully manipulated circumstances to create repeat dramas whenever possible. But the game, like all games which are played too long, proved not only exhausting but stretched Gudrun's tolerance into enmity.

"Knut, I want to speak to you."

It was not the voice of a girl who was only a few years older than myself, but an adult voice; petulant but authoritative; sounding the warning prelude to a scolding.

"Sit down."

Filled with uneasy anticipation, I lowered myself gingerly onto the edge of a chair.

"Knut. Dear. I don't know how to put this to you. And I don't want to be misunderstood."

Gudrun's hesitancy, coupled with the endearment, revealed the adulthood in which she had temporarily clothed herself was transparent and ill-fitting. I relaxed.

"You must not read into what I say . . . make significant an innocent word . . ."

Gudrun had obviously rehearsed what she wanted to say and this preparatory introduction she thought obligatory, but now that she had started, found exceedingly difficult. Even unnecessary.

"I obviously can't ask you to regard me as your mother, but . . ."

"I hate her!"

"Knut! You must not say that! Not even to me. Ever."

"I can't help what I feel, can I? And you know it's true."

"There are some things we must keep to ourselves. We have to consider the feelings of others before we give way to our own . . ."

This was part of her rehearsed speech but, because I had interrupted her, was probably out of context.

"But you know I don't like her, Gudrun. And she hates me!"

"Oh God."

She rose, with all the weight of an unwanted responsibility on her drooping shoulders and groped for the door handle. The door was swollen with damp and she had to tug it open. When she turned, I saw her face was flushed.

"I can't help it if I'm not your mother, can I? Can I?"

And she ran out of the room; weeping, I thought.

Several months later, ill in bed, propped up amongst countless pillows and too lethargic to read or turn my head, I followed Gudrun with my eyes and watched her battle with her emotional impartiality. Determined not to be over-concerned, detached but not unkind, she moved about my sick room, a stranger to her true feelings.

It was inevitable, while my illness dragged on, her determination to maintain her impartiality would weaken. Caught unawares, I saw reflected in her eyes an outflowing of concern and tenderness which she had tried to keep hidden from me. Ashamed to be found out, she redoubled her efforts to maintain her emotional equilibrium and, also, to transfer and have other support in a situation which was deteriorating rapidly and becoming intolerable, she took to summoning Mother to my bedside on the slightest of pretexts.

Far from helping Gudrun to dissociate herself, my mother's brief appearances and total lack of concern only served to underline my total dependence upon Gudrun.

Initially, it may have been pity or a sense of outrage caused by my mother's lack of regard for me, her son, which made Gudrun falter and, finally, revert to her original and loving ways. Whatever it was, it was driven like a wedge into her dammed emotions and the first trickle of endearment escaped like a single, silent tear. There soon followed such a flood of emotion that I was buoyed and carried on a tidal wave of sensations which were not only relieving but erotic.

It had begun when, after seeing I was prepared to sleep, Gudrun had laid the bell push with its long cord on the plumped pillow within easy reach of my hand and had tucked my hand beneath the clothes. I squeezed and hung onto her hand just long enough to break her will. With her hand resting on my stomach, she leaned over me and kissed my forehead. In complete silence, she sitting on the bed, I pressing her hand against me, we stayed unmoving while tears of relief stole down our cheeks. Unmoving, still, we remained in this attitude until our tears had dried on our contracting cheeks and our breathing had become even and quiet. Roused by the rustle of her clothing, I raised my bruised lids and saw her withdrawing from the room; smiling and loving; blowing me kisses.

That night, I slept as never before; secure in the knowledge I was loved.

Administered spoonfuls of love, which I sipped or gulped depending on how I hungered, I soon recovered and, allowed out of bed, felt safe in Gudrun's embrace when I took my first tentative steps towards the window.

I had acquired bed sores, and Doctor Borg had instructed Gudrun to rub soap into them in order to dry and harden the skin and I was duly undressed and turned onto my face. Doctor Borg had demonstrated to Gudrun how it was to be done, so on the first occasion, while he was present, she had shown no signs of embarrassment. But on the next day, alone with me and standing with a bar of sweetly-scented soap in her hand, Gudrun, to conceal her anxiety, was unusually flippant. The banter gradually ceased while she worked the soapy lather into my flesh and I detected in the cumulating silence the massaging taking on the moodiness of caressing. Excited, I languished under the sensation, not realising my sensuality was not private but was being shared, indeed, initiated by a Gudrun who was struggling with a quickening desire. It was only when, like an unsolicited bonne-bouche, she kissed me in the small of my back and, under her breath cried, "Oh God," before hurrying from the room, I realised the extent of the strain she was under.

She never soaped me again nor was it ever referred to by either of us, even though my sores persisted for some considerable time afterwards. And, although we did not shrink from physical contact, neither of us allowed a situation to arise which would test us needlessly, irritating a frustration which both of us, and certainly I, could not have coped with.

Of sex I knew nothing and Gudrun was probably not insensitive to this so, although I was made timid by the brink from which my sensations threatened to cast me, I did not have to struggle, like Gudrun, with a desire which she knew well enough how to satisfy. To her, all credit is due and accounts for the affection I still hold as memory. At the time, it was love. A real love and one which I depended upon if life was to be lived out.

Two months after the incident arising from my bed sores, I was sat indoors on a summer day. A day when it was bright and warm and the trees so full of sap they thrust skywards, enveloping the landscape with profuse growth. Gudrun came silently up behind me and laid her hand on my shoulder. I had a rug about my legs and was sat gazing out of the window overlooking the lake and lawns. Though much improved in health, I was still succumbing to breathlessness and found at times I had to sit perfectly still in order to recover. Behind me, Gudrun stood unmoving with her hand on my shoulder. When I placed my fingers over Gudrun's, she brought her cheek down and rested it on the top of my head.

The picture we made, silhouetted against the window, was one of utmost tenderness and tranquillity; to some perhaps grotesquely sentimental, to my mother, it was black and disturbing.

"Gudrun! Stop fussing around that boy! Haven't you any work to do?"

And my mother laid her crop across the back of Gudrun's thighs, making her flinch and buckle at the knees before she hurried out.

"It's about time that wretched girl had a child of her own. It's disgusting the way she fawns over you all the time. She's not been up to anything, has she? Has she? Serving girls generally do. They're very adept at corrupting young boys. Well? Has she?"

"Has she what?"

"Obviously she hasn't. That's a relief. Give your mother a kiss."

The cold flesh of her face and her pursed lips came slowly down towards me. I spat into her eye.

Her slap knocked me out of the chair.

Having become overfond of a canary which she called Orila, (originally she had christened it Maximilian but because she was not certain of the bird's sex she had re-christened it Maximilian-or-ila which became shortened to Orila), my mother got into the habit of taking it with her wherever she went. At table, on walks, in the bathroom, the bird in its wooden cage accompanied Mother at all times.

While my mother's attachment for the bird grew and being estranged from Nanna Axell, she found comfort with Helga down in the kitchens. They seldom held conversations because Helga's deference for Mother made continuous dialogue impossible. However, this did not seem to upset Mother, who would wander about the kitchens, birdcage in hand, nibbling sultanas and speaking about anything and everything which entered her mind.

Granoise disapproved of my mother's presence in the kitchens, being distrustful of anyone who behaved as wish and fancy moved them. (Having been brought up in the belief that each class had a rigid but different standard of conduct, Granoise would have reasoned that my mother's familiarity with the staff was a breach of propriety. But, more to the point and in all probability, she believed my mother was spying on her; finding out if she was capable of work and still employable.) Pretending to be busy, Old Granoise muttered and threw dark looks from under her dirty brow. Mother was not insensitive and, either because conversation with Helga was monosyllabic or the black looks of Granoise clouded the kitchens, she suddenly stopped going down into the basement. Everyone sighed with relief when it became known, and seem to relax, including Marcel, whose embarrassment at my ageing, limping mother had turned into silent contempt; but not Helga.

"A person can go daft without companionship. Especially a woman and at her time of life."

So she left out the utensils for Mother to make herself a cup of hot chocolate in the mornings when the rest of the household were still fast asleep.

On the morning she died, my mother had come down into the kitchen as usual. Because it was so cold, she had put Orila in his/her cage on top of the stove to warm. About to fill the saucepan in which she boiled the milk, Mother suffered a heart attack and fell to the floor dead.

It was an hour later when Helga shuffled down into the kitchens to open up the vents and draw the fires. Not only did she find my mother stretched out on the floor but Orila, its feathers singed, fluttering about in the top of his/her cage which was smouldering on the stove and rapidly being reduced to charcoal.

The shock of my mother's death was because it was unexpected but I did not grieve because I was so relieved.

When Borg came the second time, and with the death certificate, he remarked that my sister had aged in the last two days.

"She has matured considerably, but I doubt if she can cope on her own."

She didn't have to, both of us were drowned by a tidal wave of relations who swamped the house, each a potential foster parent and each intent on treachery.

Wisely, as it turned out, Nanna Axell retired to her bed and stayed there until she was nearly a hundred years old but always, and from her bed, effectively in control of situations with an authority, compassion and a knowledge of human nature which was to surprise me.

The elders who returned for my mother's funeral soon had their black mourning clothes unpacked. It would be cynical of me to suggest they did not don masks of grief because their sallow faces were already and perpetually moulded in gloom, but it would be true to say the bitterness which soured their complexions had nothing to do with Madlin's death. It was their disillusion with life which marked them. Confined and narrow in their outlook, they stole laughter and hid it in their innumerable, black, brass-studded trunks as if joy were some shaming fetish. Because of their bigotry, sincerity had become an expediency for the justification of their irrationality and it showed on their grim faces as well as in their crabbed movements. That they had returned to peck at the remains of the Strobl estate, to become parasites of a decaying corpse, I only surmised because of the liquidity of their condolences. Katya arrived at the same conclusion.

"Greed, of any kind, produces an excess of spittle. Next time, watch them lick the overspill from the corner of their mouths and swallow it down. They pretend to be overcome and dumb with grief but really, they're all very excited. And mark my word, Knut, pandemonium will fol-low, the moment the period of mourning for Mother is over."

Shortly before her death and unknown to all—on a whim, totally without justification, although the romantic would applaud such a caprice —my mother had told Gort, the family solicitor, it was her wish to be cremated and her ashes scattered over the Northern wastes. When Gort, creaking in every limb, told us, I thought he was referring to the wilder-ness in the north part of the estate, but Katya corrected me.

"Goose! Beyond Arvhed."

It was such a ridiculous proposition, because there was no way of reaching Arvhed in winter, I thought Gort would secretly empty the ashes into a dustbin. It had not occurred to me the ashes would not deteriorate if kept.

"She expressly stated it should not be done from an aeroplane, so, come the spring, I will make the journey myself, Herr Strobl."

He did, and sent confirmation of the fact when we had forgotten all about it. When I started to read his letter, I had an image of him, bent and stiff, walking awkwardly amongst the fir trees scattering the ashes like a farmer broadcasting seed, but he went on to describe the land as bleak. "I'm glad to have had the opportunity to visit that part of my country as ordinarily I would not chosen to have visited it." That he had done the scattering efficiently and as instructed, I had no doubt, but I would not have held it against him if, in a landscape which was waste and bald and tumbled with rocks on which a few mosses clung, he had crouched down behind a boulder and let the sharp winds whip the ash off his open palm. The letter was dated July, and in it he not only described the area in detail but enclosed a sketch plan—"should you contemplate a visit to lay posies." Pleased as my mother would have been with his diligence, she would have been annoyed to know he had paid a man to bury the empty casket and roll a boulder over a shallow grave because the ground was very stony. "You cannot mistake the spot for the boulder has the look of a bearded gentleman."

From such slender beginnings a myth could have been written, telling of a youth who wandered the North in search of a bearded giant who was guardian of Pandora's fabled casket. I wanted to throw the letter away but Katya insisted it be included in the family records.

"We may have children of our own one day who would like to know what became of their grandmother." I blushed and dutifully filed the letter away.

Uncle Godric, when told Madlin's body was to be cremated, was indignant.

"That's what comes of being so damned scatterbrained. Didn't she realise she was breaking with tradition? What can we mourn over? Dammit, the headstone need only have been modest."

The rest of the elders agreed she had been thoughtless and concluded that before her body was sent to Haggstianstad there must be a service in the house chapel.

I had not been in the chapel since my father's death. Cold and mouldy, it seemed preposterous that a service could be held in such a bleak cavern. But Karen and Katya, helped by Uncle Ira, and Gerda, his autumnal wife, worked hard and, with the aid of heaters from the stables, evergreen boughs, some moth-eaten flags and a considerable amount of scrubbing and polishing, decorated and warmed the cleaned but bleak interior. From somewhere, a white altar cloth was found and several pieces of silver polished and set either side of the cross. To me, this effect made the altar look like a dining room table, but Ira seemed well pleased; possibly because he was to read the lesson, which meant the whole of the fifteenth chapter of Corinthians, not part, as is usual.

Once again, Mogudo officiated at the service. He wore his mittens and would have kept them on throughout the service if Godric, failing to catch his eye, had not gone up to him and in a loud whisper ordered Mogudo to "take off those tatty gloves and show some respect, man." Mogudo had done so and, after blowing on his chilblains, had given Godric a look which only a priest officiating at a Black Mass could have cast, then he found his place and continued. Katya was separated from me by the aisle and the coffin which stood between us. Whenever I happened to glance across at her, she seemed to be deeply moved, whereas I was suffering the ritual in boredom. Somewhere behind me, Helga stifled a sob which later Ira turned to weeping with his sonorous voice when he dramatised the reading of the lesson. He managed the moment so well and heightened the tension in the small chapel to such a degree that I thought I detected in the look which Mogudo gave him afterwards just a touch of envy. It certainly moved Aunt Estrild to play the small harmonium with verve and compassion, despite the fact mould, and perhaps mice, had rendered a few notes silent. But she played "round" them and none of the elders noticed or remarked upon the odd and occasional puffs of air which should have been C natural.

Afterwards, alone with Nanna Axell, for we were the only two who did not accompany the coffin on its long journey to Haggstianstad, I was admonished for my levity. I suspected Nanna Axell, despite her demeanour, was secretly in agreement with my unnatural sentiment but, as senior elder, was merely doing her duty in rebuking me.

Later, lying back in her bed, she said, "Knut, a herdsman will sometimes beat his favourite cow. Prod a stick under her tail and thoroughly abuse the animal. It is not that the cow has been particularly obstinate, or her yield low, but because, the night before, the herdsman's wife had shewn herself unreasonable. For that, the poor cow is made to suffer." It was an odd analogy for Nanna Axell to make, but it was not lost upon me and I tried, sympathetically, to equate the pain it cost her to make such an apology for Madlin who, difficult as it was for me to imagine, had been her only child and daughter, with the bitterness of my keen disaffection; but I could not. The remorse I felt was the guilt of happiness.

When Katya and the elders returned on the following day from Haggstianstad, other relatives arrived with them. Some to pay their respects and who left the next day, others for an indefinite stay. These funerary rooks spread their meagre possessions about the rooms they occupied as if to delineate their claim to territory, and straight away began wresting from one another the various manageable objects which they swore Madlin had wanted them to have when she died. Neither I, nor Katya, whose prediction had proved correct, took any part in the tussle and our wordless contempt for their greed embarrassed but did not stop them. It was finally Nanna Axell, from the throne of her majestic bed, and whose authority they mutteringly acknowledged, who succeeded in bringing them to heel, but not before various and prized heirlooms had been swallowed up in outsized trunks which the carriers discreetly came to collect. In later years, I learned from Tetty, the lodge housekeeper, the exact amount of plunder which had been removed. Ill and overcome by remorse, she confessed to having accepted bribes from the more avaricious of the elders and, in the dead of night, had taken trunks of valuables and pieces of furniture from where they had been secretly piled in the stables under straw and carted them on her wheelbarrow to the lodge to await collection, far from the prying eyes of others.

During all this time, Katya worked hard and ceaselessly, like a young mother, but she was unable to assert herself over the elders who made all the decisions round the dining room table, excluding Katya and me from their conversations although we were both present. They seemed content to let her undertake the arrangements they had made but not willing to burden themselves with the work it entailed. As a consequence, during the following months, Katya became pale and her wide, mauve eyes sank lifelessly into her head. On the verge of tears one evening she confessed she could no longer cope.

"The longer they stay, the more determined I am to leave. Come with me, Knut."

I reassured her and, not a little disturbed by my own cowardice, persuaded her to go to bed earlier than was usual. The role of optimist was very alien to me and the last of the relations to arrive did nothing to dispel this notion.

A month later, puffing and panting, Aunt Sidony waddled into the house. Marcel had never seen her before and she frightened the life out of him when she rumbled past him with a clean, white handkerchief draped over her head and covering her face. Suffering from cancer of the nose and jaw, she hid her disease and, uncomplaining, lived a serene life in a small flat in the capital near to the Spordon hospital. From time to time, since I was a child, she had paid us short visits, so I had become familiar with her disconcerting appearance yet, because of the kerchief which perpetually covered her face, had no idea what this plump and odiferous aunt of mine really looked like; even some of the elders confessed to having forgotten. "I wouldn't recognise her in any case. She has put on so much weight", was Ira's only comment. Nanna Axell produced a brown snapshot, but the skinny child, her eyes screwed up against the sun, hands behind her and standing on the outside edges of her feet, bore little resemblance to the fat and waddling Aunt Sidony I knew. Being, as some of the elders suggested, over-imaginative and told that this was a failing, I nevertheless thought I knew what Aunt Sidony's face looked like in the darkness under her handkerchief.

One day, taken in the trap on one of my rare outings to the little village of Lindehult, Gardol had reined the horse just as we were passing a yard and from which a wagon was awkwardly turning. Standing in an open barn door a knacker had turned to see who had come trotting down the lane. In his bloody arms, he held the flayed head of a horse. Wet and red, stripped and raw, it was a gory lump from which the dead eyes stared out with an expression of gaping terror. From that moment, Aunt Sidony's face beneath the kerchief was known to me and I would run a mile rather than be picked up and jigged on her satin lap. She would try and tempt me with the gelatinous sweetmeats she ate by the box, her hand mysteriously disappearing under the kerchief to feed the jelly cubes into the raw edges of her mouth, but I wouldn't be coaxed. Dusting the powdered sugar off her bosom, she rubbed the tips of her fingers together and told me it wasn't every child who got offered sweeties from foreign parts; forgetting I could read the gold labels on the boxes she was continually giving me to keep my crayons in. To watch the monster feed and hear the frayed lips slop together and the little gurgles she gave, had not been the least of my terrors. She had a habit of belching and the kerchief would breeze outwards like a curtain in a gust of wind. When this happened I was terrified in case I would accidentally see under the kerchief when it lifted away from her face. Once, when she had accompanied me on a walk in the grounds, we had turned the comer of the house to be met by the full force of a wind which would have whipped off her kerchief had she not made a sudden grab at it. But even as she clutched it, the wind moulded it to her features and I thought I saw the void where her nose should have been.

Soon after her arrival, Aunt Sidony cornered me in the pine room and, holding my hand to condole with me for my loss, began to talk wildly and with the disconcerning frankness of the lonely. Part of her confession was to admit to a love for my father.

"I don't bear your mother a grudge, Knut, especially now she's dead, but it was a dirty trick she played on me. Of course Katya would have been a bastard, so I had no alternative but to accept that Onan should marry Madlin. But think, you might have been *my* son."

Knowing she could see the blurred outline of my grey face through the cotton, I tried not to reveal my disgust but said that life was very cruel, hoping she would interpret my remark as sympathy while I eased myself from her clamp grip. When I told Katya that she might have been a bastard, she replied she would have welcomed the notoriety if it had meant she wouldn't have had to cope with the elders. "If I had known death was so exhausting for the living, I'd rather have not been born." Appreciating she was emotionally extended I did not tell her I would have been unbearably lonely without her.

A month after Aunt Sidony arrived, she foolishly, but possibly out of curiosity or being bored, ventured into the north wing. This part of the house had been emptied of nearly everything and the swollen doors locked because a wide and alarming crack zigzagged up from the foundations to the collapsing roof, making the structure unsafe. Wandering through the rooms, gazing at the desolation through the mist of her kerchief, she trod on a patch of rotten flooring which collapsed under her weight and she fell through to the foundations. Her screams alerted Marcel who, with Ira, myself and Katya following, hurried into the north wing. There, in the farthest room, trapped, with only her head visible above the boards, was Aunt Sidony. It was strange to see her balloon head, seemingly disconnected from her body, lying on the floor lit by the pale sun which filtered in through the shutters. Seeing her like this, I thought of the imprisoned traitors in the region of Judecca who had been embedded up to their necks in ice and which Dante had described so vividly in his Inferno. The handkerchief which had covered her face had fluttered away and as we cautiously approached her, she turned her great watery eyes upon us and whined pitifully. Gaudily rouged, her mouth a mess of lipstick and her eyelashes mascara'd, she had the bloated face of an overfed trollop. There was no sign of the cancerous growth; only the ravages of excess puffed her otherwise baby-faced complexion. A blush of embarrassment rose on her rouged cheeks and she squeaked apologetically when the four of us eased her up, out of the hole. Katya handed back the handkerchief but Aunt Sidony stuffed it into her cleavage.

"I shall leave tomorrow. First thing", and we allowed her to walk ahead of us out of the north wing.

When Sidony left in the morning, she held her head proudly to weather the silent contempt of the elders who had congregated to gloat over her departure. Touchingly, she bade goodbye to Katya and, thanking Katya for her kindness, added, "Don't worry on my account, Katya dear. I intend to lead the apes in Hell a very pretty dance." As she was a spinster,

I have no doubt that is what she intended to do, if not sooner. I told Katya so but she was cross and said I lacked compassion for the poor old dear.

"Who knows what terror drove Sidony to hide from everyone? I only hope that when my reason crumbles, you will not snigger so openly."

Six months later, according to a Captain Groenderblat who wrote to us from the port of Carlsingbrod in the South, Aunt Sidony had boarded a cargo boat bound for the Middle East and had left owing him money. Katya surmised that Sidony was living with the gentleman but was too proud to write herself. "Send it, Knut, only don't tell the elders she is short of money." I did as I was bid but later received a note from Sidony which had been hastily scrawled on the back of a Hotel Splendide menu card, saying on no account should I send money to anyone using her name. Katya was heartbroken, imagining Aunt Sidony, at an age when circumspection is paramount, had thrown herself into a love affair which had become unmentionably sordid. "And it is all our fault, Knut!" I failed to see that it was but to please Katya I wrote to Aunt Sidony saying she was welcome to return to us if she was in difficulties.

We never had an answer and to this day, I do not know whether she is alive or dead or in some foreign port; a greasy encumbrance in some dreadful brothel. An idea encouraged by Katya who believed women were susceptible to the will of men, long after they were of an age when I reasoned they were of no interest to anyone.

After Sidony's departure, the house settled down and became still. Only the activity in the kitchens gave any hint of the number of mouths which had to be fed, for the elders, either because of their infirmities or to avoid those with whom they were quarrelling, kept to their rooms or sat over the fire in the pine room. The only time they met as a body was at dinner and the conversation, thankfully, because of the feuds, was fitful and never amounted to more than reminiscing. This I did not mind except when a parallel was drawn and Katya and I seemed implicated by default for the apparent lack of moral fibre which our forebears had been more than amply endowed.

Although Katya helped about the house and was sometimes assisted by Gerda or Estrild, the bulk of the work, of necessity, fell upon Karen who could always be seen walking at a trot, her hair plastered to her forehead, in answer to one or all of the jangling bells. When Katya insisted Karen rest, the house filled with shrill calls from the rooms where plaintive voices enquired querulously if they had been forgotten, so making Katya run the gauntlet for several days on end. Marcel condescendingly shared in some of the chores which he thought did not impinge upon his dignity, but he was so deliberately slow and the elders' patience short that it helped very little to have him moodily play the reluctant housemaid. Notwithstanding these minor ructions, time and routine numbed the elders eventually and the house became an oasis of calm.

During the short summer which followed, my health improved and the colour returned to Katya's cheeks and together we would wander round the grounds. Uncut for several years, the lawns had taken on the appearance of meadows and vigorous weeds obscured the brick paths. Although Gardol worked hard and kept the main drive clean and the banks cut short, he was too overworked to sort out the jungled flower beds where only the hardiest of plants which had the fecundity of weeds struggled up through the choking tangle. If by chance a tender plant blinked in the matted undergrowth, Gardol, more from surprise than compassion, would clear and weed round the flower, but invariably the petals would cringe and wither away as if in protest against the exposure of its secret blooming.

It did not bother me that the formality of the grounds was lost, and perhaps for ever, but Katya argued it was by the very manner in which man ordered and asserted himself over nature, one could tell to what extent he was civilised. Slighted, I never failed to comment how cultured she was when we passed the little patch of soil she kept clear of weeds and planted with flowers. "I refuse to be provoked, Knut", and we would have to stop while a few weeds were lifted and the dead blooms pinched off. Occasionally, on our walks, we would come across a relative sat in the weak sunlight, but seen from a distance, he or she could be avoided. However, we were often surprised by Ira and Gerda, who were the only two besides ourselves who regularly went for walks, but the four of us would pass each other in silence—even though we trod on the same, narrow path and neither party deigned to step into the long grass to let the other pass. Despite these embarrassing moments, Katya and I enjoyed our walks and both longed for the summer to continue for we were happiest when, alone, we could turn our faces up to the sun and luxuriate in its warmth.

We had hoped to spend some of our time on the lake rowing. Besides being thoroughly enjoyable, the exercise opened my lungs. But the boat was waterlogged and when Gardol helped us drag it out of the weeds he declared it was too rotten for him to repair. Disappointed, we continued on round the lake.

"If it wasn't for Felix, I'd go in for a swim." For some mysterious reason, Felix had spent most of the summer on the edges of the lake jabbing at the bushes with his cane. "I'll not have him see me naked," and Katya kicked at a tuft of grass to show her annoyance.

Always in summer, Katya went swimming. When I was with her, she would make me turn my back while she undressed and slipped into the water. I would turn to see Katya, like an otter which noiselessly and unexpectedly noses its way from the bank, swim away from me and with the same effortless ease. In the middle of the lake she would turn luxuriantly, wave and make her way slowly back. The sound of the water chuckling at her body, the slow rills which quietly spilled over the surface of the otherwise still lake, her rhythmic movements and her pale green flesh below the water always affected me in the same way. I would sit gazing at her until, crouching in the mud below me, her arms over her breasts, she implored me to let her get out.

But it was a different Katya who returned to be teased when I stood above her. With her hair plastered to her skull, her eyelashes matted into stars, it was a Katya I didn't know. Seemingly, I was looking at the bone beneath the flesh which, because of the perfection of its structure, made her strikingly more handsome. It was the real Katya I glimpsed beneath the flashing smile, the Katya she possibly felt herself to be.

Invariably splashed, I would turn away while she put on her dress, gathered up her underclothes and then together we would make a mad clash for the house. These races she always won and would be leaning out of her bedroom window chaffing me while I was still labouring across the lawns.

If she was feeling particularly happy and the water warm, she would stay in the centre of the lake and, like a duck grubbing weeds, turn turtle and disappear, leaving ghostly rings on the surface of the lake. When these finally dissipated and the water became still and she was nowhere to be seen, I would panic, imagining she had become entangled in the weeds. But always, there was a sudden surge of water and she would re-appear some distance away, give a toss to her head and plunge beneath the surface again. It was odd to see her white body flash and turn, seemingly liquid and one with the water, for her suppleness, when she effortlessly jack-knifed, and the final flick she made with her feet, gave her the look of a silver-bellied fish; a mythical fish which all lakes skimmed with mist have lurking in their depths. But no fish however exotic, or be it a plump trout or river salmon, could give me the same rush of joy I felt when watching my sister play in the water. That she swam with me as on-looker was partly habit and because, when we had been younger, a cousin had drowned in the lake. After a search for him the whole night, the lake had been dragged the following morning and Ghalin's body found. Ever after, Madlin insisted Katya should always have someone with her when she swam. This seemed eminently sensible, but for the fact I could not swim; nor for that matter, could anyone else, although Gerda said that at a pinch she might be able to rescue someone from drowning. Even Karen, who sometimes accompanied Katya if time and duty allowed, could do no more than dog paddle. I had come across them once, attracted by their squeals. Katya was stood waist deep in the water endeavouring to hold up a wildly splashing Karen, but I had been ordered not to watch to save Karen from further embarrassment. When I asked later how Karen was pro-gressing, it was obvious that Katya had given up all attempts to instruct her and, like me, Karen was to be a landlocked observer.

"Knut, I'm going to swim. Damn Felix." She seized my hand and pulled me towards the boat. "It'll stay afloat long enough to get us to the island!"

The "island" was a clump of bushes and a single tree which stuck out of the lake. It marked the spot where my great-grandfather had tried to build an island but, because of an insufficient foundation, it had settled down and disappeared, leaving only the lone tree and a few bushes sticking up out of the water.

The idea of rowing to the island in a boat which was already partially sunk terrified me and I said as much. But Katya was adamant, and, when we had tipped the water out, we set off with an oar apiece to make our journey as rapid as possible. Even so it took, or seemed to take, an age before, as Katya had predicted, we reached the island without sinking. All the way across I had watched the level of the water rise in the boat and although safely bumped against the island, I couldn't help but wonder about our journey back.

Standing on the island was a question of balance rather than taking one's ease lying full-length because the shrubs took up most of the hillock and the large tree. the rest. In a moment Katya was stripped, and behind me I heard her give a great whoop of delight. She must have jumped or dived because a great wash came rolling back, wetting my ankles as the water swilled about me. She is mad, I thought, and stood holding onto the tree feeling miserable. For a while, Katya larked about in the water giving squeals of shivering delight while I, with my toe, tried to prevent her wet clothes from drifting away.

"Oh you should come in, Knut, it's delicious!"

Just in front of where I was precariously perched, the ground must have fallen away in a slab, for when Katya swam towards me she put up her arm to be hauled out. "I must dive, Knut. I simply must try to dive this once."

I eased myself round the tree to give her room and stood looking out across the lake. From the centre, the bushes round the edge seemed peopled with eyes and I felt very exposed. When there was still no splash I called out for Katya to hurry, thinking Felix might be watching while she still stood there, her arms raised and poised to dive. But from above me, not behind, there came an exclamation when Katya, climbing the tree, barked her shin.

"Ouch. No, don't look up. I'm all right." With my hands on the trunk I felt the old tree groan while she worked her way up and out onto a branch above me. I yelled out that she was mad, but she sniggered while the water from her body dripped onto my head. Suddenly the leaves rustled violently when, as she dived, the bough released of her weight sprung back shuddering. In front of my eyes, a white form, buckled and ungainly, smacked into the water and a wave swept over the island. I made a grab for her clothes but saved only her dress, the rest, slowly tumbling, sank with her shoes. It seemed an age before her head reappeared and she gasped her way to the bank, groaning. She had evidently struck her head for soon, mixed with water, a trickle of blood flowed from beneath her hand. She insisted I did not fuss and after a while hauled herself out. When she had struggled into her wet dress, we found it was impossible to empty the boat so we embarked in a craft which was already perilously near to being totally waterlogged. Inevitably, we sank, but not before Katya had said in a very tired voice as we sat, up to our waists in water, "I think it's about time we grew up, Knut. Our childhood is over." Tumbled out of the boat, Katya, who was as calm as she was reassuring, took hold of me and swam towards the shore.

When we staggered out of the water Felix confronted us. Stabbing the ferrule of his cane into the soft earth, he upbraided us for our foolishness. "I saw you both. The pair of you. Misbehaving like children. Disgraceful!" In our wet clothes, we half walked and half ran back to the house while Felix stood his ground shouting after us that we deserved to be beaten.

"Did you notice Felix had a pair of opera glasses with him, Knut?" I hadn't and hurried shivering into the house.

The immediate consequence of our misadventure was that I caught a chill and had to go straight to bed while Katya nursed a large bump on her forehead, the size of a pigeon's egg, which she couldn't refrain from touching with her forefinger and wincing.

Sat on my bed that same evening while I sipped the hot milk she had brought me, Katya, dabbing her bruise, said she thought Felix, knowing she bathed nude, had hung about the lake all summer hoping to catch a glimpse of her naked. I was not convinced he had been acting the voyeur. "Oh, come, Knut. You know what old men are like. They'll do anything to glimpse bare flesh." I buried my blush in the glass of hot milk, and for my sins, burnt my tongue.

I had taken advantage of my privileged friendship that afternoon and sneaked a look at Katya. Despite the mishaps, I had carried away with me a lasting image of a Katya grown into womanhood; emphasised by the mysterious bush, lodged like fuzz in the fork of her legs, and as blonde as her hair. This tantalising triangle glistened with droplets which fell through the tangle to stream from it as from a bull's pizzle and there returned an image from childhood when she had squatted above the dry straw in the stable. I baulked at the memory while this selfsame girl sat beside me on the bed unaware of my dark thoughts and the grinding of my teeth.

"I've a good mind to have a word with Nanna Axell about him, Knut." I protested more in defence of my own shortcomings, that it was not necessary and besides, Nanna Axell would only send him away with a flea in his ear. "I'm not so sure. When I was a little girl, he used to get up to all sorts of strange things." When asked what, she told me Felix had several times enticed her into his room under the pretext he was a magician. "An escapologist, I think he said." Having closed the door, he would manoeuvre a large trunk into the middle of the room and get into it. Instructed to sit astride the lid when it was closed and count up to a hundred, Katya had obliged. "Of course, he never escaped, although there was a lot of grunting and scrabbling about inside the trunk. But I wasn't to know, was I?" I did not understand. "That's what I like about you, Knut. You are so innocent," and she kissed me goodnight. If only she had known.

Before sleep overtook me, something which Uncle Mungo said came back to me. We had been watching Felix walking about the grounds switching the heads off flowers with his cane. Mungo had turned to me and said, "It's a pity he would enjoy it so much, but someone really ought to break that damned stick over his back."

My chill had been only slight but when I was well enough to get up again the summer seemed to have passed and already at night the valleys were filling with autumnal mists. So, long before the snow came, I had already withdrawn into the house and had abandoned the landscape to the grip of frost.

When winter came, isolating and massing chilled and crisp drifts of snow up against the house, Katya and I were reminded of our mother when the anniversary of her death drew near and it occurred to us how little she had occupied our thoughts during that first, and what should have been painful, year.

"I would not like to think, Knut—to know now, that when I die, I shall not be missed." My brotherly affection she seemed to think inadequate. "I mean, really missed."

When I told her I would pine away, Katya agreed I would be lost without her but doubted if I would grieve with the despair of lost love. I protested and said that on the contrary, I would be likely to make a far more significant gesture than merely knocking my brow and weeping.

"Kill yourself? How foolish." I was crestfallen. I had made the supreme offer to dramatise my proof and she had rejected it out of hand. "It would please me much more to know you thought of me every single day. That way, I would know I was still—alive."

I asked on impulse if she would mind if I was buried alongside her in the same grave.

"Well if you promise not to fidget." I reminded her that she snored and got punched for my beastliness.

For the next month I saw very little of her. When we met at dinner she appeared more than usually preoccupied with her own thoughts. Imagining it was the guilt of her filial disaffection for our dead Mother which troubled her and that she was overcome by remorse, I respectfully left her alone to work through to her own solution.

I eventually approached her when I felt she had been in the grip of this sullen mood for far too long, but she turned her back and said she had no time to chatter. "And please stop following me everywhere."

It was not true I had been clogging her heels. The fact of the matter was that when I went looking for her, she was nowhere to be found.

Left on my own, I began to mope. Full of self-pity, I would sit staring out of the window, day after day, wondering what was to become of me. Often in the past, a stay in a sanatorium had been suggested. Whether this was the "bogey man" which other children are threatened with, I do not know, but I suspect it was. "You will be amongst others of your own kind, Knut," Mother had said, as if she thought I was a mongol or backward child. And I would shrink from the phrase, "boys of your own age", as I did from her monotonous, "don't be so selfish". How could one hoard a disease? But when the time came for me to leave and I had worked myself into a state of exhaustion with nervous apprehension, my admittance was cancelled for any number of unexplained reasons. From overheard conversations it appeared that "the Germans", "Gerda's opinion" and the "unfortunate suicide of that child" were responsible. Each year the threat of a stay in a Sanatorium was raised before me like a spectre and with equal regularity it was cancelled, so that in the end I came not to believe in this Valhalla and forgot all about it. That is, until Katya paid me an unexpected visit one evening before dinner.

"I've been thinking about you, Knut. You ought to go to the Fraujunga Sanatorium in Uppevalla." The name brought memory flooding back and I groaned out loud. "For a while at least. The money is ours to spend how we see fit. And your good health comes before the elders' comfort. What do you say?"

I asked why she was so suddenly anxious to get rid of me.

"Don't be so silly, Knut. Besides, I shall come and stay in Uppevalla. and visit you daily."

But I wasn't convinced my removal to this mountain sanatorium was not a pretext for some scheme she had for leaving. Telling her I did not wish to talk about it and that I wouldn't go, I asked her what she had been doing with herself as I had seen so little of her.

"Things." When asked to be more explicit, she became cross. "Just things. The house doesn't run itself you know!" Before she slammed out of the room she turned to me and said how selfish I was being for not realising she was only trying to do her best for me. When I told her those were the very words Mother used, she stamped her foot. "I hate you!"

I wanted to believe it was because she was so busy that when I went in search of her she could not be found, but when I went to the rooms where she was most likely to be and there was no sign of her, I began to think she was deliberately avoiding me. It wasn't that I was going to go back on my decision but I could not bear to war with my sister and live with misunderstanding as a treacherous division between us. Knowing Marcel never neglected to keep himself informed of what everyone was doing in the house, I swallowed my pride and asked him if he knew of Katya's whereabouts.

"I—know where Katya is? I? Your sister is in so many places doing so many things. I do not know where she is."

I did not believe him and, for the first time in my life, gave way to temper and called him a bloody liar. I would have walked past him but he put himself in front of me and so close, our clothes touched. I had never before realised how swarthy he was, and hairy. He smelt of fish oil and lemon.

"I beg your pardon, Herr Strobl?" His menacing attitude forced me to apologise and I withdrew, concealing my anger.

The opportunity to turn the tables on Marcel occurred sooner than expected. Two days later, rounding a corner into the passage which ran past Katya's room, I saw Marcel stood outside her door. He was quick but not quite quick enough but that I had surprised him was obvious.

"You are mistaken, Herr Strobl, I was not listening. I was about to knock." I had not accused him of listening so I presumed he had been about to look through the keyhole. I waved him away and he went meekly.

When I knocked on the door, it was Katya's voice which bade me enter. "Did you know Marcel was looking through your keyhole?"

Katya was not shocked but coloured slightly. When I suggested it was about time we had a family conference to decide what should be done with him, Katya said she would deal with the matter and not to go troubling the elders.

"You're just in time for tea, Knut."

I asked her how long she had been taking tea in the afternoons.

"To tell you the truth, this is the very first occasion. And don't let on, because Karen stole this scented tea from Nanna Axell." Karen, who stood holding a tray, giggled and the cups and saucers rattled.

"Have a cup, Knut. Go on." I refused. "You have no understanding or appreciation of the more subtle tastes, Knut. You will end eating mustard by the spoonful." Katya's detestation of mustard was a family joke and she boasted to having tasted it only once in her lifetime. "The tongue has two uses. For talking and tasting. If you burn it you can't do either."

To prove it had a third use and because it was my only party trick, I touched my nose with my tongue which always annoyed Katya. "Karen has my full permission to call you pig if she wishes. And to your face." Karen demurred but could hardly hold onto the tray for laughter. "You're reducing my nice sedate tea party to a 'barn up'. Please leave."

Katya's friendliness for Karen seemed to have ripened considerably over a period of several months, although judging from their tendency to giggle, it had not matured into a stabilised and adult relationship. Several times the elders complained that their afternoon naps were being disturbed by unnecessary laughter and frivolity, but I sided with Katya because her increased confidence and the flushed and, at times, the serene look she was acquiring, was sufficient justification for the "malarky", as Godric put it, to continue. Only when I observed that Katya was becoming subject to sudden and alarming changes of mood, which was most unlike her, did I think a more sobering influence should be brought to bear. But when approached, she turned her back saying she wanted to be left alone to think. This new habit of turning her back was a gesture which hurt me more than spiteful words, and it did not become her. "I can't bear your doleful eyes, Knut," was one of many excuses.

One afternoon, seeing she had been crying, I gently asked if I could be of any comfort but she pushed me in the chest and shouted, "Fool!" Stung, I was astonished by how rapidly my momentary anguish turned to tenderness and seriously began to wonder if my eagerness to earn and enjoy humiliation was a form of perversion. My doubts were not set aside when, on another occasion, slapped quite unnecessarily for suggesting she could not hold my gaze because she was frightened of what I might see, my anger, warming to the stinging blow, glowed into a love I was quite unprepared for. I think that Katya too was somewhat taken aback by the calmness with which I accepted her uncalled-for attack.

"I really don't deserve your love, Knut. I have been so beastly to you recently."

But as to the cause of her electric temperament, I could not coax it from her.

On an afternoon as dark as the night, when we were sitting on the window seat in a passage above the ballroom, and had sat for some considerable time in silence, Katya wormed her way towards me asking to be held closely. Like a child, she curled into my arms but begged me not to speak.

"I'm in such a mess Knut," and she gave a great sigh. "I don't know which way to turn."

I suggested that perhaps it was at such moments she missed Mother.

She sat up. "I am meant to be the mother now—and look how inadequate I am." I tried to gently ease the reason for her depression out of her but she would only assure me it had nothing to do with how the elders treated her. "There seems no point to life."

I protested.

"But, Knut, what if you think you see the purpose, if you see a glow, and however dim, walk towards it expecting it to show the way, and it lights up something so contemptible, so utterly. . . ." But she was lost for words and relapsed into silence. I was patient and stroked her hair.

"We all want to know who we are, Knut. Why we are. That is very necessary. It gives us confidence. But do we necessarily like what we are? I want to be me, but find the me I am revolting. So what do I do?"

It was unthinkable there was anything she did, said or thought which could be repugnant.

"But you don't know the real me. I'm horrible."

Because she would not take me into her confidence and be more explicit, I had to confess I could not help her.

"Oh, but you have. You do. You reassure me by just being. You never rage. You never complain—well, rarely. You never criticise me." But I interrupted her and said her cataloguing was making me out to be a passionate lump.

"Do you have passions, Knut? Oh, I'm sorry for you then. How awful. I didn't realise. Do forgive me."

Those few words stunned me. For the first time in my life, I saw myself as Katya did. As an invalid whose whole life was doomed and bound by the four walls of his sick room. Lying on my side, my tap root severed, she saw me as a vegetable waiting for an inevitable decomposition. I suddenly wanted to break out, to push against the confining walls and wreck the imprisoning house; to stand astride the rubble and beat my chest and declare to the world that I was a man. But even as the adrenalin pumped a wild determination through my slim veins, I knew it to be wishful thinking. Katya must have noticed my sudden dejection for she laid the back of her hand on my cheek.

"You see? You have helped me. I was being dreadfully selfish and hadn't realised. In the future I will be much more considerate."

I then made a ludicrous and pompous speech during which I severed all claim to her affection. I freed her from any obligation and urged her to flee. I would, I told her, under no circumstances whatsoever, tolerate her being chained to my sick bed because of some vague, sisterly duty. But she knocked my head and called me "nincompoop ".

"No one, least of all you, will make me feel obligated to do anything I don't choose to do. What I am and do, stems from here," and she pressed in her stomach. "When all passion is spent, maybe as an old lady, I will come if called, but everything I do before my heart grows cold, I do from love."

I warned her against the pitfalls of misguided charity, when love's heartbeats become a joyous humility. She considered this for some moments.

"Those who I cannot bring myself to touch, deserve my love. Those who I touch, already have my love. But when one spurns it or the other demands it—and you may interpret that whichever way you wish, but when that happens—life is over. Even you won't get me to your bedside!"

If that had been the end of it, if she had got up and walked away, I would not have been forced to dwell upon the intenseness of my affection for her; but she stayed, to kiss me. It was a long kiss, an unusual kiss which penetrated my mouth and tasted of scented jam. After her leave-taking—in retrospect innocently roguish but not a mocking farewell—and the longer the sensation of the kiss persisted, the more certain I was that my innocent enchantment was undergoing a metamorphosis, the magic of which was turning my brotherly affection into an unnatural love. Despairing of what to do, I locked myself into my room and lay on the bed.

It may well have been that my sister's kiss was meant to tease because she took delight in the devil she raised; equally, it could have been a deliberate but rash experiment. Katya, like myself, was isolated from the opportunity of exploring the dark complexities of the sexual labyrinth and, lacking friends of her own age, denied the chance to experiment or, in discussion, resolve those areas of mystery where ignorance and misinformation joined forces to confuse and frighten a developing mind. That some of my own preconceived notions on sexual activity were droll, others monstrous—such as the certain fact that babies emerged from the bowel—only served to convince me of Katya's daring experimentation in the light of those absurdities. However, because I was much more concerned with the effect her kiss had upon me rather than her reason for kissing me in that particular and exhilarating manner, I did not take offence nor blame her for the consternation it caused me. On the contrary, being naïve, I even failed to take into consideration the possibility of her own excitement or, and which was unthinkable, that her kiss was a prelude, intended to precipitate further, more intimate familiarities between us, but held myself to be at fault for succumbing to indecent thoughts after such a trivial incident.

However, while I lay smouldering on the bed, I found it increasingly more difficult to discount the act when the longing it created had no definition, no shape which I could pin down or hold up like a lurid illustration before my mind's eye as had been the case with Gudrun shortly before she had been dismissed. That relationship had grown from a desire to be mothered into one of sexual curiosity. The former had been an infantile hunger—a breast fixation, a desire to recapture the oral contentment I had experienced at the milky bosom of my wet nurse Granoise and which Gudrun unwittingly satisfied when, in response to my tears or at her own urging, shrugged me to her; the latter, a vague admixture of anal or vaginal curiosity—amorous crimes unthinkable in association with my sister Katya, but which probably had their origin in Gudrun's habit when I was young, and in order to keep me in view when I was particularly obstreperous, of not closing the lavatory door when she went to seat herself. Unfortunately, when it became increasingly obvious because of my curiosity that I had grown too precocious or old to witness such goings on, she slammed and bolted the door against me, fixing my curiosity for all time. Hence my obsession with the untidy view beneath her skirts, glimpsed when she lay along the bench in the conservatory.

Aged twelve, I did not associate my first, infrequent nightly emissions with desire for the reason that the bizarre dreams which saturated my sleep were totally unrelated to the world in which I awoke and where there was no cause for such alarming phenomena. Later in my development, perhaps aged fourteen, very occasional but deliberate masturbation, whilst still unrelated to images, was solely because the outcome was a pleasurable experience. Any guilt attached to it did not stem from lewd associations—as was to happen later, but from the mess it made; accentuated and made permanent by Gudrun stripping the sheets and saying I was naughty for dirtying my bed. Looking back, her flippancy and the chiding I endured were not to hide her embarrassment while she bundled the sheets but to conceal her calculation of my potential masculinity and setting it against the inadvisability of taking advantage of my excitability to satisfy her own frustration. From her mercurial and unpredictable temperament, her tears and sighs, I would have realised this was the case had I, at that early age, an understanding of women's moods. So, too, if her seduction of me had been successful, I would have had revealed to me the lodestar towards which, in my relationship with Katya, I was being inevitably drawn so that, like a mariner, I could have steered my frail craft away from the rocks and disaster and my sister and I need not have drowned. As it was, my timidity and inhibitions made me flee Gudrun's embrace but encouraged a surge of orgasms now dependent upon an image of her lying prone upon the bench. Paradoxically, years later, when I understood what it was I wanted to do to my sister, I could not masturbate to relieve my longing because, at such moments of crisis, the act itself could not be dissociated from Katya's image and the eroticism so essential to procure the desired result. Had I given way to my desire in secret, it would have engendered the continuation of a passion I struggled to terminate and soiled a love I wished to keep pure, so I refrained. However, this was in the future and on that particular, late afternoon, stretched out on my bed, susceptible to instinct, that ethereal phenomenon which does constant battle with dour reason, I acknowledged the disturbing alarm of love but was ignorant of its form.

Up until the moment Katya had kissed me, I had not consciously longed for her embrace; kissing and touching had been a natural, domestic show of affection between us. Now I desired it for its own sake, for the thrill it brought about and could not be satisfied with less. However, I would have been shocked if told I lusted after my sister and no amount of argument would have convinced me I did. Ignorant and virgin, how could have it been otherwise? Not knowing the outlet through which adult love found expression, I imagined the pain of yearning was the ultimate sensation of a person in love. The other, embarrassing fancies—mostly of an uncertain scatological nature, exigent hallucinations peculiar to me and which were best suppressed—had, or so I thought, no connection with love whatsoever. In retrospect, I have cause to be grateful for my ignorance. Had I known, as I lay on my bed, my desires were carnal, had I been told of what one did or had done to one in expression and fulfilment of this desire, I would have taken up my cutthroat razor and severed any

number of arteries to forestall the possibility of such disgusting behaviour.

As it was, like all young and innocent lovers, I sighed and stretched,
yawned and was troubled by a heart grown so swollen I felt my breathing
restricted. In a panic of mysterious dull aches, excited but maudlin, ener-
gised but listless and tingling from head to toe while Katya's kiss lingered,
I came to the difficult conclusion that the only way out of my dilemma,
other than avoiding Katya altogether, was to remain aloof and taciturn
when we met. My face set, but my heart thundering, I took my temperature and discovered, much to my delight, that I was feverish. Restriction to
my room would make my resolution that much more easy to accomplish.

But Katya, in the days which followed, became petulant. Feeling spirited and especially affectionate, she fussed round me and was somewhat
taken aback by my remoteness. To see her sad and wince when I rebuffed
her and to know I was the cause, was a bitter experience. But Katya soon
brightened and, thinking tolerance and an increased display of fondness
would win me round, renewed her attentions with fresh candour until I
was reduced to a state of hysteria.

"I understand, Knut. I understand. Don't fret so."

And I would go rigid with anguish, feeling my body had a will of its
own and my mind subsidiary to its needs. Her "I'm always near if you
want me" made me want to lean over and be sick, as if the only way to ex-
purgate my unwholesomeness was to vomit it out. At other times, my de-
vious mind alerted me to the possibility that a confession would so shock
her that, thereafter, her disgust of me would make the longed-for and irrevocable schism, but when she came smilingly towards me, treachery
and betrayal were the two words which sprang to mind, and, shrinking, I
remained mute. How could I possibly wound the one person I loved and
leave a scar which, despite time's sutures, would not heal but leave the
edges raw to suppurate?

My torment was worsened when Karen accompanied her.

"We've come to cheer you up." And they would sit throughout the afternoon, sometimes the one resting her arm about the other or, becoming

boisterous, pushing one another, all the while giggling and chattering ceaselessly and girlishly about nothing of any consequence. I would tie myself in knots to avoid imagining myself in Karen's close proximity to my beloved and would end by scattering them, like twittering birds, with loud handclaps and shouts of "enough!"

With Karen in attendance, the silliest things had begun to pain me for, jealousy, that whorish handmaiden of frustrated love, had begun to loom large. I began to detest Karen and was jealous of her innocent friendship with my sister. I found myself resenting the fact that Katya had lent her a pair of white stockings, and became distracted when she tried on Katya's shoes to see if they had the same sized feet. I was even jealous when Katya patiently mended the torn frill which edged Karen's apron, and was jaundiced to see her sprawled on the floor reading while Katya sat quietly sewing. It seemed that the more trivial, the more empty the gesture, the worse was my anguish. A borrowed pin to secure her maid's cap became a significant token and I coveted the giving of it or, and worse, I was jealous when she borrowed Katya's handkerchief to blow her nose! What finally made me realise the thin, membraned bladder in which I kept my lunacy had burst, was when an unspeakable urge came over me to steal some of Katya's underclothing. Although I was still taciturn, my jaundiced eyes stole glances and would greedily fidget over her form. It was like eating as I noted the flesh of her arm, the tucked-under leg or watched the turn of her neck. All were absorbed through my eyes and I digested them with the relish of a gourmet. I had forbidden myself to touch her, and the idea insinuated itself that the next best thing would be to possess one or other of her garments. Just as the piece of the true cross has significance for the Christian, my miserable minikin of silk would have been reverenced. It wasn't a fetish to be drawn through the fingers and sniffed for an erotic transference but, lain in a drawer, be symbolic of a love which would forever remain an unholy secret. But even as I schemed, disgust and then revulsion broke into my reverie before I was committed and, thankfully, I was able to rescue a bedraggled conscience and slam the door against further obsessions.

Tumbled into the passage, the two women were alarmed by my aggression, but the door locked, I was able to beat my head against the hard edge of my desk and in a room I would turn into a monastic cell.

But on the third day Katya came knocking at my door and her persuasion guided my trembling hand to unlock it.

"Don't give me cause to worry, Knut. Please. Let me share you."

Apparently she believed I was in the grip of an hallucination and was spending my desires secretly in the velvet-lined rooms of my imagination. It shocked me to think she could be jealous of my seduction by an illusory concubine, even if it were true.

"Well, who knows what goes on in that head of yours? It hurts me to think you are peopling a world in which I have no place. Besides, it's unhealthy." How could I explain to her the corridors of my mind had only one, slim figure which ran opening doors as quickly as I closed them? Whom I never caught, nor could, but if I ever did, would strangle.

In this mood, and feeling that nothing but a full confession would rid me of my desire, I decided I must write it all down, from the beginning and, using this excuse, kept the door shut against her. As I began to write, and in some odd way, the disgust I felt for myself turned into a passionate tirade against my mother, as if I was trying to vindicate myself by casting the blame at her feet.

It is these scribblings which I gave Katya to read although I was most careful not to let her have those which were too explicit of my feelings for her or those which told of Gudrun. Of the sections she read, many are lost, the remainder in no proper sequence. The first she eased from my grip one late afternoon whilst I sat recovering in front of an open window; perhaps a month before I began my vain attempt to reorganise the family's large collection of books.

PART THREE: FOLLOW UP

One afternoon, for want of something to do and bored with writing, I was browsing through the disordered books in the library when I suddenly decided to catalogue the entire collection. I had no idea how to set about such a task except it seemed essential I should separate the books into categories and list them by title and author. Clearing the shelves was not an easy task, especially as it meant innumerable journeys up and down the ladder, which quickly exhausted me. But I stuck to my Herculean labour and relished the slight fever it brought on; pretending to myself it was the sweat of honest toil I dabbed with my handkerchief.

As the days passed and the library became more and more disordered with the piles of books I was raising like a complicated labyrinth all over the library floor, I began to doubt the wisdom of my initial enthusiasm; especially as the quantity of books appeared to increase in number once they had been removed from the shelves and stacked in piles. To begin with, my simple system worked well. History books I put in one neat stack, autobiographies in another, and so on. A difficulty arose when I came upon the biography of a General Edric and didn't know on which stack it should be placed. The more I tried to define and subdivide within my original broad categories, the more of a muddle I got into. Despairing, I decided that if I was ever going to make order out of the chaos, I must stick to my original concept and use cross-indexing in the catalogue I was compiling for the more subtle subdivisions. I braced myself and laboured on. With weeks of work behind me, the majority of books heaped on the floor and on the chairs and the two tables, it was inevitable I should come across a most beautifully bound and exquisitely handwritten catalogue which suggested that my job had already been done for me and much more efficiently—only time and thoughtless borrowers of books having disarranged the shelves. I checked and found that this was so and nearly fell backwards off the ladder with laughter.

During the weeks I had worked in the library, I had acquired a smell. It was the odour of old, damp books and dust. The smell made it obvious to everyone what I was about and the elders took the opportunity to comment and sniff the air about them, lampooning my industriousness. Even Marcel, a master of subtlety, flinched slightly when he came near me, and stiffening, left me in no doubt, though he did not utter a word, that he found my aroma distasteful. I had wanted the elders' approbation and had hoped the ingrained dirt on my hands would seem to them symbolic of my new determination to be useful and industrious. But the elders took it to be indicative of my eccentricity and an unbecoming identification with the lower working classes. I smarted under their contempt and kept secret the fact I had to wash my hair each night to prevent soiling the pillow. Katya thought I looked happy with my smudged face and clothes which gave off a grey dust when they were patted, but I seldom saw her because she was occupied with more feminine chores and spent much of her time with Nanna Axell to whom she read. for I often heard her soothing and hypnotic voice coming from Nanna Axell's room whenever I passed.

"How much longer are you going to be messing about in the library? Your grandfather Sven—and he was a scholar, although it never did him any good—he catalogued the books."

"It will be a matter of weeks rather than months."

"Days would be preferable. All that dust will get down into your lungs. And then where will we be?"

Uncle Ira, who liked to be thought of as the original, true Christian, bore everyone else's cross with an irritability which made one suspect he found his own shortcomings intolerable and, like a guard dog, kept his hackles perpetually raised lest one pass and discover the straw in his kennel was fouled with cack.

"I suppose you know what you're doing. You're not a child anymore. Still, it must be damned cold in there."

My hands in my pockets and my shoulders hunched, I went down the dark corridors towards the library. It seemed that as a child I had been resented for not being more adult and now I had reached my majority, they wished I had remained an infant. I slammed the library door behind me and looked at the chaos with some feeling of affection. The mess was me and I wouldn't have had it otherwise.

The previous week I had begun, painstakingly, to dust the books prior to placing them back on the clean shelves, and to check each one against the elegant script in the catalogue I had discovered. I mounted the ladder and began to arrange an armful of books neatly. Damned cold, Ira had said, and I supposed it was. It had always been. I recalled a snowball I had made long ago and had brought into the house. It had taken two weeks to melt and even then was as large as an egg when Gudrun had thrown it at me and it had rolled under the bed. I knew it was inconceivable that it was still there, but I wouldn't have been surprised. As usual, my legs were numb and felt encased in lead and my body hairs raised like a porcupine's but I felt fit and, despite the dust which came out of my nose like soot from a chimney, I was coughing less. Having patted several books into position, I leaned back to admire the gilt spines. It was then I caught sight, through the window below me, of Katya, standing in the snow trying to entice what I took to be a lame pigeon, with crumbs of bread which she was scattering in front of her. I leaned down and tapped the window. The bird, startled, rose awkwardly into the air and flapped away, up, possibly onto the roof. Katya followed it with her eyes and then turned to me with a cross expression on her face. I shrugged and spread my hands apologetically. Katya stuck out her tongue and walked away.

A little later, having decided to clear and clean a space on the shelves to the left of the window in the corner, I moved the ladder and, mounting it yet again, took down a book from the topmost shelf. My shock can be imagined when, purring the pages with my thumb, I saw a kaleidoscopic tumbling of naked flesh the colour of tinned salmon and sliced pears. I was open-mouthed in disbelief. Flattening the book, I turned first to one page and then to another in quick succession. On alternate pages, all in livid colour, were depicted the erotic obscenities which I could not conceive staining the mind of the most degraded man or woman, for it seemed to be a panoramic vista of the turmoil which could only exist in the middens of hell. And I took them to be that, for even the fact I was looking at photographs of real people did not penetrate into my innocent belief that such monstrous couplings were beyond the imagination of any person living. When Katya held my hand I thought of nothing but the thrill of the moment. If she leant across me to reach for something and her breasts moulded to the shape of my shoulder my thoughts did not progress beyond that moment of ecstasy or as when I inwardly swooned under her pecks of kisses or sudden hugs. The satisfaction, the ultimate discharging of desire as expressed in physical terms was a remote and blurred objective. Its attainment seemed improbable, even not wholly desirable, and it spent itself in longing and created an ache which at times became almost mystical.

Childish as this view seems in retrospect, romantic and nauseous to those who claim that a deeper relationship exists in the natural coupling of bodies, my innocence was a painful enjoyment and had an exquisiteness which expressed itself in trembling and blushes. As an incestuous desire, it was an adoration, and as such, could not be punishable or seen as sin by the most vindictive of Gods. Any sinfulness one could attach to my desire was because of its intensity, not the object of my passion.

Or so it seemed until that moment. Gazing down at the book, all my undirected passion seemed to be funnelled, all my longings focused upon a carnality I had been too innocent to suspect. Not that I was being unwittingly corrupted, but my innocence had been snatched from me in a fashion so beastly as to havoc my already tottering stability and to load me with a guilt and horror I did not deserve. The graphic sundering of flesh and the commingling of gross muscle which erected itself before me on nearly every page and in such perverse attitudes and combinations, I could never have imagined nor wanted to, had now become part of me; of my experience. I was reminded of the time when I was violently sick after watching Gardol slit the stomach of a stunned hare and, with his hunched fingers plunged into the warm buck, grapple out the pink and purple viscera which steamed in the gaping hole he had made. Even as I gazed at the book, the scent of the hare's bowels, faint but pungent, like sweet dung, seemed to tint the air so that a new nausea swept over me and I had to grip the ladder for support. Even as I clung swaying, I tried to conceive what urge drove people to foul each other in such desperate acts of obscenity and betray the fragile sweetness of true adoration.

"Beast!"

I jumped with fright and slammed the book shut.

"You frightened off my pigeon!"

My haste and embarrassment made me clumsy and the book tumbled from my hands and plummeted to the floor, mashing one corner. Katya bent to pick it up.

"No! No!" I cried, and clattered down the ladder, desperate to regain the book before she opened it. "No!"

"What are you trying to hide from me?" And, clutching the book to her breast, she ran round the table piled high with books, putting it between us.

"Katya. Don't open that book. Trust me. Don't open that book. For the sake of your sanity," I pleaded, "do—not—open—that—book."

Filled with devilment and determined to tease, probably to pay me back for having frightened away her pigeon, she shook her head.

"You will have to catch me first."

I tried; chasing her between the avenues of books, knocking some over and destroying hours of patient work, round the tables and chairs, under the ladder, but I had no hope of catching her. Katya laughed, giving great whoops if I accidentally came near to clutching her dress. Coughing eventually reduced me to an hysterical heap and I was forced to slump over a chair while I retched and swallowed alternately and the thin barrel of my ribs caved and struggled with my breathlessness. Katya, concerned because I was overcome and had been reduced to a gasping wreck, came towards me. When she was near enough, I made a last desperate effort to snatch the book but she held it up high and backed away.

"Play fair. Are you all right?" I nodded and held out my hand. "Are you sure?" I nodded.

"Don't open that book, Katya. Please," I said in a whisper. But she had.

The silence was unbearable while she stood flicking over the pages with her moistened finger. I buried my face in my hands and waited.

When I heard the book snap shut, I looked up. Katya was staring at me, her mauve eyes wide and round but her face expressionless. I struggled to swallow down a dry cough and felt on the point of vomiting.

"So this is why you spend your time in here—cataloguing." She threw the book to me and I caught it. "No wonder you smell like a dirty old man."

"I came across it for the very first time just a second before you came in!"

"Can I believe you?"

"Katya, you must! I'm not lying!"

"To whom does the book belong?"

"I don't know. Father, I suppose," and I put the book on the edge of the table.

"Are there any more?"

I spent the next few minutes up the ladder looking. In all there were nineteen, mostly foreign and nearly all German, including a four-volumed encyclopaedia. As I found them I handed them down to Katya.

"Don't look at them, Karen—I mean Katya."

Katya glowered up at me.

"You called me Karen."

"It was a slip of the tongue."

"What's that little bitch been up to? Eh? What's been going on between you two?"

"Nothing! Nothing. Don't be so silly. And for God's sake don't look at the books when I hand them down to you. Stop it."

With the last volume in my hand, I began to descend. I paused when I recognised the binding of the volume I was holding. "Do you remember Lechner, Katya?" She tensed. "Lechner, our first tutor. It was this book . . ." Katya snatched it from me and turned her back. "Oh Katya, don't be so disgusting. Give it back."

"I'm not a child, Knut." She stood off from me and chewed her lip while she looked through the book. When she tossed it onto the pile of other books we had collected, a small cloud of dust rose into the air.

"You should be ashamed of yourself, Katya."

"Ashamed? Oh no." She began to draw looping patterns in the thick dust which had gathered on the table where the books did not stand. The designs were figures of eight or the numbers six and nine joined together. "I think I somehow feel purer for knowing." She glanced up and smiled, dazzling me. "It would appear, Knut, that I am not inhibited after all. Only lacking in invention."

I was shocked.

"You can't be serious, Katya."

"Never more so. Have you any string?" But she saw and drew out a long, hairy piece from an open drawer. "I think it best to make a bundle of them and consider what shall be done with them later."

While she tied and knotted, I wandered down and round the avenues of books, setting them straight without any notion of what I was really doing.

"They must be burnt, Katya."

"Not necessarily. They are evidence."

"Of what?"

"That remains to be seen. The elders could be embarrassed if they were confronted with them. At precisely the right moment, of course." The bundle was weighty and she stood holding it like a bucket of water, with her hip thrust out to counterbalance the weight and receive the crook of her arm.

"I originally came to say how cross I was with you for frightening away my little pigeon. I think it must have escaped from one of Gardol's snares and broken its leg." She walked past me. "I do wish that man wouldn't set traps. I know one must eat but it seems cruel to tempt them with the promise of food, only to kill them. Far better hunt," and she moved awkwardly towards the door with her dusty bundle.

"Where are you taking them?"

"To my room. For safekeeping." And she left.

I stood for some moments before I too crept out of the library and, as always when I was depressed or confused, went to the stables, this time to hide from myself.

The discovery of the books destroyed all my enthusiasm I had had for re-organising the library. I tried to complete the task I had set myself but, having no heart for it, I allowed the work to lapse. As week followed week, it became increasingly obvious I would never finish. And I didn't. The room was still in chaos two years later when the library was unlocked and all the books sent away to be sold at auction.

My difficulty during those months was to dissociate the images which kept presenting themselves to me, like rapidly changing lantern slides, from the feelings I had for Katya. The two became inseparable. Like a magnifying glass which gathers the sun's rays together and focuses them into a single, bright, burning spot, I felt my desires were being concentrated in much the same way, only the magnifying glass was the soft, erupting plasma in my head and the heat a burning sensation in my loins. Because of the state I was in, I had only to glimpse Katya's bare arm or leg, or watch the undulation of her retreating figure, to find myself embroiled with erotic images which brought me to such a pitch of excitement, sweat and confusion that I was continually having to stun myself by senseless activity to divert my mind. I would shred paper, set myself mathematical problems which I had no hope of solving, walk aimlessly about repeating out loud idiotic phrases, hoping the repetition would drive away the visions of desire, and, the most idiosyncratic of my attempts to divert my mind, eat until I could no longer stuff food into my mouth without being sick. As I had to steal the food, mostly bread, I was overcome by shame and suffered my indigestible surfeit with an added feeling of guilt. That I didn't masturbate, I have already explained, so I struggled on, creating other diversions to blanket that part of my mind which seemed to have control of me, until the day I discovered myself pacing a corridor and slapping the wall with my palm, repeating the words "boiled eggs", over and over again, I decided something positive must be done because I was in danger of losing my sanity.

Instinctively, I sought the advice of Nanna Axell. Although it took a great deal of courage, I found myself knocking at her door and entering. Lying in bed, her wrinkled head looking like an old crab apple which had lain shrivelling in the loft for years, she looked like an unearthed pharaoh.

"I am not an oracle, Knut. I am human, and therefore much more practical. Age has made others think I am wise."

After we had exchanged pleasantries, I nervously broached the subject of my sister. Cowardly in the extreme, I did not confess it was I who was in love, but spoke in the third person and posed the hypothetical problem of what should be done when a brother and sister find that an adolescent attachment has developed into a passion which was in danger of becoming an incestuous union.

Although I had been very circumspect and chosen my words with care, I expected my grandmother to be alarmed that I should concern myself with such problems. She merely clasped her jewelled fingers together and nodded attentively.

"Knut, my dear, I don't believe God made laws, rather that man made laws so that he should come to know his God the better. They are laws which enable him to live without conflict with his fellow men. They are to protect the ignorant, the unselfish from the greedy, the meek from the strong, the daughter from her father—as much as to save her from his will as a genetic understanding of the weakness, some say madness, of incestuous heredity. You come to see me so seldom, Knut . . ." I squirmed uneasily, "that I must conclude it is of yourself you speak. That you have become overfond of your sister. Have you spoken to Katya?"

I shook my head.

"Well, do." I could not conceal my look of astonishment. "Katya has an understanding far beyond her years. She will know what must be done.

And, but more important, she will be gentle. In all probability she will say much the same as I would, only, coming from her, you will believe it."

Nanna Axell must have gathered from my air of disconsolation that I was frightened of approaching Katya.

"In all probability, Knut, Katya already knows. But speak to her. And be sure you do. When next she visits me, I shall bring the matter up with her to make sure you have. Now kiss me goodnight for I am very tired."

I crept out of the room and closed the door quietly behind me. From somewhere, I would have to find the necessary courage to confront Katya.

To Katya's credit, her attitude towards me during the months after the discovery of the books in the library, helped considerably. Cold and distant, she seemed preoccupied and had divorced me from her company and chatter. Naturally, I mistook her coolness for disdain but reasoned it could equally be her own preoccupation with the traumatic upheaval initiated by the erotic pictures, hoping I suppose, that a shared experience would somehow alleviate, although not wholly, part of my burden. But when I overheard her chattering to Helga and witnessed her ease and self-confidence when in Karen's company, I came to believe her disinterestedness was a deliberate rebuttal and was forced to the conclusion that she did, after all, despise me.

Made miserable, friendless, bowed under the weight of an unmentionable aberration, my only recourse was to tears and, my spirit broken, a feeling of wickedness oozing from every pore, I became a prize example of a penitent acolyte eager for a hirsute torment to punish his unforgivable sinfulness. That I longed for such scourging and that such a punishment would have given me great pleasure was, in itself a sin and it was in this state of mind that I had gone to Nanna Axell.

When I had walked away from her door, my first instinct had been to seek solace in the darkness of the stable loft and there to sit looking out through the broken tiles to a landscape warming to spring until I had come to a decision. But as I had to pass Katya's room some force compelled me to stop and enter.

Not pausing to knock, I walked straight into her room and was brought to a sudden stop by what I saw. I turned and fled.

Katya's room was white. Every single thing in the room was white, down to her ivory-backed brushes and combs. She also had a passion for delicate drapery so not only was her bed strung about with a frothy white lace-like material but the windows had looping curtains with added frills like her dressing table and other furniture. She had even used white velvet to swag the large mirror which stood over a white marble fireplace and screened off the doors with similarly made curtains. On the floor was a fitted white carpet over which were scattered rugs of white fur. So white and light was the room that in winter it seemed like an extension of the snow landscape outside although the room was incredibly warm and her jasmine scent hung in the air like a barrier of mist, tickling one's senses. It was a room I adored but; seldom visited because it was so intensely feminine. Besides, I felt clumsy and alien in it, like a toad which has hopped up and sat on a newly-iced cake.

When I had entered unexpectedly, Katya had been sat sideways at her dressing table. It appeared to my confused senses that she was naked. Behind her, brushing her hair, stood Karen.

Having slammed the door I stood unable to move. When I did, I moved in the wrong direction and had to double past Katya's door. Halfway down the corridor, I heard Katya's door open and I cringed, waiting for a knife thrust in my back.

"Knut! Come here, you silly boob." I hesitated, undecided. "Come on! It's freezing."

I turned and slunk back, keeping my eyes on the narrow strip of carpet. When I drew close, she took my arm and pushed me into the room. Karen was stood in the same place in her neat cap and crisp apron, carding Katya's blonde hair from a brush.

"In future, Knut, knock and ask if you may enter." She had wrapped her body in a long white diaphanous robe which could have been transparent but I dared not look because of what I might see. "Now, what is it you want?"

I was so tongue-tied, I stood knotting my fingers and trying to fight down a blush which was making my cheeks uncomfortably hot. My heart was thundering so loudly, I felt sure Katya could hear it.

She turned to Karen. "Thank you, Karen. That will be all." Karen bade us both goodnight and slipped out of the room. "Now what is it, Knut?" She sat down on the bed and laid back, taking great care not to reveal her flesh. From under the pillow she took my manuscript. "Come and sit down."

I shook my head.

"Please yourself." She purred the edges of my notebook and then threw it on the bed. "I haven't quite finished it yet. Did you want it back?"

"No."

"You don't write truthfully, Knut. I mean, you're not honest with your-self. Or are you writing it just for my benefit? It would be a pity if you were." She turned her great mauve eyes upon me and all my resolve evap-orated. Between us, there built up a silence which became indestructible. "Did you want to tell me something?"

"No. That is . . . No. Nothing."

"Well, I have something to tell you. I'm not leaving. I'm going to stay."

I was stunned by her unexpected news. All along, her going had seemed the most sensible solution to my problem. That I had not con-sidered it seriously was because she had repeatedly put off the moment, presumably because I would not go with her. Also, but more important, I did not want to be the reason for her leaving. To have forced her leave-taking would have been to have lost her forever. With the clarity of a brass trumpet, her shattering announcement literally heralded my depar-ture. To leave the house, to venture into a world which would engulf me and for which I was totally unfitted, was like a death knell.

"May I ask what has decided you?"

"That's none of your business." I was crestfallen she should have a secret and not share it. "Don't look so glum."

"Well, if you have made up your mind, perhaps it would be better if I left."

"Oh, don't be so ridiculous, Knut! Who would look after you? You'd end up in some miserable attic, lonely, unhappy and consumptive."

"Am I any better off here?"

"I abhor self-pity, Knut. Stop it. You're staying. This is your home. It is also mine and I am staying. I thought that was what you wanted."

"Of course."

"Then try and look a bit more happy. Now off with you. My bath has made me sleepy."

In my room I fell like a dead man onto my bed and lay spreadeagled hoping that if sleep ever came I would wake to find myself nailed to a cross from which I would never rise.

I stayed in my room for the rest of the week and had Karen bring me up a little food. Attentive as ever, she enquired closely if I was well and generally fussed about me showing her concern. Seeing I was depressed, and knowing full well I succumbed to moods, she was tactful and, in her quiet way, very comforting.

"What you need, Knut, is a walk in the woods to reassure yourself that the world you want exists."

I rolled onto my side and stared at her. Never profound, always in agreement, as if in the avoidance of an argument she hid her true thoughts, Karen was normally enclosed and not forthcoming.

"And if it doesn't? If the birds don't awaken my spirit or the buds reassure me of eternity, what then? Do I hang myself from the nearest branch?"

"The moment to make a dramatic gesture is when it is expected of you. In that way, it shows that you have thought about it."

"Are you so calm in the face of your own problems?"

"I am a fatalist."

"Then you will never rise above your spirit," and I lay back exhausted.

When she had gone, my mind dwelled on what she had said and I could not help but recall how little I had been aware of her rapid maturing from a spindly-legged little girl into a wholesome, goodlooking young woman. I thought back to all the times I had paid so little attention to her and had, unwittingly, slighted her. It was natural I then began to recall our lives spent together and wondered how she thought of me and if my development had been equally significant. It was possible she only tolerated me. I had not deserved her respect. If we had not been kept apart I would probably have come to know her as well as I did my sister Katya, although I could not conceivably have had the same affection for her.

My musing had brought me circuitously back to thoughts of Katya and I groaned out loud.

There was a tap on the door and Katya walked quietly into the room. I stared up at the ceiling and became rigid. She closed the door and came to the side of the bed and stood looking down at me. I avoided her eyes.

"I see Karen has left her little offering." On the bedside table was a single apple. "How are you?" and she sat down on the bed.

"Did Karen send you?"

Katya "mmm'd" and lay full length beside me. I made to move but she restrained me.

"It's quite like old days, me lying here."

And it was. For hours we used to lie, side by side, on our backs until the gloom in the room was finally extinguished and all about us was black. In the darkness we talked and talked but I cannot recall a single conversation, only that we were extremely happy. It was not unusual for one, or both of us, to fall asleep and awake fully dressed in the light of a morning that was particularly dazzling. At other times, Katya, awakening suddenly in the middle of the night, rather than steal back to her own room would crawl with me under the blankets and we would fall into a deep sleep. These nightly sharings of my bed were a secret. It was an innocent joy but one which, unfortunately for me, bonded me to an unnatural need long before I became awakened to its significance and by which time I was securely addicted.

I was startled out of my reverie by Katya.

"Nanna Axell and I have had a long discussion."

I groaned and sat up. Katya pulled me back.

"Now speak."

I lay rigid and silent, hardly daring to breathe. When I tried to roll off the bed, she grabbed me.

"We're going to have this thing out, Knut. I don't care how long I wait. All night, if necessary. But you are going to tell me in your own words."

There was a long silence during which I began to count while I clenched my teeth together.

"Knut, I know. I've known for years. I'm not cross. Or indignant. Not even outraged that it should have happened. I'm not insulted. But I want you to tell me about it. Please."

After a long while, lulled by her motionlessness, I began my confession.

At first my words came with difficulty and, like an apprentice builder with odd-sized blocks, I constructed a crazed and uneven tower of words. Frightened it would topple before I had finished, I laboured like a madman to set my topmost stone to the lunatic folly. Whether Katya's silence teased my tongue or the relief of confession ordered my mind, I do not know, but my babbling quietened and I became an unhurried master builder of words.

While I spoke of my love, my heart seemed to lighten and the unburdening became a mesmerising poetry. Drunk with eloquence, I could not believe there existed a love more pure. But as the time passed and the sweetness of my feelings became unbearable, because of the hopelessness with which it would conclude, light sobs mixed with the words until I was unashamedly weeping and seeking the comfort of Katya's hand and shoulder.

"My darling baby," Katya whispered, and stroked my hair. "My poor baby. What you have suffered because of me."

I began to speak again with a voice checked and half-stifled by emotion.

"Shush. Shush now. My baby does not have to explain. It is sufficient that it is. That I know. That I am here."

Cradled in her arms, I curled myself small to snuggle into her cosiness. Her hot cheek against mine, our warmth glowed while she smoothed her hands over my back comfortingly, patting and shrugging me to her. Imperceptibly, her grip tightened and the longed-for well-being of security flooded my body, making me limp. Nestled safely, and succumbing to a feeling of peace, my mind emptied of everything save the outline of a word fluttering like a timid bird on the edge of my consciousness. I couldn't recognise the word to shape it with my lips, but it was a word I longed to say. In and out of the silence, my mind, as in a dream, went chasing it with feet of wool up a hill of honey which stuck to my insteps, cloying my progress. It seemed important I should grasp it and present it like an exotic butterfly to my darling for her admiration. But the gossamer net of my effort was full of holes and the word drifted away.

Katya, her encircling hug feeding my stupor, stirred and slowly pulled me on top of her where I sought her lips and breathed into her mouth while my tears flowed effortlessly, bathing our cheeks.

"Oh, my baby. My baby," and she clasped me tighter, heaving her body against mine. "My little baby."

In a grip from which I could not escape, she writhed under me like a snake and began to throw her head from side to side. The urgency, and a hiss from between her clenched teeth, broke into my numbness and, disturbed, a cold awareness trickled down my spine, alerting me. I sought to free myself and pawed at her arms to escape, but my wrestling invigorated her, strengthening her determination. From the calm of an idyllic peace, I found myself crushed up against the hard pelvic thrust of desire, the carnality and vigour of which was frightening. As I struggled, all the images I had tried to repress flooded back into my empty mind with an incandescence which lit and burnt in my head with the roar of a furnace. I tried to push myself away and looked down into the groaning mouth, opened in a wide, fixed smile, of a Katya who had become possessed. One arm about me, the other on my head she began to force me downwards. I resisted with all my strength and buried my face below her breasts hoping I could slip like an eel from her arms. Wriggling downwards and, I thought, freeing myself, she suddenly clamped her thighs round me and I was in a grip from which there was no escaping. As I refused to grovel to her will, she countered my resistance by worming her way up the bed and using both her hands to work my face down to between her thighs. Gasping for air, wretched and filled with shame and horror, I began to sob. I was being held instrumental to a desire of which I wanted no part but which I was powerless to prevent. My strength flowed from me with my tears and I became pliable. Manoeuvred, I was quiescent and tight-lipped. With my face sandwiched between her legs, Katya gave a small cry of alarm and then, with a fearful groan, arched her back and becoming rigid, began quivering while she slowly eased me away and I emerged from between her legs gasping for air. It was then I cried out and Katya collapsed.

In the next instant, she had thrown her leg over me and was sitting on the edge of the bed. Dishevelled, she ran her fingers through her hair and sniffed. While she sat quietly taking deep draughts of air down into her lungs, I crouched at the foot of the bed facing her. When she turned to me, I saw a face as old as eternity but when she smiled, it vanished and before me was Katya, flushed but bright and not a little bashful.

"I'm sorry, Knut," and she blew some hair out of her eyes. "I too have problems."

My senses numbed, I was unable to register the significance of her remark but remained crouched like a bedraggled dog which had been trounced and left out in the rain all night to shiver and lick its sores. Shock, or the cumulative tension, whipped through my corded nerves and set me shuddering. Seeing the tremble, Katya took hold of my hand and drew me towards her.

"It's all over, Knut," she said, feeling my resistance. "All over. Gently, now. Gently. We have come through it safely."

I allowed myself to be pulled across her lap to lay on my back like a log and stared up at her. Katya leaned over me and looked down into my face. Her hair fell forward, darkening her features, and she blew her lipsticked breath onto my eyes.

"Oh, Katya, what have we done? What have we done?" She cradled me and began to rock backwards and forwards.

"I have just created you." And she rubbed her nose against mine. "Baby."

She suddenly sat up and, to my astonishment, with a maternal gesture, eased a breast out of her blouse and, bending over me, tried to draw my face up to it. With a cry, I elbowed her away and, scrambling off the floor where I had fallen, went stumbling over the furniture towards the fireplace. When I turned with a roaring in my ears, Katya was stood buttoning her blouse and smoothing the wrinkles out of her skirt.

"There's no need to look so shocked, Knut. It is a mother you wanted, isn't it?"

The word, which had eluded me when we had lain quietly embracing, now sprang into vision and went strutting about my head, daring me to forget. I buried my face in my hands, fearing the word was writ large across my forehead, like a brand.

"No, Katya! No! *No!*" But I was denying the word had existence, not negating a lie.

"Oh yes, Knut. Just as you have always been my baby."

Recall, when it comes unexpectedly, quietly, is as illuminating as a sudden shaft of sunlight brightening a dark corner. Depressing, too, as when a housewife, proud of her polishing, sees in the shafts of sunlight the myriad specks of dancing dust, falling silently all about her. In the glow of my memory, I saw two infants isolated in the gloom of a gymnasium sat on the floor the little sister was cradling her brother who clung to her desperate for warmth and protection. As before, and since, she was rocking him backwards and forwards, lulling him to sleep.

"I'm sorry for you, Knut, if I have destroyed some illusions. Have I?" She was using my comb to tidy her hair. "But until you recognise who I am, you will suffer the pain of wanting. I am your sister, and you may not take me like a man." She peered into the glass and brushed the tip of her nose with a finger. Wetting her forefinger, she smoothed her eyebrows. "No man may. But you," and she turned, "you have come closer to liberating me than anyone." She tossed her head and settled the hair at the nape of her neck. "You may despise me from this moment and henceforward," she walked calmly towards the door and opened it, "but my feelings of affection towards you have not changed. Nor will. But remember this, Knut.

It is as you said. We have been destroyed. Long ago. But now it is up to us how we shall live. For my part I could live alongside you quite happily. Weak as you are, I trust you and I sympathise with you more than you will ever know. Possibly because I love you."

She was about to close the door when she hesitated.

"If you find you cannot sleep and I am awake, come to my room. There will be no repetition of what happened just now. Ever."

After Katya had left me, I lay on my bed in a state of exhaustion. Bewildered, my head bursting and my brow hot, I fell asleep to a night filled with dreams. At some point I must have crawled under the covers, but did not waken. The footsteps in the corridor outside my room, the slamming of doors and the raised voices of people arguing, mixed with my dreams, to become part of a continuous nightmare. When I did eventually open my eyes, I felt strangely calm. Evidently, dreaming had worked through my agitation and sorted away those solved portions which reason, in brash daylight, would have fumbled to interpret. The only feeling I had was one of shame. To hide from it, I promptly went back to sleep.

When I emerged from this deep coma, the door of my room had been thrown open and an irate Uncle Godric stood framed, his face purple with rage.

"Trust you to be skulking in your bloody bed at a time like this!"

My head seemingly bound in felt and my skull split from front to back, I could not reply at once. By the time I had raised myself up on one elbow, he had turned away.

"The little runt's still in bed!"

I thought I caught sight of Ira in the corridor, but could not be sure. With the words "sickly brat" ringing in my ears, I fell asleep again.

It seemed I had not been unconscious long when I awoke with a start. A door had slammed. I sat up and recalled Godric's words. Always insufferably rude and bombastic, his tirades had little substance but his phrase, "at a time like this", rankled. At a time like what? The phrase had an elusive significance. What had happened while I had been asleep? I recalled the slamming of doors in the night, the raised voices and the activity in the corridors, and slowly realised they had not been part of my dream. It had all actually happened! I began to panic. Something was wrong, dreadfully wrong. Perhaps Nanna Axell had died? They would have told me. Could Mungo have suffered a stroke? No. Godric would have looked pleased. Or had—and I swayed, overcome by the idea which was dawning —or had Katya hung herself!

I struggled off the bed and tried to stand up but I was ill, "galloping ill" as Katya would have said. From the yellowed leaves of some tatty medical book, she had gleaned, incorrectly, that I had galloping consumption. "Did you have a good gallop last night, Knut?" she would ask when I was flat on my back ill and to which I invariably replied, "I galloped well, Katya." It was a silly, private language we used when together. To be "on the trot", was to be sickening, to have "got over the sticks", to have survived the "race" I always won by "a short nose", which she would touch with the tip of her finger. It is said that in moments of crisis, people react in the most ludicrous ways. The imaginative feel the impact of the bullet before it is fired, the introverted worry that their fly buttons might be open or care that a shoelace is untied as they face the firing squad. I was both, for I could clearly see Katya hanging from the banisters and at the same time was recalling the nonsensical way we talked together. Fighting back my tears, I stumbled from one piece of furniture to the next until I reached the door. Dragging it open, I looked out into the passage. It stretched in a long perspective, cold and deserted. I turned my ear into it and listened. There was not a sound. The whole house, from the high attics to the basement kitchens, was as silent as the tomb. I stood shivering, waiting for a board to creak, for some movement, but not even the faint cough of an elder drifted into the silence. If something had happened, it wasn't death. Death would have roused the house, sending shivers of excitement through the elders. Death was a calamity of weeping and wailing. This calm and silence was something else. Could I have imagined the commotion? Had it been part of my vivid dreams? Not entirely convinced it was, I groped my way back to bed and flung the covers over me. Someone would come and tell me all about it. Someone. But at another moment in time.

I stayed on my back for a whole week but, on the first day, in answer to my bell, Helga had come with some soup. When I asked her if I had been mistaken in thinking I had heard a commotion during the night, she shrugged her shoulders and told me not to bother my head about it. So I had been right, something had happened!

"It was a silly misunderstanding, if you ask me. You know what your relations are like. They go looking under a carpet for the devil's footprint, not noticing their own feet are cloven."

I was disconcerted by her reply but, when pressed, she would not be more precise. "We've got to get you well again, young Knut. That's all that matters."

While I spooned my soup inelegantly, I had a notion to tiptoe to Katya's room but, on reflection, thought it would be unwise. Being ill, to have run the gauntlet of the draughty corridors, plus the emotion of seeing Katya, would have increased my fever. When it occurred to me that the commotion of the previous evening might have had something to do with Katya being in my room so late, or worse, someone had seen us embracing, a prickling heat of fever surged through me and I was forced to fling the bedclothes aside. It passed but the sleep which followed was crowded with waxen-faced elders who, grouped round my bed, rhythmically beat me. It ended with them pushing their rods into Katya who, mysteriously, had materialised beside me on the bed, naked.

The following day, when Helga again brought me food, I asked why Karen was not doing all the running about.

"She's a cold, poor dear, and I'm not having her traipse about the house with all these draughts to cut the poor mite in two."

With Karen ill, my remaining hope of finding out the reason for the midnight rumpus before I was well enough to get up, vanished. Depressed, I turned to the wall and let the fever burn itself out.

I had hoped Katya might have had the temerity to visit me, using my illness as an excuse, but I was not unduly concerned when she didn't. I knew that at the right moment, when the mood dictated it, she would tell me all.

Yet for the whole of that long week and during the few days longer it took me to regain sufficient strength to walk steadily, my mind was constantly preoccupied with the strange behaviour of the elders in the middle of that climactic night. For some inexplicable reason, I felt it was important to know; almost as if the whole of my future life depended upon knowing. At the first opportunity, feeling light-headed and vulnerable, I walked from my room in search of Karen.

I had paused outside Katya's door, undecided whether to knock, when Karen turned the corner and walked towards me carrying a broom and pan. She looked very pale and her eyes were wide and raw-rimmed. I asked her if she had recovered from her cold. Almost on the verge of tears, she managed a hasty "yes" and, breaking into a trot, scurried away. When I saw her later, she again took, what I thought, were deliberate steps to avoid me. I was further puzzled by the reaction of the elders who, when I walked into the pine room, avoided my gaze and seemed embarrassed by my presence and made excuses to leave. I stood in the deserted room like a criminal at whom the judge had pointed an accusing finger while the court sat silent, waiting for him to plead guilty. If I felt so humiliated, so utterly dejected, what must Katya be feeling?

I hurried to her room and tapped on the door. To my surprise it was Ira's voice which bade me enter.

Stood either side of the bed, Ira and Godric were looking at a pile of dusty books tumbled onto the white counterpane.

"What do you know of these?"

Without having to examine them I knew Uncle Ira's horny finger was pointing accusingly at the pornographic books Katya had lugged from the library.

"Where is Katya?"

"I asked you if you knew anything of these? We have just found them tied up in a bundle and hidden under the window seat. Well? Answer me."

I glanced round the room and saw that the drawers had been opened and all Katya's belongings indecently searched.

"No."

Ira thought I meant, no, I wouldn't answer, and I had to explain I did not know anything about the books. But Godric turned on me.

"Then why are you blushing, young man? Eh? Have you and she been gloating over these filthy books? Have you?"

I was not sufficiently skilled to hide the embarrassment of a lie nor fool enough to confess and thereby implicate Katya who might not know of this rape of her room.

"Well, speak up, young man. Just what have you and Katya been up to?"

"I wish to speak to Katya. Until then, Uncle Godric, I prefer to say nothing."

Perhaps it was the tone of my voice which made Godric raise his hand to strike me but it was his belligerence which made my spirits sore.

"If you strike me, Uncle Godric, if you so much as lay a finger on me, you, and the rest of the elders will leave this house. And for ever!"

The effect of my ultimatum could not have been imagined. The two men's faces drained of colour and their jaws sagged open. Taken aback, there was a moment of complete silence before Godric began to expostulate.

I pointed my finger; silencing him. "You are here on sufferance. Under the terms of my mother's will, Ira ceased to be my guardian two months ago."

Katya had been the only person to acknowledge my twenty-first birthday. On my pillow when I had awoken had been a biography of Strindberg with "To my darling brother now that he is a galloping Major, from his loving sister who has been a Majorette two years longer", written on the fly leaf. Even Nanna Axell had not congratulated me but from the look she gave me I suspected she knew I was, and rightfully, entitled to be addressed as Herr Strobl. The other elders, possibly sensing their future insecurity, had remained glum and at dinner had sat with downcast eyes, toying with their food.

To see the look of consternation on Ira's and Godric's faces when I delivered my ultimatum, therefore, was a pleasurable experience. Authority tasted delicious and I wanted more. I repeated myself and finally demanded to see Katya.

"She's left. Gone. And good riddance." Uncle Godric pushed past me, followed by a snorting Uncle Ira and the door slammed shut.

I stood a full minute, unable to comprehend and then sank down onto the bed. Katya gone? Left? She had always threatened to. But without a word? And why? The reason was painfully obvious. Disgusted with herself, ashamed to face me, she had left. So it had been I who had eventually forced her to run. I, the one person who loved her, I alone was to blame.

Before I guiltily left the room, I slipped my hand beneath her pillow and withdrew the manuscript. That at least, the elders would never read.

Some three months later, despairing that Katya would ever return, I went back to her room, hoping to detect, even smell, the slightest hint of her remembered presence. Filled with nostalgia and longing, I entered to find the sinister and dark figure of Marcel sprawled in the white armchair. Open on his lap was one of the pornographic books. He snapped the volume shut, tossed it onto the bed and, sucking in his cheeks, rose and, walking close to me, passed out of the room. Before he quietly shut the door, he held onto the jamb and leaned towards me.

"What odd tastes your sister had, Herr Strobl. And in literature too."

Pierced by his leering innuendo, I was crestfallen to think that he, anyone, could be contemptuous of my innocent sister. I gathered up the books for burning and, determined that if Katya never returned, I, nor anyone, would ever enter her room again, I locked the door.

Eight months later, a fire broke out in the west wing and part of the house was gutted, including my room. Although the walls still stood and enough of the roof remained to keep out most of the snow and rain, the whole of the west wing was made entirely uninhabitable by the disaster. To lay Katya's ghost, I moved into her room but, naked between the sheets in that white and pretty boudoir, it was like indecently entering her womb. Taking my erection with me, I went and sat in the cold corridor to pass the remainder of the night, my back against the hard wall, consciously eradicating all feelings of lust.

Wisely, at Karen's suggestion, I removed myself next day to a poky room at the other end of the house, far from anyone else.

"A bed. A chair. A table. And you have a mirror. What else does a man want?"

I could have told Karen what it was I wanted, but for the fact that, with my arm around her waist, she had become another sister.

The two years which followed Katya's departure were so crowded with incident that I was able, after overcoming the initial shock to fill my time without dwelling on her absence.

On the afternoon of the day I had startled Ira and Godric with my ultimatum, I went and told Nanna Axell what had happened and asked her if she knew the whereabouts of Katya. She seemed highly amused to know I had asserted myself and patted my hand approvingly.

"I didn't say anything to you on your birthday, in case you did not feel up to shouldering responsibility. Perhaps now you do. I hope so." She removed one of the many rings she wore and handed it to me. It was a wide band of gold into which a diamond had been set. "It was your father's and was given to him by his father. Take it. It is symbolic of your authority as head of the house Strobl."

Embarrassed, I thanked my grandmother and kissed her bony cheek.

"God bless you, Knut."

The ring was too large for any of my fingers and slipped off when I let my hand drop. I picked it off the carpet and put it on my thumb. I felt very silly.

"Now as to Katya's whereabouts—I don't know, Knut. I truly do not know. But she's a sensible gal and not too proud to write if she should get into difficulties."

I pressed her for an opinion as to how long she thought Katya would be gone, and was shocked by her answer.

"Oh, I doubt if she will come back, Knut. Not ever." She saw I was overcome and squeezed my hand. "Be patient. When she is more settled, she will get in touch with you. She'll probably write and ask you to go and stay with her. You'll see."

Although somewhat cheered by this unthought-of possibility, I could not believe Katya would not be coming back. Made confident by Nanna Axell's undoubted kindness and candour, I ventured to ask if she had realised that it was my fault Katya had left. She was surprised.

"It had nothing to do with you, Knut! Nothing whatsoever. And incidentally, I understand that you never did broach the subject of your—how did you put it—overfondness? Perhaps her absence will ease the pain. It has certainly solved your problem."

I was embarrassed but not satisfied Nanna Axell had told me all she could of the affair, so I asked outright if she knew why Katya had left.

"Oh, yes. Or rather, I know what precipitated her departure. Your Uncle Godric. You know how he enjoys accusing people. Well, he went too far. Katya was indignant, and stormed out of the house. As simple as that. In any case, Knut, you know as well as I do that Katya would have left us sooner or later. It is our loss, Knut, but in the end, it will be her gain. You'll see."

When I pressured her still further to tell me what Godric had accused Katya of doing, Nanna Axell raised and wagged a warning finger.

"Katya will deal with Godric in her own way."

And Katya did, or I think she did; eleven months later.

A bulky letter arrived one morning with a blurred postal cancellation. It was addressed to Frau Axell and in handwriting I did not recognise. After it had been delivered to her room, she summoned me to her bedside.

"I've just had the most surprising letter in the post. I think you will be interested to see it, Knut."

My heart leapt, imagining that it might be from Katya. Eleven months was a long time not to have heard from her.

"I don't think it's from your sister, Knut. It may be, mark you. It may be. It's just a page torn from some magazine or other. I would read it but my eyes are bad."

I suspected from the twinkle in her eye that she had already scrutinised it carefully.

The sheet of paper was very old and had been torn from a military Gazette dated the 11th of August 1928. It took a long time to find the paragraph we had been intended to read. Briefly, it stated that Uncle, or rather, Colonel Godrie Olaf Yorg Acelin, b.1888, of the 1st Bt., 2nd Div., Bg., Mt/F., had, on the 14th of February 1928, been cashiered. The news was a shock to me because I, indeed all of us, had always believed he had been retired honourably.

"Mungo knew. He always insisted Godric had been cashiered but I wouldn't believe him. I said I wanted evidence, Now here it is. Sent by whom? Katya?"

I expressed the opinion that I didn't think Katya vindictive.

"Be that as it may, I think I will speak to Godric myself. Coming from an older person, it won't be so humiliating. He will be shocked, of course. If not entirely sincere, he is an honourable man and will go quietly."

He did take his leave of us, but not quietly. A loud pistol shot brought several of us to the ballroom in a rush. In the very centre, looking immaculate in his full dress uniform, Godric lay dead with a bullet in his brain and all his teeth shattered.

The confusion his death created was inevitable and because of the enquiry which followed, I came face to face with the man I had been brought up to dread: Hans Vetch. Deceptively bland, I was taken in by his charm to begin with but began to distrust him when, with his enquiries over to his complete satisfaction, he insisted upon accompanying me on a tour of the house. With his hands behind his back, he talked effortlessly while his beady eyes took in every detail. I had never met a man with so much confidence and I realised it was authority which gave him stature; the same authority which everyone dreaded. Standing in the high-ceilinged hall, which dwarfed most people into insignificance, Vetch towered impressively when he shook my hand, bowed and replaced his homburg.

"I'm so glad to have met you, Herr Strobl. I've no doubt we shall meet again. Misfortune has the disconcerting mathematical habit of recurring in threes. For your sake, I hope I am proved wrong. Good day."

His leave-taking had the disturbing darkness of a threat and I was uncomfortable for days after.

Godric was buried in Lindehult without ceremony. Only Felix followed the coffin and, with his cane under his arm, marched like a soldier leading a cortège.

"The man was more sinned against than sinful. But then we're all misunderstood. Aren't we?" He had looked at each of the elders in turn after making the announcement that he was going to attend Godric's funeral.

"Go heal thyself," Ira muttered and Felix had nearly raised his cane. Godric's tragic and unnecessary death had made the elders sensitive. It was as if each had a shameful secret and was distrustful of the potential Judas in everyone. A fear, which in the end, broke up the smug coterie and scattered the flotsam far and wide. Long before Godric's death, however, and while I muddled through those first few weeks after Katya's flight, Nanna. Axell had encouraged me to saddle myself with the responsibilities of running the house and what was left of the estate.

"It will prevent you moping. And besides, it is your inheritance."

Under her guidance, I was introduced to the complexities of paperwork and decision making. Shewn accounts, there was unfolded before me the tragic decline of the house Strobl. Gort, feeling he was also on the wane, rather than make the long journeys, sent a young man called Gripp.

"I have taken him into the firm and have every intention of making him a partner."

The thought of the firm being called Gort & Gripp amused me. But Gripp dispelled all sense of frivolity. Starved, unyielding, as cold as an icicle, he cast his bright, humourless eyes over the sheets of figures and took in the extent of our predicament with no show of emotion.

"Re-insure, and pray there will be a natural disaster."

I asked him if he was serious.

"Of course. Sell, otherwise. And sell as rubble. It would be more profitable. This house is a, a . . . "

I ventured the word mausoleum and he nodded. "I was going to say white elephant. Yes. It would be a complete waste of capital to try and restore it in the hopes of attracting a profit from its sale. The return would be insufficient to justify the outlay. If any."

I said I had no intention of selling.

"In that case I suggest you, one, invest your capital better. Two. Sell more land than you feel able. Three. Get rid of your pine. Outright. Not as a concession. As it stands." Gripp was referring to the forest we, or rather, I owned. "One other thing. I would be less generous."

His allusion to my generosity puzzled me until he revealed how the elders had systematically milked the estate of several thousand Kronor. Noticing another set of figures, I asked Gripp why they had been abstracted a few weeks before.

"Your sister, quite legally, claimed the shares which had been set aside for her under the terms of your father's will. Presumably she has sold them."

It was a large sum but I was more interested to know if he had Katya's address.

"Ah. Now. Yes. Old Gort will have it if she has been in correspondence with him. I'll enquire."

Three days later, he was seated opposite to me in the study again, sitting bolt upright. "It would appear that your sister came in person to instruct Gort, and later collected the cheque."

I had no reason to doubt Gripp and got him to promise me the moment he learnt of Katya's whereabouts, he would tell me.

"Presumably she did not wish us to know where she was living, but I will do my best to trace her."

I baulked at the suggestion a detective should be hired and said no. Keen as I was to know where she was living and why she had needed so large an amount of money, and all at once, I did not want the police involved, it was not improbable that she had gone abroad to live. The war in Europe was over and no doubt people were travelling again. I thought back to all the conversations Katya and I had had but could not recall her ever expressing a desire to live in any one particular country. "Like all Northerners, Knut, I crave the sun, but being light-skinned, I expect I would be unable to bear the heat." Recalling this made me doubt if she had gone far.

The outcome of all Gripp's visits was that I did as he suggested and, to add to the diminished capital, stripped the house of valuables and sold them. Stupidly, I forgot to re-insure the house so that when the west wing burnt down, there was not one öre of compensation. It was entirely my own fault. Gripp had sent me the form to sign but I had put it aside because, at that time, I was more interested in evaluating my inheritance.

In order to sell the contents, I had to make an inventory. Armed with ancient stock lists trailing cotton threads from their broken spines, I explored the rooms in which furniture and valuables were still to be found. It wasn't long before I realised the lists were incorrect. I had expected some discrepancies but did not think to discover that furniture and valuables by the van load would be missing. Not all had been filched under the cover of darkness, but had been disposed of during the many financial crises which seemed to beset the Strobl estate. When shown the lists and the two compared, Nanna Axell shook her head sadly.

"To think the Strobls were once worth a fortune. It's like a judgement on us for our worthless lives."

But, encouraged by her to do what I thought best and not heed the protestations of the elders who, when I marked down something to be sold, used persuasion and, failing that, invective, to get me to alter my mind, I carried on despite them.

In one empty room, under a dust sheet, I discovered a painting of a nude woman. Sprawled erotically on a day-bed with her back towards the spectator, she had her head turned, looking over her shoulder in threequarter profile. Blonde, with fine, sensitive features, intelligent-looking but not overbearingly arrogant, disdainful yet with a tiny, moist hint of amusement in the corner of her mouth, she was the image of Katya. The likeness was uncanny and, but for the fact the painting had been done some two hundred years before Katya's birth, it could have been her portrait. Unfortunately, the unknown lady's body, with its plump and odoriferous buttocks and the spreading rose-pink blush emanating from them, was so unlike Katya as to destroy the illusion. Despite this too obvious and provocative pose, I coveted the painting but had to admit to myself it was the saucy nudity which added to the excitement of Katya's face. I guiltily covered the painting with the dust sheet again and took comfort from the fact I knew where it was if I ever cared to look.

The gentleman Gort sent to value the possessions I had listed was a soft-fleshed man. Named Schtek, he smoked incessantly, spilling ash down his waistcoat and staining his moustache ginger. That he knew his job was unquestionable, but I was not in agreement with him on two points. The first concerned the place of sale. I insisted the auction should not be held in the house. Already I had witnessed the rape by plough of the land I had sold and could not bear the thought of watching the sale of our possessions on the premises. He grudgingly conceded, but only after I had threatened to call off the sale. The second argument was over the nude painting I had discovered. He coughed himself into a paroxysm of tobacco-smoked convulsions when I told him I had thought of cutting out the head to keep.

"But it's by Boucher, Herr Strobl, and worth . . ." But, red-faced and his eyes watering, he had to cough up his lungs in the corner and I didn't hear his valuation, but guessed it was several thousand Kronor. After he had ground his unfinished cigarette into the floorboards, he renewed his pleading not to damage the painting but to sell it if I thought so little of it. I refused but promised him I would not mutilate the picture. And I kept my promise. Instead of cutting out the head, I pasted brown paper over the body, leaving Katya's head gazing round at me. In between coughs while I walked down the drive with him, Schtek said he would send a man to look at the books in the library and, lighting another cigarette, got into his chauffeur-driven car which had crunched down the drive following us.

A week later, a very short and ingratiating man called Fischer came creeping into the house. The books disappointed him. Few were rare and the bulk he thought should be sold by the foot.

"Not weight?" I cynically suggested.

"No, no, Herr Strobl," pronouncing it "Schtrobal". "No. It is the spines they're after. They want the look of a library without the dust. Besides, who would want to read such rubbish?"

Secretly, I was in agreement with him. My forebears had not been scholarly in their choice of books, just pompous. Before Fischer went he took me aside in the great hall and, pulling at my lapels, pawed his way up to my ear. His breath was fetid and I tried to draw back but he clung like a leech.

"A library that size. A nineteenth-century library. They invariably collected certain—what shall we call them?—esoteric literature? Perhaps you've put them aside? I could dispose of them for you. Your name would not be mentioned. And cash, of course!"

I disengaged myself from his sticky embrace and, knowing full well to what books he was referring, took great pleasure in telling him there had been some very erotic books, a thousand all told, but I had burnt them. He went down the drive looking imploringly up to heaven, as if asking God to be his witness before such fools of men. It was then I noticed his shirt tail was hanging out, but I did not call his attention to it and let him drive away.

With the sales over, our financial resources a little more buoyant and the fire in the west wing not yet lit, I went to Nanna Axell with a feeling of relief. Her room had not been ravished by the whirlwind of my ruthless plundering. Everything in that majestic room had been left intact.

"They are my only possessions, Knut. Leftover relics from the days when your grandfather Joachim, whom you won't remember, was the greatest catch a girl could win for herself. As a man, he was ineffectual, but I never hurt his pride by telling him so. Nor did I expose him to the contempt of his drunken companions. But he was generous and I wanted for nothing. Nor do."

She patted my hand and I saw how the veins stood up like swollen rivers and streamed into her wrinkled fingers, cluttered with jewellery. It was odd how the elderly coveted and wore their own, their mother's and their grandmother's rings, I thought. It was as if the rings were symbolic and, by wearing them, they were able to assume the authority which the dead had once had over them.

"Katya will have my jewellery when I die and anything else she may choose to have. You, too. It is all in my will."

I told her she had a great number of years still left to live and must not disappoint me by not reaching a hundred.

"You're a great comfort to me, Knut, even though I know you only say things to flatter me."

I had made it a habit to sit with Nanna Axell each day. We either discussed the problems of the house together, or I read to her. I came to respect her judgement and found her very shrewd. While our intimacy grew, it was not unusual for me to do those little tasks generally left to Karen to perform, such as changing the stone hot water bottle she kept wrapped in lint at her feet. The first time I saw her feet, I was surprised by their youthful appearance. They seemed not to belong to the wizened old head at the other end of the bed. Nearly bald, a light white fuzz stood out from her almost naked skull like the seeds of a dandelion. Not embarrassed to reveal her balding pate, she would give it a good scratch and replace her frilled cap.

"I'd like to reach a hundred, Knut, but not if it means my mind as well as my body has to become senile."

I said that it was unthinkable her mind would cease to be active and deteriorate.

"But my body, Knut. It's gone. I don't recognise it any more. Even Karen thinks it looks like a twig floating on the water when I have my bath."

That might be true, I said, but she had the prettiest feet I had ever seen.

"They are, aren't they? Joachim used to grovel over them but his attentions seemed so unnatural that I came to detest them. But thank you for the compliment. Incidentally, have you heard from Katya yet?" She knew I hadn't but intended her remark to show she was concerned for my happiness and I was pleased. "What will you do with yourself, now that our affairs seem to be in some sort of order?"

I confessed I did not know; not daring to tell her I intended to spend as much as my time as I could with Karen.

During the first months of that hectic year, Karen had made herself indispensable. Emptying drawers, dusting, carrying, moving cumbersome furniture which I could not manage on my own, I had come to depend upon her. I also enjoyed her company. Being taller than me, although tall for a girl, she surprised me by her strength and I stood in awe of her whenever she managed the impossible. Even the odour of light sweat which emanated from her after we had been particularly active had a quality which I found attractive. Pungent, it was the scent of sour lavender and the smell of a young but well-washed body which pride and health kept active and sweet.

"It's rude to comment on such things, Knut. It is embarrassing."

The next day, she came and stood close to me. "Well? Notice any difference?"

Memory stirred, but like a mole deep underground.

"It's your sister's scent. She gave me a bottle for my birthday."

I winced as memory bit and pretended disapproval on the grounds that it was totally unnecessary. Secretly, I was disturbed by the ominous, almost tangible presence locked in the cloud of perfume, imagining it was Katya's phantom, struggling to materialise. Dogged by this spectre when we unavoidably passed or I walked up behind her and was enveloped in a cloud of scent, I was forced to tell Karen the perfume did not become her and she should not use it again.

"There is too little of it to waste on you, Knut. In any case," and she sniffed the crook of her arm, "I dab it on for my own pleasure. And then only sparingly. I want it to last." Then, deliberately, almost as if to tease me, she flounced her skirt and pirouetted. "Katya was very wicked. Did you know she used to scent the hem of her dress?"

I did not, but the idea lodged and became erotic.

Later, sitting perched on some furniture, I began to reappraise Karen. I was coming to see her as an individual, as an attractive and personable young woman. I told her as much and apologised for my previous indiffer-ence, saying it had been unintentional and blaming my previous imma-turity. She was not in the least put out and was extremely frank with me; disarmingly so, for she showed herself to be very perceptive.

"It's only because you miss having Katya fuss round you all the time. If she were still here, it would never occur to you to notice me. So I'm not flattered."

Close as Karen had been to Katya, I doubted if Katya had hinted at my unnatural attachment or that they had secretly giggled over it together. But, as when one knows one is being observed from a distance through a telescope it isn't until one realises how sharp, near and surprisingly large the image of oneself is in the spy glass, one becomes embarrassed and feels naked and exposed. With Karen's perception trained upon me like a spy glass, I was uncomfortable and made a note to be wary of her all-see-ing third eye. I asked her if she missed Katya.

She did not reply at once but sank down heavily on a sofa and stuck out her legs in front of her; very like an adolescent girl.

"Katya was like a mother to me."

I shrank and, colouring rapidly, jumped down and walked to the win-dow to hide my embarrassment. I could not understand why, with all the motherly affection Helga bestowed on Karen, she should look up to Katya as a mother figure. Big-bosomed, amply hipped, arms like piano legs and a lap broad and deep enough to cradle an enormous brood, Helga was the ideal mother earth. The clue seemed to lie in the unconscious way I had thought of Karen as looking "up" to, rather than "on" Katya as a mother figure. It had never occurred to me Katya could be adored by a girl, envied even; yet it seemed eminently sensible.

"Helga's a fine, honest, dependable woman but her fault is that she is overfond. Her frustration of my not being her daughter, of not having a child of her own, has made her possessive. She smothers me. She always has. Like a well-meaning person can be insufferable. You know? I realise I could have been fostered out on someone far less likeable. My life could have been hell. But Helga's too motherly. Naturally I feel dreadful, because she's such a good woman. Really good. Surrounded by ten children of her own, she would have been in her element and had no time for favouritism. She would have been the perfect mother. As it is, she's indestructible."

I asked if she knew who her real mother was.

"It's not Helga." There had been the usual tittle-tattle suggesting she had been Helga's bastard. Obviously Karen had heard this gossip. "I'm more likely to have been your mother's daughter."

I was shocked. Yet, hating Madlin as I had and knowing her to have been immoral, I couldn't understand why I should be offended. Then I found myself being attracted by the possibility that she was indeed a second sister but was repelled by the sheer horror of realising I was riding the crest of an unnatural attachment.

"Of course I'm not your sister, but I came very near to being related to you. Did you know I was nearly adopted by your Aunt Estrild?" I had not. "Sorry as I am for her. . . Well, you know all about that."

Karen had no need to explain. Estrild's past was never discussed; only alluded to.

Over-sensitive, grey and brittle, Aunt Estrild had led the family to believe her husband, Madlin's cousin Kisch, had left her for another woman. To make matters worse, Estrild had said she was pregnant. To win sympathy from relatives who were not given to shows of affection and whose compassion had dried up, was, I think, the reason for Aunt Estrild's desperate lie. Kisch had not left her and she was not pregnant. It was easier to convince the elders that Kisch was despicable than prove she was with child. But this she did by discreetly padding out her stomach. Once enmeshed by her lie, in her desperation she had no alternative but to see the lie through to its ultimate end; a birth. How she accomplished this was so revolting that it was only alluded to but must have been responsible for her continuing madness. In the dead of night, without anyone present until it was all over, she delivered herself of a dead child. Wrapped in newspaper, it was handed to Granoise to burn while the female elders fussed round her. Granoise, dumb but wily, before the flames in the grate consumed the secret package, curiously poked the contents. To her peasant eye, the blooded mess was a skinned and mutilated rabbit, not a human baby. At first no one knew, for none were told and no doubt it would have remained a secret if Granoise had not confronted Estrild. Whether Granoise had attempted to blackmail Estrild is only speculation, but her persistent and unusual efforts to corner Estrild ended with Estrild's nervous collapse. It was Helga who managed to restrain Granoise but only after she had been told the truth. Because no one would believe it, Granoise held her tongue and it was left to Gardol to say that a rabbit had been taken from the larder.

"I suppose if Estrild had adopted me, she would have been saved from her madness. On the other hand . . . No. The prospects are too frightening."

I agreed. Estrild was mad but never wild, although she had to be restrained from time to time. Gerda had taken upon herself the task of chaperoning Estrild and always seemed to be on hand when Estrild's behaviour got out of hand. Only twice did I witness her outbursts. Once, when Estrild had walked into the dining room and, in front of us all, opened her blouse, announcing she had cancer: "I shall have to cut them off, won't I?" Gerda had hustled her away while Katya and I had been told to get on with our dinner. The second occasion was in the pine room when I had come upon her unexpectedly. Alone in the room, she had been smearing the windows with what looked like brown mud; in fact it was excreta. Madlin had removed her, gripping Estrild's neck and taking her upstairs like a naughty child. There were other upsetting moments, but not all so disturbing. The reason why Estrild had never been committed to an asylum was painfully apparent to Karen.

"Your relatives, degenerate as they are, have a nonsensical pride. They prefer to keep their dark secrets hidden from the rest of the disinterested world. Don't you agree?" I did.

In the following months, I came to know Karen well. We talked easily together and found that we had a lot in common. Possibly because it irked me or made me more embarrassed than I need have been, I didn't take kindly to her almost obsessive and deliberate avoidance of physical contact. Often, I was forced to touch her when I scrambled by her or squeezed myself past to get to the other side of a piece of furniture. She would shrink from my contact, however accidental, especially if I unthinkingly put my elbow on her shoulder like a gardener leaning on his spade to rest a moment. Then she would suddenly twist away and, using the excuse that my elbow was painful or that she wanted to sit down, would walk away from me. There came the moment when I caught hold of her by the shoulders and held her while I stared into her pale green eyes. I wanted to establish that she existed and, through my touch, reassure myself that I too had a corporeal body at that particular moment in time. It was difficult to explain this, to convince her that it was nothing more than reassurance. How else could it be?

"I would not like to think you were taking advantage of me but that you were moved to do this."

I released her. The tension in her unyielding body and the cold rigidity frustrated the possible flow of understanding between us.

"Sometimes, Knut, the desire to overcome inhibition may result in rash behaviour. I've no intention you should have regrets."

I was irritated by her uncanny perception and shrugged off my moodiness by saying that perhaps it was because I was lonely.

"I too feel isolated but we would be courting inevitable disaster if we were impelled solely by loneliness to seek each other's company." It was not an unreasonable point of view but it implied that in our coming together a love would develop between us. Nothing could have been further from my thoughts at that moment.

I tried to explain I had no intention of doing anything which would compromise our relationship.

"I believe you. But you must give me time to adjust. You have a disturbing effect upon me . . ." I stiffened and frowned. "You make me feel overprotective towards you. It would endanger a proper friendship."

I was reassured but a little alarmed by the analysis and cold control she had over her emotions.

Towards the end of that first year after Katya had left and winter once again surrounded the house, and after a wet summer during which I hardly went out, it was inevitable I succumbed to illness. For two months, I hovered between my warm bed and the fire kept blazing in my room. During that time, Karen came and sat with me almost daily. She either talked quietly, read aloud, brought up her sewing basket and sat darning or, and more often than not, warmed her pale hands in front of the fire. It did not bother me that she remained silent, it was enough that she was there, with me, and I respected the privacy of her thoughts. The regularity of her visits and no doubt the attention she lavished upon me while fussing about the bed plumping pillows and making sure I was comfortable, made me grow very fond of her.

"It isn't love, Knut. Compassion must not be confused with love. Every man falls in love with his nurse."

I told her she went beyond what could be reasonably expected of her.

"Duty?" She was surprised and sat down on the bed. "Duty? My dear Knut, you are a fellow human who is helpless. Chance has it that I am here."

A few days later, sat in the armchair and hot from the heat of the fire I told Karen she was heartless and cold. She "poo-pooed" me.

"It's your masculine pride which is hurt. You feel you should dominate me, and don't. You're peeved, that's all."

I argued that our friendship had the quality of love and she shouldn't denigrate something so rare and innocent.

"Don't delude yourself, Knut. What is it you want of me? The same as if I were a man? No."

I had to admit that it was because she was a woman.

"You would despise me, and come to despise yourself if I became your mistress."

I shocked myself, Karen too, by what I said next. I asked her to marry me. Stunned into silence, we avoided each other's eyes. When the moment had passed when she could have struck me or, and more humiliating, laughed at such a ridiculous proposition, when she did not move, I sank back into my chair to consider the implications of my offer. Surprisingly, I could not in the consequences anything which would make me reconsider or withdraw it. Karen was the first to stir.

"D'you know, Knut, I suppose every girl, long before she is asked, considers—knows—how she will answer. Like any other girl, I thought I knew. I don't. It is a compliment and one which cannot be cruelly turned aside, yet when it comes as a surprise it inevitably begs to be rejected. Do you understand?"

I understood only too well and said I had been premature in asking.

"I doubt if time will make any difference, but I am prepared to wait and to accept what may become inevitable. I told you I was a fatalist. At the same time, I must try and exercise control over situations which are not necessarily going to contribute towards my future happiness."

I begged her to say no and have done with it, but she took hold of my hand.

"If had suspected you were so fond of me, Knut, I would have taken steps to avoid causing you pain. As it is, let's speak no more about it until we have both had more time to think."

I pulled on her hand and inched her towards me but as our faces came together, I saw her lips compress and felt a reluctance stiffen her arm. I released her and found myself fiddling with my linger ends. Karen stood up and, coming up behind me, kissed the top of my head.

"Such consideration is all I ask for, Knut."

Left on my own, I dwelled on her last remark. Had I unwittingly opened up the possibilities of a love deep inside her? If I had, I hoped it did not mean that to please her, I would have to play the neutered lapdog, sat trembling nervously on her closed thighs, impotent under caresses.

The first few days after this meeting passed awkwardly but we got over the difficulty of imagining casual remarks contained a hidden significance which had not been intended. So, settled into a deep and total friendship, we committed our lives to nothing more positive than happiness and found it in the simplest of things. Unfortunately, as in all relationships, there were times when misunderstanding, selfishness and irritability caused friction and we were reduced to quarrelling.

On our first outing in the trap, a brittle relationship was revealed by what was a very trivial incident. Feeling much better and the spring being early and unusually warm, I had persuaded Karen to take me out. Wrapped in rugs up to the chin, I sat by her side, with old Grinn harnessed between the shafts. We had gone along the lanes, rising slowly until we came to an opening in the trees which allowed us to look out across the valley. The ride had been extremely pleasant and I glowed under the rugs while my cold face smarted but alerted me to the beauty of my surrounds. Karen was equally enchanted and was unusually excited. I took no part in her seduction, for it was the landscape, the fresh, almost virile air and the birds calling to one another across the valley which enamoured her.

On the fringe of her allurement and thinking I could take advantage of it, besides being moved by her beauty, I asked her to kiss me.

"No."

I asked her again, for she had refused me teasingly.

"I don't want to, Knut."

Not put off, on the contrary, I was excited by her heady gaiety, I persisted. Old Grinn had stopped and wandered off the road to nibble grass.

"Silly. I don't want to." And she flipped my nose with her finger. "Don't spoil it for me, Knut."

I could not see how a kiss could spoil anything, especially as the moment and mood seemed made for it.

"For goodness sake, Knut! Stop it!" And she elbowed me in the ribs as I sought her face. Angered, I withdrew into the rugs until only my eyes and hat showed above them. Stealing a glance, I saw Karen's face had become pinched and white and there was a wildness in her eyes.

"Do you want me the way a man wants a woman? Is that it? Well? Do you?" I smouldered and remained silent. "Go on then. Do it. Do what you want. Go on. I dare you!"

I snatched the reins from her and tried to haunch-slap old Grinn into a trot and back onto the road. Stubborn and old, gorging himself on new grass, he refused to budge. I lost my temper and would have whipped him if Karen had not wrenched the whip from me and thrown it into the bushes.

"Don't be so silly, Knut. Have you gone mad?"'

I pushed Karen away and pulled hard on the reins to purposely get the bit to cut into Grinn's soft mouth.

"Knut! You're being cruel! Stop it!"

I turned on her and shouted it was not I who was cruel but she and, throwing the reins aside, began to struggle out of the trap saying I would damn well walk back without her. But she clung onto me and I was no match for her strength. Frustrated, I cringed and remained.

"And stay sat!"

In silence, we rode all the way back to the house.

That evening, she came to my room and stood awkwardly in the door-way. "I've brought you an apple."

I told her to get out and to take her bloody apple with her. Whereupon she flung it at my head and burst into tears.

A whole week passed before we apologised to each other. Surprisingly, we found we had drawn closer together. Probably, the tension released, we were able to see how we had both been to blame. Calmed, I asked her if she had really believed I, Knut, who loved her, would have dared to rape her, let alone contemplate such a despicable act.

"I wouldn't have cared. You would have suffered more than me in the long run. That sort of messing about wouldn't have spoiled the real me. The me which I am."

When I looked at her, what she said seemed strangely reminiscent of Katya, and I saw, perhaps for the first time, how alike they were.

We continued in friendship for some months. Although reserved and quiet, both of us, without commenting upon it, were aware that beneath this outward calm, there lurked an emotion which would be climaxed in a carnal embrace if either asserted their desire. It was the fire in the west wing and the events that followed which almost precipitated this calamity.

The fire, the cause of which was never discovered, brought the worst and best out in the elders who still remained. Greed made Ira brave in face of the flames which threatened his possessions; the excitement of lust caused Felix to dance like a jinn on the periphery of the holocaust, while Uncle Mungo shrank from his own cowardice and remained wide-eyed, far from the flames. Only Helga and Gardol were calm and practical, giving way to their emotion only when all that remained of the west wing was charred wood and the overwhelming stench of burnt soot blanketed the house. Nanna Axell had been stoical and had prepared herself to be moved out of her room if necessary after Karen had reassured her she was not forgotten. But it was Marcel who proved himself brave and reckless. To him was credited the saving of some furniture and pictures and we were all, without exception, very grateful to him. I surprised myself, not with the courage I found to drag a few bits and pieces from my burning room, but by how little I cared when, helpless to quench the flames, I stood back and hot-faced watched the building roar. By the time the firemen came, all they could do was to prevent the fire spreading and we counted ourselves lucky.

In the light of dawn, smudged with soot and kicking the warm ashes, Karen came up behind me and put her arms round my waist. She blew into my ear and said bed was the proper place for me. I shook my head and turned. We embraced and I kissed her and was kissed back. We would probably have become passionate if it had not been for our comical, black faces which made us giggle. However, the spell was broken and while we wandered hand in hand through the stinking ash, we each trembled slightly at the other's touch.

There was a considerable amount of sorting and rearranging to be done after the disaster and it was then I discovered I had forgotten to re-insure the house. Nanna Axell spread her hands.

"We are fated, Knut. But it could have been worse."

I agreed.

"Of course it could have been a judgement upon us, in which case there must still be more to come for I am sure He up there will not be satisfied with so small a conflagration." I did not believe in such divine punishment but had I known then that Nanna Axell was a prophet, I would have rekindled the flames and gladly thrown myself onto the pyre.

Ira and his wife left shortly after. I paid little attention to their long explanation, knowing they would return the moment I faltered and Ira thought there might be a chance to inherit the estate. Felix too took his leave but this was because Karen had complained to me about his behaviour and told me the disgusting tricks he had got up to in the past; none of which were overtly sexual but I now understood his perversion and could not tolerate it any longer. Told to go and pack his damned trunk, he went meekly after insisting we shake hands. Only Uncle Mungo remained. Dressed all in brown, he kept to his room and whenever I went upstairs to see him, he was always sat looking out of the window doing nothing.

The house to ourselves, I expected Karen and I, if we could avoid Marcel, would be deliriously happy. As things turned out, I was never more miserable.

The summer was the warmest I could remember and on the first sunny day Granoise died. Struggling into the kitchen with an armful of logs to feed the cooking stoves, she had fallen over backwards, dead. All of us, including Mungo and Marcel, attended her funeral in Lindehult. Afterwards I described the sad little ceremony to Nanna Axell. What was strange, I explained to her, was the nakedness I felt when I had walked through the village and had seen everyone looking at me; not with hostility but with dumb curiosity.

"Your father would go down there and everyone would acknowledge him. You have grown since then and it is a long time since they have seen you. You should visit them more often, even though they no longer work on the estate, but you have an obligation to the old and sick for they knew you as a child."

But I did not care to play the benevolent Squire.

Still in my mourning clothes and smelling strongly of camphor, I persuaded Karen to walk with me down to the lake. Standing at its edge skimming stones, I asked how much longer I should have to wait before I dared ask her to marry me. She took my arm and put it round her shoulder and gripped me tightly.

"Don't ever ask." I tried to pull away but she held me. "Listen to me. I am very happy as we are. No, listen. Hear me out, Knut. I am very happy. Marriage would not make me happier. Will you listen?" I was trying to pull away for I did not want to hear. "I know marriage means that . . . Well. I don't want to become your mistress. To become a sort of possession—not that you would regard me like that I know. But I want to be something less definite."

Depressed, exhausted almost, I asked how that could be.

"Well, if you feel strongly enough—I mean, want me, in that sort of way, I think I could." She was trembling violently.

I disengaged myself and stood away from her. I could not bring myself to speak, so took her hand and walked her back to the house. Alone in my cramped little room, I thought of all the things I could have said and was glad that I hadn't.

For some time past, I had been writing poetry. Determined it should occupy all my waking moments, I redoubled my efforts in the hopes it would distract my thoughts from Karen. But sometimes she would enter my room and, leaning over my shoulder, read what I had written or picking up a discarded sheet from the floor lie reading it on my bed.

"Must you be so sad, Knut? All your poems are so sad."

It was true; although concerned with unobtainable love, the despair was for Katya, not Karen. I had begun writing poetry because of the frustration of Karen's rejection but it had seemed so closely linked in my mind with Katya, all my old longings and aches had come back. Karen, I had to admit to myself, was really a substitute for Katya. Katya was unobtainable, Karen was proving to be, so the two became one. They were indivisible.

"Am I really like this? How you see me? Do you, Knut?"

I had prepared myself for this question and had decided to answer truthfully. As gently as I could, to risk offending her in order to hear the truth work for my own good, I told her the poems were about Katya. Karen's reaction, apart from a moment's silence, was unexpected. Throwing her arms about me, she smothered my face with kisses and held me tightly.

"Oh, I love you, Knut. Truly love you."

I would like to have believed it was a natural instinct which urged me to tumble her back onto the bed, to fumble under her apron and wedge my hand between her thighs, scrabbling to find a way through the intricacies of her underwear. I would have liked to believe this, even when, swooning and almost delirious, she groaned beneath my touch. But, and here I am not at all certain what was said, yet the sense, the implication was that she loved me—oh yes, I was her darling baby! Had she not uttered those words or their meaning held such significance, I am certain we would have destroyed our mutual virginity in a state verging on hysteria. As it was, I hesitated, became calm and turned aside my attentions—content to buss her cheek whilst apologising for my inexcusable behaviour. Inwardly I was sickened.

Surprised, but not unduly, shrugging down her skirt and sitting up, Karen accepted my shortcomings with a sniff and patted my thigh.

Solemnly, but with no hint of recrimination—for she squeezed my hand, kissed me and looked adoringly back—Karen left quietly afterwards.

Doubtful that she suffered a comparable ache, I retired onto a bed ruckled by our struggle and fell into an uncomfortable sleep, only to awake next morning with my desire still rampant and unsatisfied.

During the weeks which followed and while the summer still held, we took great care not to manoeuvre each other into a repetition of the incident. From Karen's looks and occasional sighs I was led to understand she, too, found the situation unbearable, so it seemed inevitable both of us would have to confess and to each other, it was desire, not love, which would weld us into what would prove to be a messy and shameful union. And soon.

On the twelfth of August, Helga came looking for me. It was unusual to see Helga in the main part of the house except when she helped serve at dinner. She apologised but seemed distraught, plucking at her apron and unnecessarily smoothing out the creases. Sat knee to knee with me, she came straight to the point.

"There must be a marriage, Knut. I insist. She will marry. There is going to be a proper wedding, and she will marry. I don't care who protests or how loudly, she is to marry. And I can force her to. I am still her adoptive mother and until she is twenty-one, she does as I say. And she marries. Karen—will—marry."

If she had been referring to Karen and myself, I think I would still have been shocked, but she wasn't.

"They were in bed together. That damned Marcel and my Karen. He's going to marry her and she's going to marry him."

I cannot pretend I sat composed while Helga unfolded her story. I felt I wanted to be sick but it was evident that Helga knew nothing of the fondness which existed between Karen and myself. Even while Helga rattled on, I could not believe she was telling the truth.

"But I saw them. With my own eyes. As close as I sit to you. Not a stitch on. Either of them. Karen was ashamed, mind. I'm not saying she wasn't. But that damned Marcel! Cocky as you please!"

I was beginning to believe the unbelievable and asked in whose bed they had been found.

"What does that matter? It was Karen's. But the damage is done!"

It was, indeed, but I was reassured to know Karen had not gone traipsing into Marcel's room. This somehow put the blame on Marcel and I asked Helga if she thought Marcel had used his strength against Karen.

"Never in your life. Oh, she said he had, but a girl two doors away from me, do you think I wouldn't have heard her scream? The young hussy. And to think how I have tried to bring her up . . ." Helga cried into her apron.

After a while, her eyes dabbed dry, I asked if it would be any use if I talked to them.

"She's going to marry. Nothing else will satisfy me. And I want you, Knut, I want you to make it a nice wedding . . ." And she wept like a mother who sees her daughter's will as defiance and whose own wise but common sense as vandalised. A snook had been cocked at her authority and the experience was bitter.

Saying I would not decide before I had first spoken to Marcel and Karen, I helped her down to the kitchens and went up to the attics where she said Karen had locked herself into her room.

It was difficult to persuade Karen to open the door but when she did, I stood aghast at the change in her. Pulled and swollen, her face was unrecognisable and her once pale green eyes were tiny red, watery holes which blinked and spilled tears. I gave her time to recover from another prolonged outburst of sobbing and asked her to tell me what had happened. It was as Helga had said. While I listened, her shame turned my pain into compassion and I went to take her hand. Karen snatched it away and shrank from me. I asked if it had been on my account, for there persisted the idea her action had been deliberately planned and was intended to goad me into jealous pursuit. I did not believe this, yet could not credit Karen giving way to frustration; I preferred to think Marcel had forced his attentions upon her. However, I asked if I had been to blame. Karen threw her arms about my neck and sobbed that I wasn't. When she was calmer, I explained most carefully all the alternatives that were open to her, but she seemed determined to be obstinately contrary. She would not marry me; would not run away but would stay and marry Marcel.

"Don't you see? I'm fated to marry him! Fated!"

I could not see, and to stun her into the realisation of her predicament, asked her what she would do if she found she was pregnant. She vomited, and the next ten minutes I spent clearing up the mess.

It was just after this, while I was rinsing my hands, Marcel pushed open the door with his foot and leant against the jamb.

"Are you going to congratulate me, Herr Strobl?" Marcel's arrogance was menacing. He was so self-confident and Karen so bowed and meek I knew he had a hold over her which could not be broken.

However, I made my protest, hoping it would encourage Karen to stand up and denounce him, but she remained silent and passive, almost as if she wanted to be broken on a rack in the belief that her suffering would in some way compensate her for the shame she felt. Upon Marcel, my ranting had no effect whatsoever. His amused tolerance infuriated me, so, impotent to vent my fury, I withdrew; feeling myself to be an intruder. The marriage would take place.

As in the days when I was less adult, I found myself once more compelled to seek out a place to hide and climbed into the loft over the stables. But here too I felt an intruder, and into my own childhood which had passed. Labouring back down the ladder, I saw I had no alternative but to accept my role as an invalid hermit and could look forward to nothing more than endless days spent in solitude. But what seemed important at that moment was to avoid Karen in the weeks before her marriage and to keep in check the desire I felt for her. And I did, although I took her in my arms to dance at her wedding feast and months later clung to her desperately while between us lay a corpse.

Helga, naturally, made the arrangements for the wedding. The chapel was once more swept and tidied and the ballroom thoroughly cleaned and polished. I was not sure I had seen the ballroom ever put to use but had been told how it looked and so accepted the transformation. Brightly lit, the chandeliers reflected in the hundreds of mirrors, it looked like a heavenly nova. Even to walk in it made me light-headed and I experienced how easily one could become irresponsible and gay. Nanna Axell had wanted to see it once more before she died, but I thought it too risky to move her so far away from her room, so I described it to her. Sighing and shaking her head, she reminisced until the tears came into her bright blue eyes.

"Silly old me. But they were wonderful days, Knut. And your grandfather danced *so* well." She knew I was upset by Karen's forthcoming marriage, but not that I was in love with her. "I must admit that Marcel is not a good choice, but marriage may change him. I'm surprised Karen is so reticent to talk about it. You would think she would be more, more gay. Or is this how the young today behave when they are in love? It seems most strange to me."

Without telling me, Nanna Axell made them both a present of some money but shrewdly made certain Karen would not be robbed of her share by an avaricious Marcel.

"I don't trust the man, Knut," she said later. "Anyway, a gal has a right to be independent. Gives her confidence in herself. So I'm glad I did it."

As the wedding drew near Helga, helped by some women from the village, became unbearably overexcited. It was infectious and made me irritable. I had carefully avoided Karen and made certain I was never cornered but the little I saw of her, in the distance or at dinner, convinced me her brave face would have split wide open if her anguish had been temptingly cosseted. The evening before the wedding she had obviously wanted to speak to me and made every effort to do so but I dodged her on each occasion. It seemed cruel but necessary for I knew I too would have broken down. Going to my room and locking the door, I turned to discover on my writing table and in the very centre, a brightly-polished apple. I flung myself down and wept. But as I wept I took the apple and, with ungovernable passion, devoured it until the juice ran off my chin. Core, pips and stalk, I devoured it all with the passion of a rapist.

The next day, dressed in my best and feeling dandy with a buttonhole, I welcomed a strange and assorted company of men and women into the house and showed them through to the chapel. There were surprisingly many guests but, as Helga explained, most were cronies from her past, all villagers, a few friends but mostly old workers from the estate that was. The men wore large boots and seemed uncomfortable in their best clothes. Weathered by the winds and snow, their turkey necks and clubbed hands poked raw and awkwardly out of their stiff clothes.

The women, too, appeared ill-at-ease in their finery and all were unnaturally deferential towards me while they elbowed their husbands to be likewise. There were perhaps half a dozen young people, a few younger than myself, who passed nodding and silent, embarrassed by their own clumsiness. Of the girls I saw, all seemed to be suffering from colds and had adenoids yet had bright wide, toothy smiles. I would not have blamed them if they, and their elders, thought me arrogant when I walked stiffly ahead of them unable to smile, but it was my defence against a body of people who had one thing in common and which bound them together like the clay of the earth, alienating me. As individuals, I discovered later, they were simple and honest and given to shyness like myself. Where we differed was in our outlook on life. Whereas I might have picked up a stone because I was attracted by its beauty, they would have loaded it into their slingshot and brought down a pigeon; whereas I would have sat gazing fascinated at a running brook, they would have washed their feet in it. Because I envied their total confidence in the correctness of their lives, my pretended indifference was really a mute admiration. Had I confessed to this, they would have thought me mad.

All sat in the chapel, the guest list checked, they ceased their coughing and shuffling of iron-clad boots and sat in expectation while I went to fetch the bride. Persuading me against my better judgement, Helga had pressed me to oblige her.

"You are head of the house, and it is proper."

I thought it most improper, but acquiesced.

She stood at the top of the main staircase, obscured by her white veil; it was like meeting the ghost of my childhood. Like a tinselled sprite with candles on her head, Katya had looked as striking and virginal when, as a child, I had sat wide-eyed while she had walked about the table at Candlemass. Both of us trembled when, holding her gloved hand, I led Karen downwards, towards the altar and the dark figure of Marcel. It was only when she threw back her veil defiantly, after Mogudo had pronounced them man and wife, I saw how ill she looked, and dead, under her thick, unnatural make-up.

It had been intended that following the ceremony, a feast should be held on the terrace outside the ballroom, but a sudden summer thunderstorm released a torrent of rain and the tables were only just got inside in time. After we had eaten and drunk a little, the cake cut and speeches made, which, and thankfully, were very short and unemotional, four men produced instruments and, unable to be persuaded to go up into the tiny minstrel gallery, stood at the far end near to the barrels of beer and began to play. The young flautist I thought had a strange quality to his playing. It was enticing and thoroughly immoral, and his eyes while he gazed over the top of his thin flute seemed to be daring us to folly. But it was some time before the drink we had provided made the men loosen their collars and the ladies to give a twist to their tight corsets. Only then did the old ballroom shudder when they rose in a body to dance in their boots.

Leaving the festivities and with a piece of cake Helga pressed me to take, I went up to see Nanna Axell. She was fast asleep. From her room the hullabaloo below sounded only like an indistinct murmur of thunder. I withdrew after leaving the cake on her bedside table and went to sit on the stairs, but Helga, searching for me, pulled me back down to the ball-room. I protested that I couldn't dance but she paid no attention.

"D'you think they've come all this way and will leave before they have danced with Herr Strobl?"

I wished they had when I lumbered through dance after dance with every woman in the room. I felt caught up in a whirling insanity but got through it all with much back-slapping and hurrahs. Red-faced before, the guests now had faces like boiled beetroots. I had never in my life talked so much and it seemed, with their tongues loosened by drink, the guests would never stop. Thinking I had done my duty, I was prevented from leaving before I had danced with the bride. Half swooning, I was pushed towards her and she came reluctantly. When the clapping died away and the rest of the mad throng jumped and jigged and buffeted us, Karen's smile remained fixed and wide while a tear stole down her caked cheeks. We spoke not a word but gripped each other's hand so tightly I could not distinguish our individual fingers. The dance over, we separated and turned our backs on each other. Marcel, always moody, now that he was securely wed and with drink inside him, became hideously cocksure, although I detected under the swaggering façade an insecurity which pin-pointed his quicksilver duplicity. He was a Machiavellian tomcat whose nocturnal schemings drew wails of despair from his victims. I made an oath, when he walked towards me, I would catch him out one day and, bundled into a sack, would drown him.

But he came to take his farewell of me and in front of Karen I had no choice but to wish them both a long and happy life together.

"Thank you, Herr Strobl. I'm sure you wish us that and more. Without your blessing Karen would not think herself married." He bowed low, but being drunk and to Karen's embarrassment, he stumbled. Presumably the guests thought it a proper state to be in and cheered his departure while Helga patted her bosom and wiped away a tear.

Long after I had gone to bed, I could hear the sudden laughter and con-tinuing drone of the party in the ballroom. Above it, was the thin, mes-merising sound of the hypnotic flute beckoning forth thoughts and painful memories.

My present to Karen had been an eighteenth-century gilded frame and mirror. To Marcel I gave an ivory and silver-backed toilet-set which had belonged to a grandfather but had never been used. So that they could set up house I gave them a considerable quantity of furniture and the promise of two rooms on the second floor if they decided to return. I also told Karen that had Katya known of her wedding she would have wished her to have something and suggested she should go to her room and perhaps take one of Katya's many dolls. She did not decline, but when I checked later I discovered none had been taken.

It never crossed my mind that they would return so, when I bade them goodbye on the following morning, it was with the feeling I would never see Karen again

Both Helga and I had a card each from Baros where they had gone to honeymoon. Karen, who had written them, was noncommittal; not even saying she missed being with us. A month later they returned, with no explanation and, taking the two rooms I had promised them, became servants once again.

I expected Karen to have changed. She had not. If anything, she was more reserved and seemed content to serve and wait upon me—but as if it was a penance she were undertaking. Marcel, on the other hand, piqued but contemptuous, took to lounging in my room as if he had been a lifelong friend, so I was forced to lock the door against him. It was also not unusual to find him in the pine room with his feet up and smoking, masquerading as an elder or a longstanding guest. I told Karen I disapproved but it had little effect and I was forced to the subterfuge of making my presence known before I entered a room to save me from the embarrassment of finding him sprawled out on a sofa. But it seemed his actions were deliberate and intended to provoke. He also took great delight in unnecessary familiarity with Karen when I was present and was quick tempered when she rebuked him for his shamelessness. Karen could not hide the fact she cried most days but when questioned would answer brightly she was quite happy.

Matters carne to a head when, in the middle of the day, I came across them on the back staircase. Karen was struggling while Marcel had his hand up her skirt. When he stormed off up the stairs shouting abuse at both of us, I made off in the other direction, shocked by what I had witnessed.

Two days later, and after a considerable amount of thought, I had them come before me and told them I would not tolerate such behaviour and if it occurred again, I would not hesitate to dismiss them both. Marcel sneered but Karen suffered her humiliation in silence.

I visited Nanna Axell daily. She saw a great deal of Karen and although I told her nothing of Marcel's behaviour, she knew something was amiss.

"That gal's dreadfully unhappy, Knut. Isn't there anything you can do?"

When I told her there wasn't and that I had been in love with Karen and had asked her to marry me, she nodded.

"I thought you had become fond of her at one time. Perhaps it's wrong of me to say so, but I'm glad she refused you. Don't look surprised. I understand her better than you suppose. Not just because I am a woman, but because I know how people are. Karen is a twilight child. She is a child in a woman's body. Oh, I know she's intelligent, but she has not matured. She has turned her back on adulthood and has not progressed beyond her first youthful adventure. And you, Knut, are the last person to help such a gal over her difficulties. A marriage between you two would have been a disaster. I expect you asked her out of kindness. Or was it desperation? It's a great pity you cannot meet other gals. It must bother you at times. That's why I wish that sister of yours would write. She must have made friends by now. Amongst them might be a sweetheart for you. A gal who could grow as fond of you as I am."

I kissed her and she held up her hands burdened with jewellery. "And another kiss because I am also your grandmother." I bussed her cheek and she held onto me for just that little longer.

"Now, have Karen run a bath for me. I feel the need to be refreshed."

It was Karen's shouts which brought me running. Abandoning my book, I ran to the bathroom. There, in barely five inches of water, Nanna Axell lay dead. I calmed Karen and between us struggled out the bony creature which bore little resemblance to my beloved Nanna. Nude, her head was grotesquely large and rolled loosely on a body which was so emaciated it looked too weak to articulate without falling to pieces. I had not expected her skin to be so white, so transparent, revealing the rivers of veins beneath; nor her breasts to be paper-thin and flung aside like spaniel's ears; nor her genitals to be so puffed and sparsely growing long white pubic hairs; nor her knees to be so incredibly wrinkled. Embarrassed by my searching look, Karen dropped a towel over Nanna after we had laid the brittle corpse on the floor.

"Oh, isn't it awful, Knut. That's what we'll become. What we are."

I looked into Nanna's black mouth where her top row of teeth had fallen, lodged across her jaw, and saw the ugliness only death reveals. Death which, in a quiet wood amidst the tumbling leaves, tiptoes respectfully through the rustling undergrowth or, upon a hillside, is blown before the wind and has the dignity of eternal nature. But in the cubicle of the bathroom, amidst the hard-edged porcelain receptacles and the stark light reflected off the bright, white-tiled walls, death seemed obscene, accentuating man's frailty in the clutter of his bits and pieces which had become inadequate and useless.

Death had robbed Nanna Axell of her dignity but it was her nudity which stripped Karen and me of pride, and the humiliation became an acid which burnt into the core of our substance. We became nonentities, a conglomerate pulp which cringed before its own insignificance and bewailed the ineffectiveness to control a destiny it was forced to suffer.

I waited for my tears to come, but none came. Then I knew that grief is the realisation of one's own irrevocable end and that the tears fall inwardly, splashing a protesting heart while one remains numb and dry-eyed.

I would like to think it was to comfort me Karen opened wide her arms and pulled me to her, and I did not resist. I wanted to be close to her, to have the warmth of another human being encircling and sharing the discomfiture of insignificance. It was only when her lips slid over my cheek to suck on my lips, I became aware of a contradiction in my emotions. The unreality of the situation, while her tongue slid easily in and out of my mouth, prevented the stimulation of my excitement, until I had overcome reason.

And reason at such moments is a poor loser because it does not have the experience to argue beyond the fact that death is inevitable. Isolated, it is attacked from all sides by the dark, protesting parts of the mind which will not accept death or, to placate fear, cry out in contradiction of reason, that death is but the beginning. In this conflict there bubble to the surface unimaginable fears and disquieting emotions which the brain, activated beyond reasonableness, scums with a soothing oil so that in the emulsion one swims as much from an instinct to survive temporarily, as to deny the existence of death. The rock towards which one swims is embedded in the instincts and one copulates upon its slippery side in an ecstasy of continuation for the life now, or in infinity. Hope becomes a religion because pride cannot accept the inevitable. Doomed, man becomes fragmented and his actions inexplicable.

So it was when, urged and guided by Karen to embrace over the corpse, grief took the form of a positive rejection and the impropriety became an ecstatic but primitive triumph. Trembling with lust, I shuddered and at the very moment our knees quaked and weakened, Marcel walked into the bathroom.

Seeing him, I burst into tears. Frustrated lust and the shock of death clashed together to produce a copious flow and I wept unashamedly. Marcel was not unduly disturbed to find his wife embracing me, imagining she was comforting the bereaved grandson, whereas she was clutching to her lost hope and shuddering with unrelieved tension.

After I had been calmed, we all three hauled Nanna Axell's broken body into her room and laid it on the bed. Karen covered her with a sheet. Mungo was fetched and, with his hair standing out from his head like a golliwog's, knelt sobbing and buried his face in the bedclothes. Helga, too, gave way to grief and the room was filled with an unearthly wailing.

It was Marcel who eventually persuaded us to leave and Karen who led us down into the warm kitchens where, sat silently round the bare table, we drank a glass of brandy each while Doctor Borg's assistant was sent for.

Long past midnight, and after he had gone, Karen walked with me up to my room. I took her arm but she withdrew it. While we stood looking at each other it occurred to me that we had become strangers again and the only thing we had in common was guilt. Saddened, we turned away from each other and went our separate ways. The moment had passed so we crawled like victims into the isolation of our individual cells to slake our thirst on the chill waters of our confinement. And, when I slept, in my dream I saw doors shutting one after another while the inmates busily stuffed the keyholes with wax.

In the morning I went back, down into the kitchens and, sitting at the scrubbed table, drank a bowl of milky coffee. With Helga sat next to the grate staring into the flames, the room was peaceful and silent. I watched her pick up the poker and settle a log. A puff of smoke went up the chimney and a flame billowed out and licked the wood.

"I've sent for Katya."

At first I did not register the significance of her remark. When I did, I was dumbfounded.

"Before she left, Knut, she said I was to get in touch with her only if Frau Axell was ill."

I protested at her deceit and of keeping Katya's whereabouts secret.

"I never break a promise, Knut. Ever." I was not so easily placated but Helga was unruffled. "I have telephoned her and she will be on her way by now."

Taking the stairs two at a time, I ran to tell Karen. I found her in the pine room. Her bottom was higher than her head while, on all fours, she tried to blow a flame into the thick smoke of the fire she had just lit. I told her that Katya was coming back but she went on blowing into the grate. Devilled, I took hold of her waist in my hands and squeezed as an expression of my excitement. She looked over her shoulder and stared. It was a disconcerting look and one which I was not sure if I understood. Despising but yielding, it was an admixture of hate and subservience. I withdrew my hands, releasing her, but, stupidly, patted her flank. It had been intended to be a gesture of understanding and reassurance, but it turned into a stroking pat one gives to a faithful dog.

Ashamed, I withdrew.

PART FOUR: AT MY DICTATION

I do not remember how I passed the time waiting for you. I think my first reaction had been to unlock your room and instruct Marcel to light a fire and have Karen put fresh linen on your bed, dust and tidy the room generally.

I can remember spending hours stood at the window looking up the drive while the rain poured down, hoping to catch the first glimpse of you running towards the house. But I was impatient so, periodically, I wandered into Nanna Axell's room where Mungo was keeping a silent vigil after Helga had washed and prepared Nanna for burial.

Time, I know, did not pass quickly enough and I remember at lunch my unnecessary anxiety made Helga irritable. She upset me by saying that you might not arrive that day. When night came and you still had not made an appearance, I went up to bed but could not sleep.

I was up early in the morning and went straight to your room, but it was empty and the bed had not been slept in. After spending the whole morning with my face pressed to the window and playing childish games with the raindrops which trickled down the glass, huffing on the panes to write my name backwards and drawing silly pictures, I began to despair of you ever coming and went up to my room and threw myself onto the bed. Imagination played her usual pranks and I saw you lying in a ditch, dead. Refusing to believe this, I saw it was the floods which prevented you reaching me. Each road was blocked by an enormous lake and I stupidly imagined that if you really wanted to come back to me, you would swim. In my more rational moments, I thought of harnessing Grinn, but I could have gone off in any number of directions and missed you. So, I just lay on my bed, listening. But every footfall alerted me and I would go into the corridor, only to find it was Marcel or Karen; and once Mungo, on his way to the lavatory. The afternoon dragged on endlessly and my ears filled with the irritating ring of silence.

In the evening, having been reassured by Gardol the generator would not break down, I switched on as many lights as I was able so that in the darkness when you approached, the house would shine brightly and be more welcoming. I even begged extra candles from Helga and, having arranged and lit the last one in the great hall, I sensed someone above me. I turned to look, and there, at the top of the stairs and dressed in a silver suit was you, my beloved sister, having spirited yourself as if by magic into the grim castle of your wicked brother. For one moment I thought my eyes deceived me because the glitter of your clothes danced on my retina with the hallucinatory effect of a tumbling kaleidoscope. Only your calling of my name convinced me you were not an apparition in my demented mind.

I think we met halfway up the stairs; I know we hugged and kissed until our cheekbones were bruised. I remember my tears spoilt your make-up and while you applied fresh colour and powder, I sat next to you on the sofa in the pine room and feasted my eyes on a changed Katya. You were very much thinner, but not gaunt. I suppose you had absorbed your puppy fat and during the metabolism had acquired a maturity which revealed the bone structure of your face and made you strikingly handsome. Beautiful. Also, you had an added sophistication. Your movements were now controlled and adult; your head sat proudly on your shoulders with the authority of an amazon. Your extraordinary silver suit, your severe hair style, cropped like a boy's, and the fact you smoked, all contributed to your aura of feminine maturity. You had the look, too, of a girl who had lost her virginity and had been given the key to the mystery of mysteries, the secret of which you kept behind the serenity of your smile. If I had not come to know the inflection of your voice and the mannerism of your gestures so well, I might not have thought the girl sitting next to me was my sister. But it was your mauve eyes which revealed you and reflected the twenty years and more, we had spent together. Twenty years which, if we had been married, we had managed more successfully than most loving couples who grow insensitive to each other's needs and despise each other's failings.

I remember you settled back on the sofa and took my hand. You said you would stay for the funeral, but no longer, and I was heartbroken. I tried to persuade you to stay but you explained you were only permitted to take a few days off. And you squeezed my hand. "Besides," you said, "what is there to keep me?" How could I tell you that my love was unchanged? How could I justify a love which must have appeared to you to be so shabby and neurotic, meaningless and without a future? An infantile love, from the union of which would have been born a child for the satisfaction of the regressive playing of your mother to my father? To dandle our child like a doll and wheel it in a fairy pram would have been to have become the children of our child; never outliving our nursery days. Of course, had I known then you were retarded, my conscience would not have hindered my efforts to drag you down into a mutual destruction. When I did discover, I had already been betrayed.

You must have realised I was dejected, for you gave my knee a reassuring squeeze and explained you had not written because you hoped time would have erased my feelings. When you said this, all the old passions moved uncomfortably, rumbling in my stomach as in some dreadful midden. For an instant, I was gripped by an acute desire to ravish you; to rape that bright tinselled sister sat breathing and glowing warm beside me. To have done with my unnatural desire, once and for all, and, like a butcher, wallow in the gore of your viscera. But it passed; like a temper one swallows down, to be digested until the anger disperses naturally.

In the conversation which followed, I learnt very little of how you had spent those two years away from me. Life had been very easy, you said, during the first exhilarating months. You had made friends. Too many friends. You said you gorged yourself with them, and it was frightening. You told me how you had grown dissatisfied with the shallow relationships because they were transient and how, feeling your life lacked purpose, you had removed yourself to Malhagen and given away all your money to a hospital foundation. You admitted it was an impulsive gesture and one which, at moments, you regretted. Unskilled, lacking qualifications, you said idealism lay like a stone in your stomach and you were very unhappy. It was not until you met Olga Lebus as a customer in the corset shop where you worked, that life changed dramatically and you were happy again. It was she who persuaded you to go into prison service. I was shocked when you told me but you said it was not how I imagined it. "I am not a wardress, more of a house matron. Or will be." You told how you helped rehabilitate young girls who were in your care for periods of not more than two years. I remember laughing nervously because it struck me as ludicrous that you, glamorously dressed in silver brocade, could even be considered suitable for employment in a prison. You were indignant and went to great lengths to explain what you called your purpose in life. The girls, you said, were, for the most part, mentally backward. That, plus the pressure of society as a whole and, in particular, the tragedy of their upbringing, had forced the girls to become socially delinquent. They were not criminal. Just girls. Young girls who had been broken by their parents and the unthinking adult—which was every one of us. You and me, you said. We all contributed to a person's humiliation and destruction. We robbed a person of pride to establish our own superiority. We were contemptuous of another's feelings because we were ashamed of our own. We corrupted whom we touched for the satisfaction of our own desires. And you asked me if I could fault you, and I couldn't. I could not because I was filled with shame and saw how I had almost infected you with my crime.

I deliberately changed the subject, hoping to cover my unease, and told you that Karen had married. You did not seem surprised and asked if you knew the man. When I told you it was Marcel, you sat motionless with a cigarette held up to your lips. When you did finally draw on it, the end glowed bright red and, like a fuse, the fire crackled down the paper until I thought the whole of your cigarette would be consumed and would end by burning your lips. But you blew out a long, long cloud of streamed smoke and had to take a second breath to expel it all. How disgusting, you said, and I agreed that Karen's sudden marriage was inexplicable. You had your suspicions why, but were cross with me for not, as you said, "protecting the poor child from herself". I was hurt you thought I had failed in my duty but did not see where my duty lay and did not dare hint at my affection for Karen. I asked what you thought I should have done, bearing in mind that left on my own to cope had been difficult enough. Your exact words were, "I suppose I do owe you an apology". And that was all.

We sat in silence for a long time, I remember. When the fire collapsed and a shower of sparks was spirited up the chimney, the logs burst into flame and spat out cinders. While you were brushing them off the carpet, you said my greeting on the stairs had been much more affectionate than you had expected or deserved. I couldn't understand why you deliberately chose to return to the subject of our uneasy intimacy, and sat rubbing my sweating palm with a finger, making rolls of dirt and unable to answer. You went on to say I had every reason to despise you. When I asked why, because I had supposed you had left on my account, you gave me a curious look. At first, I took it to be a frown of doubt but saw in it later the shrewdness of silence, when things are best left unexplained.

Although I do not blame you, looking back, none of what subsequently happened need have occurred if you had been truthful with me then. I cannot imagine how I would have reacted, but as you were always so sensitive of my feelings, I would have trusted you to have been circumspect and broken it to me gently.

As it was, when I pressed you to explain, you stood up and, throwing your cigarette into the fire, said you were hungry. To distract me still further, you asked for my opinion of your suit and slowly turned for my inspection. When you lifted the jacket and showed me how the trousers hugged your bottom, I confess I could have fallen on my knees and grovelled with my cheek pressed against you. Disgusted with myself, I stood up. I think you thought I was about to take hold of you, and you stiffened, imperceptibly. It was as if you had controlled an instinctive reaction so as not to offend me, but it was your eyes which betrayed your aversion. You were not unaware and saw how I had been wounded. You squeezed my arm saying you had forgotten how gentle I was and asked to be forgiven.

At moments like those, I cursed civilisation for having branded me with guilt.

In the dining room, you were unbearably rude to Karen, and harassed her continually. I would have protested had Karen caught my eye, but she ignored me, being bound slavishly to you by the atmosphere you had created. I was disturbed to see her subservient but, in turn, I was dominated by your hostility so did nothing. As she stood next to you, trembling on the edge of your irritability, I saw how she did not resemble you. The imagined likeness had been an illusion. Her skin was greasy round her nose, her colour pallid and her hair dull and lank. She looked oppressed and worn; bitter and resentful. I was ashamed to find, while comparing you, a diminishing regard for the Karen I had almost come to love in your stead. It was only later, when she left the room, I realised anyone matched against your glitter that evening would have appeared tawdry. When, after the second course, we sat waiting for her return and Marcel had come in response to your persistent ringing, your mood changed to one of outrage and anger. Marcel had come into the room carrying our sweet on a tray and you shouted at him, upbraiding him for his slackness and his contemptuous look; saying you were not a tart of a scullery maid whom he could abuse and dominate. I had expected him to strike you. Instead, he turned the tray upside down and left the room. I chased and caught up with him at the head of the stairs, but he turned and punched me in the shoulder. When I returned to the dining room, you had gone.

Passing your room on the way to bed, I noticed your light was on but did not knock, for I heard you talking to Karen.

In the night, I thought I heard a door bang, but was not sure. I know someone ran down the corridor in bare feet. I did not bother to investigate because I was too tired; besides, I wanted to get as much sleep as possible because the funeral was next day.

Originally, as you know, I had tried to arrange for Nanna Axell to be buried in the mausoleum, in the remaining niche which had been set aside to receive my mortal remains. Failing that, to have a portion of the floor dug up for her grave. Gripp, informed of Nanna Axell's death, said she was to be buried in Gottod, alongside her husband.

Gottod, I remember, was bleak and deserted. The stone buildings with their uncompromising small windows and featureless façades were unfriendly and appeared to have their backs turned on us like old men who huddle together when strangers are passing down the village street. We caught a glimpse of Nanna Axell's old house on the outskirts of Gottod. Stuck atop a hill, it too was unwelcoming and had the chill squareness of a block of granite.

The church was severe and damp, and the churchyard starved of monuments, save for stone slabs which were so thick and heavy they seemed to bear down, crushing the bones beneath, making impossible the resurrection of such totally crushed souls.

Fortunately, the service was short and, because it was so cold and the rain fine and gusted, no one wept but stood petrified in their overcoats which slowly absorbed the drizzle, making them heavy and releasing a pungent odour. As a group, we resembled scarecrows propped up in a field wearing mouldy black which flapped in the breeze. You were the odd one out. You were smartly dressed. I had never seen you in black high-heeled shoes before and, to be truthful, it was these and your silk stockings which absorbed my attention throughout the service and while we stood round the grave. Disrespectful perhaps, but I was fascinated by the seams which ran up the back of your legs and disappeared under your skirt.

Of course you will remember the disaster with the Collin. Gardol, old and his joints swollen with arthritis, Mungo, myself and Marcel were the pallbearers. I did not actually see Mungo stumble but felt the coffin slide away from me. It fell on its edge with such a crash that I thought it would burst open. I know that in the confusion and with everyone's concern for Mungo, I watched some of the contents of the coffin swill out through the distorted corner. With Mungo sat in the vestry, and with the help of the verger we manhandled the coffin to the grave and buried it after more words were said.

One other thing I noticed was the mud. Everyone's shoes were caked with it and there was that awful moment when I had to shake the trowel repeatedly before the earth, in a wedgelike clay, shot off the end and thumped onto the coffin. I wanted to laugh, but did not.

As we were grouped round the two cars, I remember how you persuaded Mungo to go on to Borsund to see a doctor. When you promised to travel with him, I felt it was a ruse to make your escape and not return. I was even more convinced that it was a trick when you insisted you went alone.

The rest of us squashed into the remaining car, and with Helga and Karen squeezed on either side, I returned home determined that if you failed to show up on the following day, I would force Helga to give me your address and go after you before you had time to pack and cover your tracks.

I did not hear you return, for I slept late, the cold wind in the cemetery having brought on a slight fever, but when I saw you in the hall, I knew I had worried needlessly. You told me how Mungo had been admitted to the hospital in Borsund and that, in all probability, he would die there. Although you looked tired and kept leaning forward and pressing your stomach, I had no idea then that you were ill. You told me your stomach was troubling you and that I was not to fuss. It was, you said, not at all unusual. I did, however, persuade you to go to your room and lie down.

Late that same afternoon, I tapped on your door and, entering, found you fast asleep. Your scent once again hung in the air but, mingled with smell of charred wood which still lingered from the fire in the west wing, it seemed strangely sour.

When you did not appear at dinner, I asked Karen to see if you would take anything in your room. She told me she had already taken you up a glass of warm milk and that you could not stomach more. Asked if she thought you were ill and if the doctor ought to be sent for, Karen replied you had already seen a doctor. And Marcel walked in to clear the table.

Before I went to bed, I approached your room on tiptoe but, seeing the light did not shine under your door, I went to bed.

For two days you kept to your room and would see no one. On the third day when I walked in you sat up and said you were better; that you had been more tired than you had supposed. You also said you had had time to think. I had hoped that you were going to stay but you disappointed me by saying you would be leaving on the Sunday. I think it was unkind of you to get out of bed while I was still in the room because while I waited for you downstairs it was almost more than I could do to rid myself of your image.

Washed and groomed, you seemed less vulnerable, and during the conversation which followed you did your best to dominate me; probably for my own good, but at the time it seemed unnecessarily cruel.

I do not remember in detail what we said to each other, only that after failing to convince me it was in my interest to stay in a sanatorium for a while you said under no circumstance would you allow me to become a millstone round your neck. I think that was said after I had suggested I came to live with you—or near to you—but you said the further away from me you were, the happier you would be.

I left the room to lie on my bed. If you hadn't regretted what you said and come to my bedside to stroke my hair and beg forgiveness, I have no doubt we would have parted in enmity and I would have been forced to forget you. As it was, you stayed and stirred hope, and the hope swelled into love. It was a kind unkindness you did to me but I would not have wished it otherwise, even though the pain which was to follow was made worse.

Living with a landscape which grew up to the very walls of the house and spending most of my time when not writing, looking out over it, I had come to enjoy certain times of the day more than others. It was the quality of light which moved me. The seasons too. Winter, summer, autumn and spring, all were different; each had a distinct light or darkness which separated it from the others. Evenings in spring were distinct from summer twilights, whereas in winter to detect such a change was almost impossible. It was too subtle or else one was deceived at midday into thinking night was falling.

As the evening of the day which was to be our last together was rapidly dulling the landscape, I got up to stretch. My chest was dry and sore and my back ached. The writing I was engaged on had come to a standstill because thoughts of you and the imminence of your departure intruded into the rhythm of my working habits. I went and stood close to the window. The landscape was sodden and unable to absorb the water which lay in pools everywhere. Even the lake had flooded into what had once been a meadow. It was impossible to imagine the land would ever dry. Partly because of the rapid thaw, but due mainly to the weeks of rain, the landscape had been turned into a marsh. Little did I think, while I stood looking out over it and noticing how the water reflected the even grey sky, that I would spend that night, the whole of the next day and another night, trying to make my escape through what turned out to be a muddy hell.

One odd fact I recall is the quietness of the evening. I had not noticed the birds quit their singing, but suddenly everything was still and unusually quiet. While I stood straining my ears, it began to rain and, in the gloom, I imagined the birds, with their feathers fluffed, sat on bare twigs to wait out the night. I even imagined the occasional bird, its crop empty, slowly tumbling, spiralling to the ground, dead and already cold from hunger, its feathers matted and spiky, bedraggled and ugly. When an owl circled lazily in front of the window, scattering the bats in all directions, I turned away before the last light was squeezed out of a sky which had become the colour of gun metal.

From habit, rather than being able to see clearly, I made my way along the corridor, intending to go downstairs to see if you were in the pine room. It did not concern me unduly that none of the lights had been turned on, for I knew Gardol was finding it increasingly difficult to prime the generator. I imagined him cursing and kicking the old-fashioned mechanical contraption and wishing he could persuade me to go back to using oil lamps. Musing as I was, it was not that the door stood ajar which made me turn back but, in passing it, the white dust sheet covering the painting blinked in the corner of my eye. Recalling the painting of a woman who looked like you was beneath the dust sheet, I turned and went back. I still do not know if I intended to close the door or to look at the painting to see if the likeness of the woman to you was still justified. So, I was neither entering nor leaving, but had my hand round the cold door knob when I heard the sound. It was not the rustle made by mice nor the squeak of one rat greeting another. Neither was it the flurry of a bird trapped in the room. If anything, it was the sound of moths fluttering against a light; or again, of elastic being stretched. Above all, there was the whistle of breath. I paused for only a moment before looking round the door.

Silhouetted against the darkening window panes was a black form. Even as I approached it, I was not convinced it was human, for I had a preconceived notion it was some forgotten object covered by a dust sheet and that the frantic scratching and squeaks were made by some mice racing round beneath it. My intention had been to frighten them away, knowing full well they would return the moment I had left the room. But my curiosity had to be satisfied, so I moved closer, walking on tiptoe. It was only when the form split in two and I saw the white flash of flesh, I recognised the figures of Karen and you embracing.

Your surprise, I imagine, hinged upon the impossibility of knowing how long I had been stood watching you together. In fact, the instant I realised what I had stumbled upon, I fled. It was only while I was running, my head ballooned with images, filling out the grotesque details of the dark wedlock I had witnessed.

I remember you shouted out and I heard your feet following me. But I was too quick for you and had doubled back under the main staircase and had headed for the stables, long before you could guess what I was up to. You say you followed, but you had forgotten it was to the stables I went whenever my world was collapsing all about me.

I stayed in the stables until well after midnight. There were moments, while I crouched hidden, when I thought I had been mistaken in what I had seen; possibly because I wanted it to be untrue. I wanted to confront you and have you deny it, but I was too frightened. I finally discarded your possible innocence when I realised your love for Karen was the reas- on you had left so mysteriously on that night two years previously. Ac- cepting this reason, so many other things fell into place and my previous life was no longer a jigsaw but a picture of a stupid young man totally blinded by prejudice, unable to see beyond his own, miserable little exist- ence.

About one o'clock in the morning I crept out of my hiding place and sneaked back into the house. From the safe in the study, I took as much money as was there and went back to the stables. I had planned my long- delayed escape and there was no going back.

Do you remember before the stables were allowed to fall into disrepair, Mother quartered her Frederiksborgs in there? Father preferred Ardennes. It was only because of his sentimental attachment to this breed of horse, probably because it was a type much favoured in the army in those days, that Madlin allowed him to graze his stallion in the lower meadow. To me, that Ardenne stallion was a terrifying beast. I know it only stood fifteen hands high, but to a young child, and frightened as I was by horses, it was a monster. I was convinced he had been sired by the eight-legged Sleipuir who carried Odin when, armed with Gungnir and a black crow squatting on either shoulder, he had ridden back to Valhalla with Hadding bundled up on the saddle. Because childhood fantasies continue to lurk in the dark subconscious, it was understandable when this brute, which Father had christened Vilk, came under the auctioneer's hammer and was sold, I was beside myself with glee. Blutchner bought him and that meant before the day was out, Vilk would be axed, slit and carved up for his meat while his bones and massive head were rendered down for fat. I thought it a fitting end for a beast I hated. It was you who told me Vilk had been bought off Blutchner by Bostroem and put out to stud. For weeks, I looked out of the window expecting to see the black brood he had sired come galloping towards the house. I was very young and had no idea of the length of gestation required, otherwise I would not have worried myself to sleep all those weeks. But Vilk still returns in my dreams; only now I admire him and envy the potency stored in his loins.

Unlike poor old Grinn.

I often think old Grinn and I had a lot in common. A miserable but much-favoured stallion. Dun coloured. A Gudbrandsdal with a coffin-shaped head. The unnerving stare of buck eye and, as if to emphasise the black comedy, the stupid overhang of a village idiot's elk lip on which, that night I used him for my escape, grew the grey hairs of a sparse moustache.

I remember Gardol said of Grinn that if he had been human, Grinn would have been in government. I disagreed and said why should he be transformed. "Horses like donkeys for company." Gardol laughed and thwacked his thigh, repeating what I had said, over and over again. Then he poked me in the chest with his stubby finger on which a horny nail grew and told me that although I lacked muscle, I had a head. "A lad can go far, using his head." How wrong I have proved him to be!

Years before, Mother had said much the same thing. Do you remember? It was shortly before Grinn came to us.

Warning you and me of a troupe of wandering actors and actresses who were reported in the district—probably the same troupe Mother invited in for that unbelievable orgy—she cautioned us to keep well away from them because they had no morals and took great delight in corrupting little children. I can remember the exact words she used to caution us.

"With the same pleasure we take in sucking the butter off asparagus, these filthy mummers soil any and every child they entice away. You haven't got the strength to defend your sister, Knut, so for God's sake, use your head if either of you are offered a sweet or some silly trinket. And get Katya away. Use guile."

I think it was about a week later the troupe, crammed into their rickety caravan, had the audacity to come clattering into the yard to ask Helga if they could have the honour of performing for the esteemed House of Strobl. Mother, enraged, stormed down to confront them, crop in hand. Seeing the dirty white, underfed horse which pulled the overloaded caravan, she momentarily forgot the mummers' corrupting influence and upbraided them for their inhuman cruelty to a dumb animal. I remember one actor telling Mother that if she was so concerned he would not object if madam fed the beast; adding, the troupe would gladly camp out on the lawns while she fattened him up. Mother was not deterred by the man's cheek and noticed a young colt tied by a piece of rope to the far side of the caravan.

I don't think either of us heard her offer to buy the colt but I remember while the mummers haggled, you and I wandered round to the back of the caravan and stared up at the children packed and overflowing from the interior. For children who had been enticed away from their parents with sweets and promises, they looked remarkably happy and well fed. Grubby, perhaps, but certainly not corrupted. Their hair was in tangles which gave them a roguish look but they grinned down at us with such friendly smiles, we were immediately captivated. Crowding onto the tailboard, they acted out a pantomime especially for us—the well-scrubbed children of indulgent parents. We laughed, not realising we were being gently mocked, but it was when one of the older boys with eyes as blue as ice and a devilish, infectious grin, opened his unbuttoned trousers and mimed his masturbation with an organ which was so large, dark and incredibly hairy, that we ran away and hid. I remember we peeked from our place of safety—it must have been the stables—but each time they pretended to make water in our direction or turning, wriggled their bottoms in a shameless way. Why we persisted in looking, I cannot imagine, for both of us were equally horrified. The mummers' children, like star performers who had secured the undivided attention of their audience, continued to develop their insulting mime; wobbling their buttocks, poking out their tongues and getting up to the most curious antics. When Mother took no notice of our shouts, I remember you pulled me away and burst into tears. I was much too embarrassed to do more than stand with my hand on your shoulder while the blushes burnt my cheeks.

We were winkled out of our hiding place by Mother who, after the mummers had departed, wanted to show us the young colt she had bought. She said she was going to christen him Grinn but we were more impatient to tell her about the disgusting children.

"Children? There was one child. A baby. The rest were dwarfs."

We weren't able to describe what the children had done, but I remember her ruffling my hair and saying dwarfs got up to all sorts of outrageous things and I wasn't to bother my head about it. "All harmless fun," she said.

Pitiful when he was bought, old Grinn grew into a misshapen beast. Hog-backed, goose-rumped and with the most extraordinary ragged hips from which Gardol sometimes hung his jacket, Grinn grew unbelievably ugly. I think he tried to make up for his imperfections by working eagerly, and showed his gratitude by never failing us when the snow was deep. I think he was unique. Certainly deserving of our kindness. He was forever nuzzling your pocket for the scrubbed carrots you secretly fed him. He loved you, yet tolerated me, I, who, although it shames me to confess, used to eat the carrots which Helga gave me to feed him.

That night when I decided to run away, to flee, mounted on Grinn's back, there were moments when I wished I had fed him every single carrot; and more.

He did not bother to turn his head when I returned from the study and, having found a saddle, flung it over his bony back. The saddle had broken stitching and the straw stuffing stuck out in places. I think it was the saddle you had as a young girl and during part of my ride that night became unreasonably excited to think you had once sat astride it. But that was later; much later, when I came to regret my flight. Before that I had to secure the girth which, for me, who had never done it before but only watched it done, was unbelievably difficult. Sensing it was adjusted correctly and buckled securely, I ran my hand over his barrel ribs and detected the flutter of his old heart which feathered the sides in dying, unequal beats. Praying it would have the strength to last out the journey, I was momentarily disconcerted by the similarity of his captive heart to Mother's scorched canary fluttering in its burnt cage. Such a poignant memory was not good for my morale, especially when I recalled Gardol's words. "Let the beast die on straw, Knut. Let him die on straw." That was after I had suggested Grinn should be given his freedom. "It would be unkind to return him to the forests. No self-respecting stallion would choose to die defeated, nipped and kicked to death; perhaps by the very stallions he had sired." Gardol did not seem to remember that Grinn had never been put to stud and had been too young to have sired a filly before

Madlin had bought him. Unlike Vilk, Grinn had the shrivelled, dry seed of the ascetic, a wrinkled, barren loin; only his lashed eyes betrayed his passion, like mine, in a doleful stare.

I patted him affectionately. I was one with the beast. Ugly as he was, nature had taken pity on him and given him a tail which swept the ground and which any horse would have been proud to possess. Likewise, a mane. Abundant and long, it gave him the dignity of an old, battle-scarred lion. I whispered in his ear that I hoped he had the heart for such a journey and that if he had, he would live out the rest of his life in a luxury of straw and oats.

After making certain the stirrups hung evenly and were not too short, I struggled onto Grinn a much repaired head harness. The throat lash was broken but I let it dangle. Later, I came to regret I had not bothered to search about for something to secure it, but at the time I excused myself because I thought it was too dark in the stables to go hunting for the odd piece of twine or wire. Dressed in Gardol's sheepskin overcoat which I had found hanging on the back of the stable door and, holding it up like a dress because, being so long, it tangled my feet, I mounted Grinn from a block.

A younger horse would have sensed my nervousness and, being more self-willed and stronger, would have asserted himself by kicking, prancing or shying away, to show he was unwilling to be mastered. But old Grinn just turned his head when I sat down heavily on the saddle, looked at me for a long time and blinked once.

When I had blown out the oil lamp above my head, I tugged on the reins, turned Grinn's head towards the opened door, and dug my heels into his bony ribs. A full minute later, he took a step forward and I had begun my painfully slow escape from the house where I had lived all my life.

You had told me several times you had packed a case and lugged it to the door of your room in preparation for your flight. Each time, you said, when you had looked out to see if your escape would be unobserved, the corridor had suddenly appeared twice as long, the doors to be tiptoed past double in number and, quite inexplicably, all standing open. It had been, you said, the familiar corridors and stairs which had defeated you, the house you knew so well and the lawns and grounds surrounding it; not the strangeness beyond where, free, you could have thrown your hat into the air and behaved quite ridiculously. I was reminded of this while Grinn and I made our painfully slow escape. I repeatedly glanced back at the dark shape of the house and felt the powerful hold it had over me, trying to draw me back. It was as if I was joined to it by an umbilical cord and the stretching, as we moved away, was made more painful before being pulled taut it suddenly snapped and I was free but bleeding.

Twice I nearly turned back when, in the darkness old Grinn stopped, his legs astride and, hanging his head, seemed too tired to continue. What should have begun as a mad flight to freedom, undertaken at a gallop, so that the speed and dash made the severance that much more dramatic and final, was drawn out into a silent, humorous farce over which I had no control but was the star buffoon. It took an effort of will and some unkindness to stir Grinn to pick up his dishing feet. Once moving, I was wise enough to leave it to Grinn's instinctive choice of path over the muddy ground while we climbed slowly out of the valley and rode a track I had not known existed.

On the rim of the valley, I reined Grinn to a standstill while I searched the valley below for a last glimpse of the old house. I saw what I thought might be the lake but the valley was flooded and there were so many stretches of still water I could not be certain it was our lake. Giving Grinn's croup a mighty thwack, I urged him on in a loud voice and we trotted over the hill and began our long and tortuous descent into the valley on the other side.

I had no definite plan when I set off, only that by going north then making a circular detour to the east I would eventually be able to go south without having to pass through Haggstianstad or Lindehult. I did not want to be followed and suffer the humiliation of being persuaded back, so, by making this long detour, I thought I was being crafty. Unfortunately, I had not taken into account that all the rivers were in flood and I would not be able to ford even the smallest of streams.

It was soon after we had emerged from the wood I realised the drama of my situation. Picking our way between the trees had been eerie but I was comforted by the sound of the waterfall we were headed towards. When I saw the foaming water churning up over the road below us I knew I would have to turn east sooner than I had intended because the little stream which in summer one could wade across had become a torrent and was impassable. Reaching the waterfall, I looked up and was awestruck by the power and the quantity of water which surged over the rocks in the darkness above me and thundered down into the cleft. The din it made was frightening and, because it was dark, it was as if I was witness to some terrible catastrophe which would burst upon a sleeping world before I had time to warn it. Dismounting, Grinn and I made our way up the side of the waterfall, going south, until we were above the cascade. Then it began to rain.

It rained and continued to rain without interruption for the rest of that night, throughout the whole of next day, the following night, and was still raining when the dawn broke on the Monday morning. It was fortunate I had stolen Gardol's sheepskin. It was greasy and too large, so I was able to wrap it around me and keep reasonably dry but the relentless rain, flattening my hair and streaming over my exposed face, turned my collar into a gutter so that long fingers of water trickled down into my underwear chilling me. But on that first dawn, I was reasonably dry.

While the landscape was slowly illuminated by a gigantic sun, seemingly too heavy to rise, I saw we were making our way across the geological folds rather than moving along them and making our journey easier; so I turned east, hoping to find a valley which ran south. When we came to the beginnings of a forest, I saw it dipped into a deep ridge in the direction I intended to go, so I dismounted and, pulling Grinn, made for the shelter of the forest.

Sat hard up against a tree with my head on my arms, I tried to sleep while Grinn stood unmoving, being relentlessly splashed by the large drops of rain which fell from the pines. The tranquillising sound of the rain high above us as it fell onto the trees did not soothe me and I was unable to sleep. I looked at my wristwatch and saw it had stopped. I had forgotten to wind it.

Disheartened, I struggled to my feet and, walking beside Grinn, began to penetrate the forest. I walked for as long as I was able, but the soft pine needles beneath my feet tired me quickly and I was forced to hike myself up onto the saddle and let Grinn find an easy path out. For the first time, I felt hungry.

I suppose it was early afternoon when we emerged. Walking out into the steady rain, Grinn stopped dead in his tracks as if in protest. I dismounted and pulled him back under the comparative shelter of the trees.

Loping through the forest, Grinn's feet had been barely audible on the thick mat of pine needles. In the silence, the stillness of the trees impressed itself upon me so I began to sense how, in the cathedral-like atmosphere, man must have imagined an unseen presence all about him. For the time, I longed to be back home. Not because I was cold and tired but because I was strangely moved and wanted to share my feelings of tranquillity with someone, to be forgiving.

I sat for perhaps two hours before Grinn moved out towards the grass and began to graze on the little there was. The poor beast was bedraggled. His long coat was matted and plastered unevenly over his bony frame in glistening, ugly locks. His tail hung straight, shedding rain in drips, while his mane clung to his neck and looked thin and sparse. I felt very sorry for him and ashamed it was I who was responsible for his evident discomfiture but when he seemed satisfied with the little he had eaten, I caught the rein and, mounting, set off again; hunched against the rain which was being blown against me in gusts by a rising, and bitterly cold north wind.

As I became increasingly more wet, my aches began to take on the familiar heat of fever and I detected the first protest from my lungs. I longed for the warmth of shelter and a bowl of steaming soup, but each valley we came to, a swollen stream blocked our path and we were forced to make yet another detour, carrying us away, or so it seemed, from any form of civilisation. For the whole of that long day, I had not seen a house or the mark of a track which would have indicated we were not far from a fire and the chance to sit under a roof. I did not want to admit to being lost but had to acknowledge that I had become completely disorientated, and my frustration became acute. It turned to panic when I realised the darkening sky was the beginning of night; a night which would have to be spent in a wilderness of mud.

Chance had it that in the darkness we stumbled upon a clump of trees and rocks. Tying Grinn to a tree, I went in search of food for him. In the dark, each wet clump of grass slithered through my fingers and the amount I was able to collect was pitifully small. When I returned with more, Grinn had lain down, stretching the rein. I hastily undid it to free his head and saw that the saddle had slipped. While he munched on the grass I tried to get the saddle off but no amount of pushing would get him to shift so I could reach the buckle. In the end I gave up and sat down, leaning my back against his stomach. In the position we had sat ourselves, we were exposed to the northerly wind and it wasn't long before I was shivering uncontrollably. Feeling cramped and my legs strangely bowed, I struggled to my feet and after pulling long and hard on the rein, got Grinn to follow me.

In the dark it was difficult to see what lay ahead but eventually we succeeded in moving behind an outcrop of rock which protected us from the wind. Grinn flopped down and I laid myself against him, listening to his strained heart, hoping it would last out the night and be sufficiently strong to carry me in the morning to a place of safety. I was fast tiring of my adventure and wanted nothing more than to be home; to be in the warmth and safety of my bed. It was too cold to sleep and my shuddering continued until I thought I would rattle to pieces. The pebbles beneath my hip did not help and, however much I changed my position, they bit into me until I felt it was a punishment.

I did not think I had slept but I was suddenly aware that I had stopped shivering, and I snuggled into the sheepskin to take advantage of the fever which was building up a heat. When the trembling returned, I decided I had had enough and, after much urging and shouting, got Grinn to his feet. In the darkness, the saddle seeming to slip at every step, we moved forward to a slow dawn.

When a thin daylight had filtered into the valley we were in, I saw, much to my relief, that we were on a track of sorts. Sticky with mud, it meandered about, leading us downwards. I hoped it led to a road on which poor old Grinn would be able to make better headway. As it turned out, it led into a morass where Grinn was to die.

Suddenly it was light and through the drizzle I saw what looked like a village in the distance. Already palls of smoke were climbing out of chimneys to hang in the saturated air, so I knew that people were about. I encouraged Grinn with promises of oats and hay and a good towelling to dry him out. Although his nostrils twitched as he smelt the dry hay stored in the lofts, he continued to drag his feet. Had I known he was dying, I would have dismounted and stayed with him to the end, but I was eager to get down amongst the houses, to buy food and dry myself out on a welcoming hearth.

While we drew nearer and the track slowly widened, I saw that the houses, squat and low, their roofs covered in turf, were set in two rows facing one another with a wide expanse between them, evidently a wide thoroughfare for the herding of cattle. However, long before we reached the houses, old Grinn gave up and came to a stop. The mud was becoming so deep and treacherous that he was having difficulty lifting his feet out and keeping his balance. I slipped off his back and the mud came over the top of my boots. Not discouraged, I began to pull him towards the nearest cottage. I was in the morass before I realised.

It was evident that, centuries before, a stream had run between the houses which accounted for their being set in two rows and wide apart. Over the years, it had gone underground but, when the land flooded, the safe expanse between them became treacherous and deep with mud. Frozen hard and covered in snow one could cross this expanse, or, dried out in summer, it was sufficiently firm to bear the weight of milling cattle. When I approached it, leading old Grinn, it was a quagmire of mud.

The cottage I was making towards had no smoke coming from the chimney, so I altered direction and, dragging Grinn behind me, made my way between the rows of cottages towards one from which the smoke belched out of a broken chimney. Our progress was painfully slow and I had time to see that the cottages were no more than hovels and entirely neglected. They were, literally, settling back into the mud from which they had been made. However, the mud through which I was struggling was becoming deeper and deeper so that I was on the point of giving up because of the difficulty of walking. I had already abandoned any attempt to hold up the sheepskin coat out of the mud and I let it trail behind me, becoming soggy and as filthy as a sheep's tail. Grinn, resisting the tugging rein, finally stopped and when I pulled, the head harness, which I had not bothered to mend, slipped over his head and I fell backwards into the mud. I heard someone laugh. I would have turned but Grinn, steaming and his eyes staring wildly—bloodshot as if a vein had burst, filling the glassy orbs with blood—reared up, baring his old, yellow teeth. A sound, like a flute blocked with phlegm, bubbled up from his throat and he collapsed, keeling over onto his side. He went down with an ungainly splash, splattering me. I moved towards him cumbersomely and half in panic while he kicked and threshed his head. When I saw his head beginning to sink into the mud, I lifted it out of the sucking morass to prevent him smothering. The inside of his mouth was already blocked and I scooped the mud out with my hand but could not bring myself to insert a linger up his nostril to clear it. It would have been pointless in any case because, with a shudder, he collapsed and died. I let his head, weighing like a sack of corn, drop and was horrified to see his whole carcass, steaming and twitching, begin to settle into the mud which, like melting chocolate, slowly closed over his head, covering the one staring eye.

Alerted by the shouts of voices, I turned. In all the doorways stood men and women staring. I cried out that my horse was dead. Old Grinn was dead! But they smiled and were silent. I tried to make them understand, but they just looked.

In the pouring rain, with the mud up to my knees, I felt the victim of some macabre dream, the men and women I had appealed to, the black dwarfs of my nightmares. Below average stature, with skins as dark and greasy as a nomad's, their black hair looked like the wool of shaggy oxen. I appealed to them again, but my shouting went echoing down the empty valley like blown tissue to be lost in the mists and rain. Thinking reason would appeal to their sense of decency, I began to struggle towards a man in a far hovel whose white beard and hair made me think he would have an understanding of my situation.

I laboured on down the middle of the morass while the faces grinned and the black eyes followed my movements. Behind me there was a shouted hurrah, and everyone looked in that direction. I turned to see. Grouped round Grinn, up to their knees in mud, were several of the villagers. With knives and long-handled bill-hooks they were hacking at Grinn's carcass. I shouted out my protest as his belly was slit and the fluorescent guts tumbled out of him, bright and glistening against the mud. I shouted again, my voice becoming a scream, and a villager, looping Grinn's guts round his arm like a skein of wool, turned and spat in my direction.

I tried to struggle quickly towards them, but I stumbled and sank into the mud. A roar of laughter accompanied my fall, but I got up, making a last desperate effort to reach them.

One peasant detached himself from a hovel and came down to meet me. I marvelled at the speed he picked his way through the mud until I saw he was naked from the waist down. I thought he had come to help me and I turned towards him smiling and extending my hand to be helped. The man smiled, baring his rotten teeth. Someone threw him a shovel and he caught it. I turned to see who had thrown it and saw behind me another man carrying a long-handled dung fork. From the way they stood threatening me, I knew they intended to prevent me reaching Grinn. I gestured to Grinn and pleaded with them to stop their butchery. In the rain, soaked to the skin, both men looked like animals. I began to work my way through the mud to try and avoid them, but the mud, as in a nightmare, seemed to solidify round my feet, imprisoning me. I threshed about using up my strength needlessly.

The first blow was on my unguarded back. I sank to my knees in an agony. It took an age to fall and, as I was falling, I saw the shovel coming straight into my face, edge on.

That was the last thing I ever saw; that shovel and somewhere beyond, a group of dark men standing in the downpour, pulling the steaming unending gut from poor old Grinn.

No doubt I would have been murdered and my body hidden in a quickly-dug grave or, robbed and, dead or alive, buried in the mud just the same. It was, in part, your prompt action when you discovered I was missing which saved my life; that, and the coincidence of Vetch's men searching for Klmit. I suppose I should be eternally grateful on both counts, but there are moments when I doubt the necessity for my survival. I could willingly have died, there and then. I felt nothing; only experienced an unbelievable sound which entered each ear and met inside my head like the clashing of cymbals but without the resonance. It was a final and obliterating sound and I remember nothing afterwards. It was how I hope death will be. Even the fear beforehand, and which stretched to an unendurable length, was eased by the sudden and terminating blow to my face. It had the reassuring finality of a hammered nail being driven home; and then oblivion.

As you know, it was not because Vetch's men had picked up my meandering trail, but because they were making a dawn raid on that group of hovels they chanced to find me lying in the mud. Warned to be on the look out for me, they were far more interested in arresting Klmit.

As I heard the tale from Vetch, Klmit, believing Mother would institute proceedings against him for stabbing her in the thigh, had fled, taking refuge up in the mountains. Eventually, the winter had forced him down into the lower valleys. Travelling with some nomads, he had come upon that group of hovels quite by chance and decided to use it as his headquarters. An extreme socialist, but a bad communist, he had won their confidence and soon formed a revolutionary cell. Not content with that, he wandered the district converting others and setting up similar cells wherever he could and stalling them with discontented men and women. Always managing to elude Vetch, Klmit survived for almost five years and without ever once being informed upon. His mistake was to seduce another man's woman in Teoyfelte. Enraged, the husband had followed Klmit down from the north when Klmit had fled to what he thought was the safety of that wretched group of hovels. The place has no name on the map but I think Vetch referred to it as Gelgoth. This husband, who would no doubt have killed Klmit if he had caught him, met up with some of Vetch's men who were out scouring the hills for me. After telling them his tale, the jealous husband let fall that the man whose throat he would like to slit was named Klmit. By dawn, Gelgoth had been surrounded and Vetch's men moved in at the very moment I was felled like an ox.

To have engineered such a coincidence would have stretched the imagination into the realms of fancy. But it happened and I can only assume Klmit's arrest was a Divine retribution and that I was only coincidental to the master plan. And still am. We both are, until we are found out.

According to Vetch, when he visited me in hospital, Klmit had witnessed the attack upon me and had actually encouraged it. He had not recognised me, nor, as I explained to Vetch, did I recall seeing Klmit's face amongst the many who jeered. I did not see him arrested, nor do I remember being hurriedly removed to Haggstianstad. It was after I had been transferred to Uppsala it dawned on me I was still alive but in hospital.

Behind my bandages, I listened to countless kind voices, all reassuring me, but none of them was yours. I fretted and kept asking them to send for you, but you never came. It was left to Helga to grope her way to my bedside. Her voice, filled with tears, did nothing to dispel my pessimism. To be told that you had abandoned your job in Saasval Prison, and were at home and intending to remain, only poisoned the renewed hope I had for a reconciliation because the thought of you being alone with Karen made me inordinately jealous. Helga tried, unsuccessfully, to convince me you would visit the hospital, but I knew she was lying and you would not come. In retrospect, I am glad she did not tell me you were ill and in an agony of guilt, blaming yourself for the catastrophe which had overtaken me. It was easier to accept a lie and propose my own reasons for your not wanting to visit me; it fed my ego with a hatred rather than self-pity. It was more difficult to accept the fact, which the doctors believed would be less of a shock if told by Helga, that I would remain blind for the rest of my life.

I surprised myself by the calmness with which I accepted this fate. I can only assume I was still in a state of shock and that I felt I only existed in a little cone of silence somewhere inside my head. The extension of my physical being from this small zone of awareness was a chance construction and had very little to do with me. I was a slab of matter on which tourists could have carved their initials and taken pieces from for souvenirs. If I had been cut, broken and slowly dispersed, I believed there would still remain in the hollow of the indented pillow, the invisible me which was unaffected by blindness.

The operations, and there were many of them, were not entirely without pain but the drugs which they used to treat my tuberculosis had such a miraculous effect, I felt better than I had in the whole of my life. For that alone, I was very grateful. If I had remained, there was the possibility I should have been cured. But, without you near me, my good health seemed wasted. There was no point in being fit and rehabilitated for blindness if, in the meantime, I had lost you forever. But I was swept along by the efficiency of the hospital's organisation, so I am better, but not cured, blind yet not fully trained to be entirely independent.

The unbalancing of the senses, the struggle to fill the gap caused by the loss of sight was a curious one. Sight and touch are so closely linked, and with the added extension of experience which tells you how an object will appear to look on the other side, one can grasp an object without necessarily concentrating all these senses. In my sighted days, I had seen and with my experience, touched, knowing beforehand the sensation. In hospital, I did not see, but listened, turning not my eyes but my ears towards the object I discovered on my tray or beside my bed. The experience I had acquired of everyday objects during my sighted life had to be learnt all over again and the effort was very tiring. My assessment of people depended, and still does, not on their gestures, their frowns, their smiles but upon their voices and the touch of their hand.

In the hospital, behind the veil of my blind eyes, other people's hands were, at first, like spiders, unexpectedly dropping from the ceiling. Strange hands, some so plump and soft I thought they would burst if pricked. Others so hard and calloused that no sense flowed from them; they were like gloves filled with flints. Most were dutiful hands, well-intentioned but sandpapered of all affection. And there were the reassuring hands which squeezed too hard and patted too often as if they were dumb and had to repeat their gestures to make themselves understood. And there were the clammy hands which rested on my brow-toady hands hopped up from a slimy pool to sit sweating on my forehead. No hands expressed the love which your hands do and in all the ones which fluttered round me, none came to rest like a butterfly to sip at my affection.

I also slowly learnt to catalogue people's voices and to form an idea of what they looked like. I was amazed by the different dialects and found I was no judge of character from the quality of a voice but had to depend upon the sense spoken. Insincerity, without the accompaniment of gestures and an unwavering eye to make the conceit convincing, was easily detected; especially when the deceiver was forced to use up more words than would normally have been necessary for the accomplishment of this sleight of word. But these people, all patients, came and went, so I took less and less interest when they came to sit on my bed, for I knew they would soon pass out of my life. It was not cynicism for I had come to realise that those whose contact was of necessity brief, and who knew we would never meet again, struggled to leave behind an impression of themselves which would be lasting; almost with the same desperation a man erects a monument over his grave to prove he has been and though gone, has left his pathetic mark to prove he was, thus hoping to insure he will be remembered. It is the desperation which dogs man and precipitates follies—of all kinds. It is a conceit, and bedevils those who have never been but in their going protest against the futility and hopelessness of ever being.

Of the nurses, there were two I could distinguish by their walk. Both were exceedingly kind to me and treated my body as if it was fragile and deserving of their respect when they washed and dried it. Perhaps it was the sureness of their touch or their continuous and cheerful chatter; perhaps it was because they had time to listen or that their opinions could be respected; perhaps they did not see my blindness as an obstacle. Whatever it was, I warmed to them.

It was these same two, Irma and Bergit, on whom I depended when I took my first, faltering steps into the black void. Supported, I did not care where or how far they guided me beyond my immediate surrounds, but called to, I found it too unnerving to walk towards them through the intervening space, even though I was assured there was no obstacle in my path. I think they were disappointed with my progress and timidity, for they scolded me like a child. But the more they persevered, the more I begged to be allowed to retire into my shell and be left alone. It was not that I didn't trust them but, the truth was, I did not want to learn the secret of the hospital labyrinth; it was in my own home I wanted to fumble and eventually tap out a familiar route. When Doctor Bloch revealed his irritation, I countered by demanding to be sent home. He pointed out that I was still ill and could not be discharged before another operation had been performed on my eyes to remove them. Depressed, I sealed myself off and resisted all offers of help or comfort.

It was about then Jutta moved into my night life.

From the south, a city girl, she had the frankness of a milkmaid and the audacity of a fire-eater. Ostensibly, her visits to my bedside when the other patients were asleep were to confess in a whisper to her miserable and disordered life. Over the cup of chocolate she smuggled to me, there emerged from the chaos of her telling, a life story of a girl who was as shiftless as she was untruthful. However, there was some reason to feel sorry for her because, like Candide's, her life had been a series of uninterrupted misfortunes, yet none of the calamities she thought were for the best, so she lacked resilience and was very bitter.

Basically, her tale—her life—was one of humiliation, of having her dignity restored only to be rejected, of being favoured again and later spurned, and so on. Inevitably, although she did not say so, I saw she had become slowly tinged with perversion because of her efforts to please, in the mistaken belief it would stabilise the relationship she was having at the time. Karen believes, or did, that, whatever would happen, did; Jutta, that it couldn't. She didn't see herself as the instigator of all her own misfortune and did not realise she attracted calamity like a high building tempts suicides.

Unfortunately, I succumbed to her peculiar charm and she amused herself with me one night and drew cries of shame with her chapped, milkmaid hands so that I was thoroughly disgusted with myself and filled with shame.

I dreaded the next time she would stalk up to my bed but, when she had not made an appearance for over a week and I enquired hopefully if she had been moved to another ward, I was told she had been dismissed. The news was a great relief but could not be compared to the joy I felt when I was told I could return home as soon as arrangements had been made.

And coming home was a joy, a dark joy, like returning to the house at night and fumbling for the switch to illuminate a sleeping household but knowing one was safely home.

I stood in the hall for, what, a moment only? sensing the cavern of the great hall and the chill rising up from the marble floor. It was as if I had been placed in the middle of a deep quarry and left, so vast was the emptiness which surrounded me. In my mind's eye, I could see every detail, yet I sensed only space. Those who once thought the world flat, would have experienced the same feeling if they had stood on the edge of the world before stepping off into the void of infinity. But you were there, suddenly and glowing warm beside me, and the moment you touched me all my anxieties fell away while I allowed myself to be drawn into your embrace. Time, the agonies I had suffered, the loneliness, all were dissipated in that one, long embrace.

It was late summer when I returned. You took me out to sit in the weak sunlight and held my hand. You held it until our perspiration mingled, until it seemed our hands had become welded into one, indivisible joint, as if each of us had become the extension of the other.

There had been no need to talk, but I remember you insisted upon explanations, arguing that from the moment I entered the house again, there must be no more doubts.

Your frankness was a little disarming, coming as it did within minutes of my arrival home, but first I needed to know whether my looks were so repellent you found it impossible to look at me without a feeling of revulsion. I knew you would not lie, but found it difficult to believe it was not the fascination of horror which made you say no. Under my fingertips, the hollows left by the scarring across my forehead and nose were like ragged crevasses or deep fissures—a veritable cliff-face of toe and finger holds. I realised the exaggeration was a trick of my senses, very like when one's tongue searches out a hollow tooth and probes a cave large enough to contain a prune stone and one has to rely upon sight to restore a balanced judgement; but you had the eyes to see, not I. When I told you Doctor Bloch suggested I should have glass eyes inserted to prevent my lids from shrivelling, you gave a cry of alarm and, with your thumbs, smoothed them as if soothing me to sleep. It was then you convinced me, although, to be truthful, I wondered if it was courage, not love, which made you do it. Perhaps courage and love are indivisible; in our relationship they are inseparable, a necessity. However, sitting on the terrace on that first day, I was reassured by your selfless gesture. Indeed, I was given a confidence which I had not had before.

And that confidence was a curious thing and, since, I have come to the conclusion it was my blindness which contributed to it. But for my blindness, I doubt if your own confidence would have been sufficient to get you through that first, terrible hour.

Could you have confessed so fully if my gimlet eye had bored . . . doleful, you say? Doleful, then. If my doleful eyes had gazed on your red cheeks; would you have been inhibited by their restlessness; ashamed when they closed to hide the pain you were causing me; made abject when they sought the heavens for the compassion which was needed to listen to such dreadful revelations. Perhaps I would have sat wide-eyed in disbelief. I do not know. My injury made me more passive and my ear more attuned to listening and you may have been aware of this.

Whatever the reason, both drew confidence from the other and were able to be outspoken as never before.

I did not force your confession, nor did I ask for so detailed an explanation, but I must admit, without it, I might have remained in ignorance of the compulsion to repetition which governs instinct. Knowing this I can now see, only too clearly, that the preformative occurrences of our childhood, of yours especially, clinched the predisposition of our awkward adulthood. Note, I did not say tragic.

What I cannot understand is why you never complained. Mother, Nanna Axell, either of them would have had Marcel in front of the magistrate before he had time to draw breath. After all, you did complain to Mother about Herr Lechner; and he was bundled out on his nose before dawn had broken. I suppose, being infatuated, you felt you had compromised yourself and therefore the blame could not be Marcel's alone, and that you were too ashamed to confess. But Karen, too? It is almost inconceivable. But there, it happened. I should have realised what was going on because I did surprise you and Marcel on one occasion, but it never occurred to me he was doing more than straightening your apron. If any blame can be attached to us since, I think we could be accused of lack of sympathy for Marcel's own condition, although I think his subsequent behaviour negated it. But what must his upbringing have been to have made him an obligor to a childhood, impotent fantasy; what dreadful and dark influences made him prey to compulsion? We shall never know. I could understand if he had tried to rape you. Karen, too. But just to use his hand against you, as if rendering a favour and not asking anything in return; it is very odd. How many dreadful and dark corners there are in this house where he must have dragged you and which you pass daily, only to be reminded. It is horrifying to think upon. Worse, that he should have been responsible for the wrecking of two such bright and promising lives. I am glad he is dead.

On reflection, it is almost comical to think of my terrible doubts and my stricken conscience while I wrestled with my love, imagining I was the only one who had such terrible obsessions. Yet there was you, and your little Karen, struggling against God knows what temptations and thinking yourself damned. What a mess this family is; was. Was, for I am sure we have done the only thing possible; to come to terms with our obsessions; understanding why they are and accepting they have become an integral part of us like our skin and teeth. The tragedy is that it should have occurred, not that it is. The guilt is not ours. It belongs to another time, another generation. We are the children of guilt and, as such, tinged—perverted if you like—but at least we will not pass it on, infect or unwittingly corrupt others. We will live out the rest of our lives in this rotting house—which will become our memorial—and when our lives have ended, it will be all over. We have contributed nothing, taken little, but have been effectively destroyed by elders who reject us for wanting to isolate ourselves but who would not accept us, the children of their sins.

I hadn't reached these conclusions while you sat talking to me on the bench in the pale sun on the day I returned; only since, but when we entered the house together, I already had an understanding of how we should live our life if I could submerge my jealousy of Karen. As things turned out, Marcel was our only obstacle.

Karen, I remember, at first trembled on the edge of my awareness; thinking I either blamed her or held her in contempt, and she hung back. It may well have been because she was embarrassed by my blindness or because of the difficult time you had both experienced while I was in hospital, and my returning made her think I was just one more millstone to be hung round her neck. I realised it was up to me to put her at her ease. You thanked me afterwards for the manner in which I had done it. This embarrassed me because I had been untruthful with Karen when I found it easier and more expedient to be forgiving. It was only afterwards, after a long and painful heart-searching, extending over several months, my deceit bore the fruit of truth.

Did it take six months to learn to move about as much of the house as I thought necessary without one or either of you holding the crook of my arm? I know it was winter when you remarked you had quite forgotten I was blind when I walked into the pine room.

For all our apparent ease when together, it was a difficult time for me. As I said, I was jealous of Karen and would strain my ears to listen for the unmistakable rustle of your sleeves when you might be finger-talking to one another, expressing patience while I was in the room or raising a finger to your lips for silence while I was there. More but brief intimacies between you I didn't suspect, for I knew, besides decorum you feared the ever-present but lurking Marcel. That he was suspicious only served to make me more so and I confess I took to sneaking about, hoping to surprise you and Karen. But, being blind, it was as if I was in another room and guessing, from the indistinct scrabblings going on, what was taking place. Naturally, my imagination outstripped my reason and I was hard put to contain myself. Your constant reassurance allowed me to keep my sanity, but only just. It was when I was going through this period of intense jealousy Marcel began to play his idiotic games.

Although my ears were attuned to a degree which I had never thought possible before, Marcel was able to creep up and, as he told me, walk behind me without arousing my suspicions. His one mistake, that of telling me, put me on my guard and I was able from that moment on to attune my ears to the particular frequency he emitted. Not only that but, having become adept at receiving several sounds together and being able to sort them out one from the other, listening to them independently, I was able to trick him on several occasions when he sneaked up. Unfortunately he could trip me or, when he baited me, choose his spot to poke the walking stick he had snatched from me. I found that if I kept perfectly still he soon tired of tormenting me. Typically, he would throw my walking stick either down the corridor for me to find or chuck it into one of the rooms, even hiding it under furniture. At first I thought his vendetta personal and did not know he was harassing and insulting both you and Karen. I knew there were cross words between you and him, and that is why I suggested he and Karen moved into Tetty's lodge, but you pointed out that such a solution would only exacerbate Marcel. With Gardol and Helga gone and living in retirement in Svegvika, you needed someone close at hand to help cope with all the work and if Marcel and Karen were isolated at the lodge it would not be the same as if they lived in. I could understand your concern for Karen at the mercy of Marcel and away from the house, but did not believe, as you insisted, that you had sufficient control over Marcel to keep him in check. And how right I was proved to be!

I do not know what made me grope my way to the ballroom; it was certainly not because of the sounds of quarrelling, for I did not hear them until I opened the door.

Told by you to go back up to my room, I might have withdrawn if Marcel had not seized and pulled me roughly into the room, slamming the door behind me. You said, later, Marcel had not been drinking but his manner was not that of a man whose unreasonableness was due to irritability but had the heady insanity of a drunkard whose actions and speech lacked the precision and discretion of a sober man who has regard for consequences. Instinctively, I gripped my stick tightly to forestall the mean trick Marcel enjoyed playing on me of snatching it away and held myself rigid in expectation.

Having been drawn into the middle of a furious quarrel, I was at a disadvantage until Marcel, with all the crudity and vulgarity of a swinish hog, detailed what he had just caught you and Karen at and went on to accuse with the listing of unimaginable obscenities. It was not the rantings of a puritanical reformer, affronted and preaching hell and damnation, but of a rabid sensualist spermatising over the inanimate objects of his obsessions.

Activated by his vileness and thinking I knew exactly where he stood in space and distance, I lashed out with my stick, unfortunately striking Karen and losing my stick into the bargain.

Perhaps my action precipitated the tussle which followed, but I think we had all been goaded beyond endurance and, hating him, what had occurred in the past all converged and became the signal for a concentrated attack upon him.

Sighted, I might have acted the pacifist and intervened; blind, with my stick gone, the raised voices and the milling feet made me panic. I scrabbled on the floor, feeling about for my stick, my hands being trodden upon while the three of you screamed and wrestled. It was chance Marcel tripped over me and fell but the clatter of my stick told me where it was and that Marcel had been holding it and, as you told me afterwards, striking you and Karen about the head. Marcel and I seized the stick at the exact same moment, holding it with both our hands. I knew it was not my strength alone which was forcing it downwards, across his throat, but it was only when you knelt on one end with your arm about me and Karen stood on the other, I knew the three of us had Marcel powerless. That the stick was across his neck, I had no idea. For some reason, I thought it across his open mouth; possibly because he was making such peculiar sounds in the back of his throat. When his body beneath me went limp, I thought he had come to his senses and was prepared to be co-operative and that we would be able to dictate our terms. It was the silence which told me he was dead.

Looking back, I think it was a mistake to leave his body in the ballroom to decompose, but I well understood your reluctance to touch him. By the time I had summoned up sufficient courage to do something about his corpse, there was little of him left and that had to be shovelled. Like you, I was prepared to lock the ballroom after his body had reached a stage of decomposition which made it impossible for you to enter, but it was Vetch's unexpected visit which frightened me into concealing the body in the stables. Blind, I had only my imagination and my sense of smell to revolt my stomach, so it could be said my courage was suspect.

On that first night, after Marcel's death, and the three of us took refuge in Nanna Axell's old room, filled with dread for the coming dawn, we lacked courage. Like children, we crowded into her bed and succeeded in scaring ourselves like children do when they tell each other ghost stories.

But when our talking stopped and the dawn illuminated that incredible room, it seemed all our difficulties were over and, but for Marcel's body, the future looked bright and filled with the promise of total happiness.

And it was, but, if I remember correctly, only when Marcel's body had been finally concealed in the stables and the ballroom scrubbed.

Vetch, unaware he filled us with dread by his unexpected visit, must have thought our nervousness due to our isolation in this crumbling mansion, otherwise he would not have suggested we moved into town, into a flat and lived as other young people do. Telling us Klmit had been sentenced and that the charges against the man who had attacked me had been dropped because of his death in prison, he must have been relieved I was not to be called into the witness box when he saw me dressed in a frock. I think your explanation, that it was an old dress of yours I used as a nightgown, must have convinced him that I, like all Strobls, was as eccentric as an Englishman. I nearly gave myself away by chuckling but I am certain he left without his suspicions aroused.

How long ago that seems in retrospect, yet not much more than five months have passed. Five months of unbelievable happiness for the three of us. Who ever would have thought, when we were children, how happy we would become?

It unfortunate Gudrun and her bastard child called yesterday. Although she said it was because she had heard I was blind and wondered if she could be of help in the house, I am sure it was to see Marcel she came, to get him to contribute some money for the child. Making her an allowance was a wise thing to do, but I am not entirely convinced we have seen the last of her. The four of us could not possibly live in harmony; not without taking her into our confidence. She would baulk at joining our little ménage if she were told the truth. On the other hand, if you remain in bed for very much longer, I feel it would only be fair on Karen if she had some help. What if I too should fall ill?